PATRICIA WENTWORTH
THE ANNAM JEWEL

PATRICIA WENTWORTH was born Dora Amy Elles in India in 1877 (not 1878 as has sometimes been stated). She was first educated privately in India, and later at Blackheath School for Girls. Her first husband was George Dillon, with whom she had her only child, a daughter. She also had two stepsons from her first marriage, one of whom died in the Somme during World War I.

Her first novel was published in 1910, but it wasn't until the 1920's that she embarked on her long career as a writer of mysteries. Her most famous creation was Miss Maud Silver, who appeared in 32 novels, though there were a further 33 full-length mysteries not featuring Miss Silver—the entire run of these is now reissued by Dean Street Press.

Patricia Wentworth died in 1961. She is recognized today as one of the pre-eminent exponents of the classic British golden age mystery novel.

By Patricia Wentworth

The Benbow Smith Mysteries
Fool Errant
Danger Calling
Walk with Care
Down Under

The Frank Garrett Mysteries
Dead or Alive
Rolling Stone

The Ernest Lamb Mysteries
The Blind Side
Who Pays the Piper?
Pursuit of a Parcel

Standalones
The Astonishing Adventure of Jane Smith
The Red Lacquer Case
The Annam Jewel
The Black Cabinet
The Dower House Mystery
The Amazing Chance
Hue and Cry
Anne Belinda
Will-o'-the-Wisp
Beggar's Choice
The Coldstone
Kingdom Lost
Nothing Venture
Red Shadow
Outrageous Fortune
Touch and Go
Fear by Night
Red Stefan
Blindfold
Hole and Corner
Mr. Zero
Run!
Weekend with Death
Silence in Court

PATRICIA WENTWORTH

THE ANNAM JEWEL

With an introduction by
Curtis Evans

DEAN STREET PRESS

Introduction

BRITISH AUTHOR Patricia Wentworth published her first novel, a gripping tale of desperate love during the French Revolution entitled *A Marriage under the Terror*, a little over a century ago, in 1910. The book won first prize in the Melrose Novel Competition and was a popular success in both the United States and the United Kingdom. Over the next five years Wentworth published five additional novels, the majority of them historical fiction, the best-known of which today is *The Devil's Wind* (1912), another sweeping period romance, this one set during the Sepoy Mutiny (1857-58) in India, a region with which the author, as we shall see, had extensive familiarity. Like *A Marriage under the Terror*, *The Devil's Wind* received much praise from reviewers for its sheer storytelling élan. One notice, for example, pronounced the novel "an achievement of some magnitude" on account of "the extraordinary vividness...the reality of the atmosphere...the scenes that shift and move with the swiftness of a moving picture...." (*The Bookman*, August 1912) With her knack for spinning a yarn, it perhaps should come as no surprise that Patricia Wentworth during the early years of the Golden Age of mystery fiction (roughly from 1920 into the 1940s) launched upon her own mystery-writing career, a course charted most successfully for nearly four decades by the prolific author, right up to the year of her death in 1961.

Considering that Patricia Wentworth belongs to the select company of Golden Age mystery writers with books which have remained in print in every decade for nearly a century now (the centenary of Agatha Christie's first mystery, *The Mysterious Affair at Styles*, is in 2020; the centenary of Wentworth's first mystery, *The Astonishing Adventure of Jane Smith*, follows merely three years later, in 2023), relatively little is known about the author herself. It appears, for example, that even the widely given year of Wentworth's birth, 1878, is incorrect. Yet it is sufficiently clear that Wentworth lived a varied and intriguing life that provided her ample inspiration for a writing career devoted to imaginative fiction.

It is usually stated that Patricia Wentworth was born Dora Amy Elles on 10 November 1878 in Mussoorie, India, during the heyday of the British Raj; however, her Indian birth and baptismal record states that she in fact was born on 15 October 1877 and was baptized on 26 November of that same year in Gwalior. Whatever doubts surround her actual birth year, however, unquestionably the future author came from a prominent Anglo-Indian military family. Her father, Edmond Roche Elles, a son of Malcolm Jamieson Elles, a Porto, Portugal wine merchant originally from Ardrossan, Scotland, entered the British Royal Artillery in 1867, a decade before Wentworth's birth, and first saw service in India during the Lushai Expedition of 1871-72. The next year Elles in India wed Clara Gertrude Rothney, daughter of Brigadier-General Octavius Edward Rothney, commander of the Gwalior District, and Maria (Dempster) Rothney, daughter of a surgeon in the Bengal Medical Service. Four children were born of the union of Edmond and Clara Elles, Wentworth being the only daughter.

Before his retirement from the army in 1908, Edmond Elles rose to the rank of lieutenant-general and was awarded the KCB (Knight Commander of the Order of Bath), as was the case with his elder brother, Wentworth's uncle, Lieutenant-General Sir William Kidston Elles, of the Bengal Command. Edmond Elles also served as Military Member to the Council of the Governor-General of India from 1901 to 1905. Two of Wentworth's brothers, Malcolm Rothney Elles and Edmond Claude Elles, served in the Indian Army as well, though both of them died young (Malcolm in 1906 drowned in the Ganges Canal while attempting to rescue his orderly, who had fallen into the water), while her youngest brother, Hugh Jamieson Elles, achieved great distinction in the British Army. During the First World War he catapulted, at the relatively youthful age of 37, to the rank of brigadier-general and the command of the British Tank Corps, at the Battle of Cambrai personally leading the advance of more than 350 tanks against the German line. Years later Hugh Elles also played a major role in British civil defense during the Second World War. In the event of a German invasion of Great Britain, something which seemed all too possible in 1940, he was tasked with leading the defense of southwestern England. Like Sir Edmond and Sir William,

Hugh Elles attained the rank of lieutenant-general and was awarded the KCB.

Although she was born in India, Patricia Wentworth spent much of her childhood in England. In 1881 she with her mother and two younger brothers was at Tunbridge Wells, Kent, on what appears to have been a rather extended visit in her ancestral country; while a decade later the same family group resided at Blackheath, London at Lennox House, domicile of Wentworth's widowed maternal grandmother, Maria Rothney. (Her eldest brother, Malcolm, was in Bristol attending Clifton College.) During her years at Lennox House, Wentworth attended Blackheath High School for Girls, then only recently founded as "one of the first schools in the country to give girls a proper education" (*The London Encyclopaedia*, 3rd ed., p. 74). Lennox House was an ample Victorian villa with a great glassed-in conservatory running all along the back and a substantial garden--most happily, one presumes, for Wentworth, who resided there not only with her grandmother, mother and two brothers, but also five aunts (Maria Rothney's unmarried daughters, aged 26 to 42), one adult first cousin once removed and nine first cousins, adolescents like Wentworth herself, from no less than three different families (one Barrow, three Masons and five Dempsters); their parents, like Wentworth's father, presumably were living many miles away in various far-flung British dominions. Three servants--a cook, parlourmaid and housemaid--were tasked with serving this full score of individuals.

Sometime after graduating from Blackheath High School in the mid-1890s, Wentworth returned to India, where in a local British newspaper she is said to have published her first fiction. In 1901 the 23-year-old Wentworth married widower George Fredrick Horace Dillon, a 41-year-old lieutenant-colonel in the Indian Army with three sons from his prior marriage. Two years later Wentworth gave birth to her only child, a daughter named Clare Roche Dillon. (In some sources it is erroneously stated that Clare was the offspring of Wentworth's second marriage.) However in 1906, after just five years of marriage, George Dillon died suddenly on a sea voyage, leaving Wentworth with sole responsibility for her three teenaged stepsons and baby daughter. A very short span of years, 1904 to 1907, saw the deaths of Wentworth's husband, mother, grandmother and brothers Malcolm and Edmond, removing much of her support network. In 1908, however, her father, who was now sixty years old, retired from the army and returned to England, settling at Guildford, Surrey with an older unmarried sister named Dora (for whom his daughter presumably had been named). Wentworth joined this household as well, along with her daughter and her youngest stepson. Here in Surrey Wentworth, presumably with the goal of making herself financially independent for the first time in her life (she was now in her early thirties), wrote the novel that changed the course of her life, *A Marriage under the Terror*, for the first time we know of utilizing her famous *nom de plume*.

The burst of creative energy that resulted in Wentworth's publication of six novels in six years suddenly halted after the appearance of *Queen Anne Is Dead* in 1915. It seems not unlikely that the Great War impinged in various ways on her writing. One tragic episode was the death on the western front of one of her stepsons, George Charles Tracey Dillon. Mining in Colorado when war was declared, young Dillon worked his passage from Galveston, Texas to Bristol, England as a shipboard muleteer (mule-tender) and joined the Gloucestershire Regiment. In 1916 he died at the Somme at the age of 29 (about the age of Wentworth's two brothers when they had passed away in India).

A couple of years after the conflict's cessation in 1918, a happy event occurred in Wentworth's life when at Frimley, Surrey she wed George Oliver Turnbull, up to this time a lifelong bachelor who like the author's first husband was a lieutenant-colonel in the Indian Army. Like his bride now forty-two years old, George Turnbull as a younger man had distinguished himself for his athletic prowess, playing forward for eight years for the Scottish rugby team and while a student at the Royal Military Academy winning the medal awarded the best athlete of his term. It seems not unlikely that Turnbull played a role in his wife's turn toward writing mystery fiction, for he is said to have strongly supported Wentworth's career, even assisting her in preparing manuscripts for publication. In 1936 the couple in Camberley, Surrey built Heatherglade House, a large two-story structure on substantial grounds, where they resided until Wentworth's death a quarter of a century later. (George Turnbull survived his wife by nearly a decade, passing away in 1970 at the age of 92.) This highly successful middle-aged companionate marriage contrasts sharply with the more youthful yet rocky union of Agatha and Archie Christie, which was three years away from sundering when Wentworth published *The Astonishing Adventure of Jane Smith* (1923), the first of her sixty-five mystery novels.

Although Patricia Wentworth became best-known for her cozy tales of the criminal investigations of consulting detective Miss Maud Silver, one of the mystery genre's most prominent spinster sleuths, in truth the Miss Silver tales account for just under half of Wentworth's 65 mystery novels. Miss Silver did not make her debut until 1928 and she did not come to predominate in Wentworth's fictional criminous output until the 1940s. Between 1923 and 1945 Wentworth published 33 mystery novels without Miss Silver, a handsome and substantial legacy in and of itself to vintage crime fiction fans. Many of these books are standalone tales of mystery, but nine of them have series characters. Debuting in the novel *Fool Errant* in 1929, a year after Miss Silver first appeared in print, was the enigmatic, nautically-named *eminence grise* Benbow Collingwood Horatio Smith, owner of a most expressively opinionated parrot named Ananias (and quite a colorful character in his own right). Benbow Smith went on to appear in three additional Wentworth mysteries: *Danger Calling* (1931), *Walk with Care* (1933) and *Down Under* (1937). Working in tandem with Smith in the investigation of sinister affairs threatening the security of Great Britain in *Danger Calling* and *Walk with Care* is Frank Garrett, Head of Intelligence for the Foreign Office, who also appears solo in *Dead or Alive* (1936) and *Rolling Stone* (1940) and collaborates with additional series characters, Scotland Yard's Inspector Ernest Lamb and Sergeant Frank Abbott, in *Pursuit of a Parcel* (1942). Inspector Lamb and Sergeant Abbott headlined a further pair of mysteries, *The Blind Side* (1939) and *Who Pays the Piper?* (1940), before they became absorbed, beginning with *Miss Silver Deals with Death* (1943), into the burgeoning Miss Silver canon. Lamb would make his farewell appearance in 1955 in *The Listening Eye*, while Abbott would take his final bow in mystery fiction with Wentworth's last published novel, *The Girl in the Cellar* (1961), which went into print the year of the author's death at the age of 83.

The remaining two dozen Wentworth mysteries, from the fantastical *The Astonishing Adventure of Jane Smith* in 1923 to the intense legal drama *Silence in Court* in 1945, are, like the author's series novels, highly imaginative and entertaining tales of mystery and adventure, told by a writer gifted with a consummate flair for storytelling. As one confirmed Patricia Wentworth mystery fiction addict, American Golden Age mystery writer Todd Downing, admiringly declared in the 1930s, "There's something about Miss Wentworth's yarns that is contagious." This attractive new series of Patricia Wentworth reissues by Dean Street Press provides modern fans of vintage mystery a splendid opportunity to catch the Wentworth fever.

Curtis Evans

Prologue

I

THE JEWEL LAY upon the shrine. Darkness covered it, the darkness of absolute night.

James Waring stood with his back against the rock, and felt, as the slow minutes passed, that this gloom was like a weight pressing down upon him with a steady and relentless force. Since he had entered the cavern he had seen nothing, heard nothing. The silence was as dreadful as the dark. Not once, but many times, his hand sought and closed upon the candle and the matches which lay in his coat pocket; but each time the hand withdrew again, and he told himself fiercely what kind of a fool he would be if now, on the very brink of an undreamed-of success, he were to yield to panic and jeopardize everything.

He shut his eyes. One kind of darkness was like another if one's eyes were shut. Standing thus, motionless, almost rigid, he forced his mind back over the details of his journey. How long ago since he had left the ship? He found that the ability to gauge time was gone, lost in this vastness, this blackness, this silence. There it was; one came back to it, one could not escape. Yet they said that the mind was free.

He made another effort. Henderson and Dale—when had they discovered that he had given them the slip? The girl had drugged their liquor. He wondered if they would guess. The girl—he thought with a little flicker of scorn of the abject terror in her eyes when she realized how much she had betrayed. Well, if he got the Jewel, he would make a point of rewarding her handsomely. He began to think of how it might be done. Not till some months had passed, lest she should be exposed to suspicion. Just for a moment he saw her eyes, wide, startled, full of terror. Little fool, who would hurt her?

He began to reckon up the time that had passed since he had parted from her at the entrance to the hidden way. It must have taken him half an hour to crawl inch by inch along the slippery downward incline. He still thought with a leaping heart of the moment when his hands went out over the edge and found nothing. It must have been five minutes before he had nerved himself to stand upright on the brink of that unseen precipice, and feel for the rope which she had said was there. Then the descent of the rocky face—if the rope were to give I Heaven knew how long it had been hanging there; it felt dry and brittle. Sometimes his foot slipped on worn, shallow steps, and all his weight was on the cord. He tingled now as he thought of it. The descent must have taken him twenty minutes. How long ago since he had slipped from the last step on to the rocky floor of the cavern and waked those echoes which he remembered, shuddering? He could not tell. It seemed so long that time was meaningless. How much longer must he wait? After all, why wait? What was it the girl had said? "The way must be trodden in darkness, and in darkness the seeker must wait." The whole thing was nonsense. Of course she believed it, and to pacify her he had promised; but, after all ... His hand went into his pocket for the twentieth time.

He was about to draw out a match when the astonishing thing began to happen.

He stood arrested, the match half in, half out of the box. Very far away—or so it seemed to him—the blackness, that dense velvety blackness, had turned grey. The darkness was thinning away; it was like seeing water poured into ink. In the middle of the greyness there appeared a jagged line enclosing an irregular circle.

James Waring understood that this was an opening, a window in the rock, letting in the growing light of dawn. He looked away, and could see nothing. Then, fascinated, he looked back at the light and watched it grow.

Long ago his fingers had snapped in two the match which they had held, but he continued to grip the fragile splinter without the least consciousness of what he was doing.

The greyness became light, and the light focussed into a ray. The ray came to rest on the Jewel.

James Waring took a step forward and drew a long sobbing breath.

There was a pillar of rough stone, unwrought. It was about four feet high and a foot across. James Waring stood a stone's throw from it, and saw it in the light of the ray. There was something upon it like a carved lotus, and in the centre of the lotus, raised above the petals, was the Jewel.

It was true then—true or else he was dreaming now. He had not really believed what the girl had whispered to him, her breath caught by terror; but it was true. He saw the Jewel, the only one in the world. He saw what no white man had ever seen before the sacred thing which only the eyes of the purified might behold.

The Jewel shone in the ray. He saw the sapphire blue, the fiery crimson, the green-like flame, and the inmost golden heart. Exultation swelled in him. He was not afraid of the echoes now. He strode forward, and suddenly those echoes woke into hideous life. The dark corners of the cavern rang as if to the beating of brazen gongs.

James Waring saw a movement of many figures. A thrown dagger flashed through the ray and went singing past his ear. He whipped out his revolver and fired, and the rock walls gave back the sound of the shot, magnified beyond endurance. He fired again as his left hand closed on the Jewel. Then something caught him by the ankle, and he went down, fighting like a wild beast that is trapped.

II

James Waring opened his eyes. Everything had happened long ago, very long ago. He opened his eyes and saw the sunlight. It hung like a dazzling curtain across the mouth of the little cave. He was in the cave, lying on sand. The cave was in shadow. Outside he could see sun-flooded air a-quiver with heat. He shut his eyes. A long time passed. When he opened them again he saw the man.

The sun had crept round a little, and the light fell upon the man, bathing him from head to foot. He sat cross-legged; his hands were hidden in his robe; his eyes were downcast; his head was shaven. His skin was of the colour and consistency of very old parchment; there were no lines upon it, and it had a certain strange transparency.

James Waring shut his eyes again. He did not sleep or wake, but remained, as it were, at a fixed point between the two states. At last something shocked him into full consciousness. He did not know what it was. He only knew that he was awake, alive, and that his whole being was tingling as if from some sudden blow.

The man was still there. The sunlight now streamed right into the cave. The man's eyes were resting upon him. They were queer, mild eyes, of the nondescript colour of mist.

James Waring spoke, and his voice sounded very strange to him.

"Where am I? What are you going to do to me?" he said.

The mild eyes dwelt upon him. James Waring spoke again, and as he spoke he got upon his feet.

"You can't keep me here," he said. He strode to the mouth of the cave and saw the cliff fall sheer and trackless. There were rice fields far below, green as slips of emerald, green as the flame of the Jewel.

For the first time, he remembered the Jewel, the glory of it in the ray, the cold, hard feel of it in his hand. With a quick movement his fingers slipped into that inner pocket, and felt again the coldness and the hard, smooth contour. Was it possible?

With a jerk he had it out. His pulses drummed. The Jewel lay in his open palm.

He had forgotten the man until he met those misty eyes. They looked at him, not at the Jewel. Then a voice said, speaking slowly with a pause between each word:

"Is it well?"

He started. Of course he had yet to get away with it. Then he laughed aloud. What was an old man? It would be easy enough to dispose of him—and, miracle of miracles, they had left him his revolver.

He advanced threateningly.

"Show me the way out," he said.

The eyes did not waver from his. Something checked him. The voice went on speaking.

"Look upon the Jewel," it said; and Waring looked. The thing dazzled him. The greatness, the glory of his success dazzled him.

The voice said:

"The blue is the Celestial Heaven; the red is the Elemental Fire; the green is the Living Earth; and the gold at the heart of it is the Ray of Wisdom. Are these things to be taken by violence? Look upon the Jewel and tell me this, O violent man."

"The Jewel is mine," said James Waring.

"Take it and go," said the voice. "Thou hast betrayed, and thou hast slain. Is the Jewel thine?"

"It is mine," said James Waring.

The man rose slowly to his feet. There was a coil of rope in a recess. He fastened it carefully to an iron hook, and moved to the mouth of the cave. Waring followed him.

Chapter One

THE WIND DROVE the rain against the nursery window. It came in gusts, drove against the panes with a splash, and then withdrew, leaving them drenched. The nursery floor was covered with green oilcloth, very old, very shabby, very much stained. The fire had gone out.

Rose Ellen, eight years old, sat cross-legged on the hearth-rug. Her eyes were screwed up tightly, her fat little hands quivered as she pressed them against her ears. All the bricks, all the toys, and all the nursery books were also on the floor.

Peter, aged twelve, had constructed an admirable gallows with the bricks. This occupied the centre of the floor, and against it, in a huddled attitude, there was propped that luckless criminal, Laura Augusta Belladonna, commonly known as Augustabel, and dear beyond words to the lacerated heart of Rose Ellen. The books had been built into a grandstand with three tiers, and all the remaining dolls and toys had been accommodated with seats from which a commanding view of the impending execution could be obtained. There was a bear without a head, a mutilated donkey, a jack-in-the-box with a broken neck, and a monkey with a scarlet coat and a permanent grin. There was also Maria, the wax doll, who appeared to have swooned.

Immediately opposite the gallows sat Peter Waring in an upright chair with twisted arms. He wore a scarlet flannel dressing-gown, and was endeavouring to balance a square of black cloth upon the top of his head. "Hanged by the neck until you are dead," he was repeating with unction. The criminal appeared unmoved, but Rose Ellen gave a wriggle and a sniff.

"Peter," she said, in a little soft voice, "isn't it over? Oh, Peter de—ah, I really, truly, can't keep scrooged up any longer. Oh, Peter darlin'—"

"Rose Ellen!" said Peter in an awful voice. Then he addressed the prisoner:

"Laura Augusta Belladonna—" he began, but in an instant Rose Ellen was on her feet, eyes and ears wide open. She snatched Augustabel from the gallows foot, clasped her to a much stained pinafore, and fixed Peter with a glance of most deadly reproach.

"Not my Augustabel—I never said you might have my Augustabel," she said, the words hurrying with just the faintest suspicion of a lisp. "You said Teddy, and it wouldn't hurt him, because he hadn't got a head at all. And then to go and take a dreadful advantage like that just because of my eyes being shut and—and my ears, when you know perfectly well that I can't possibly bear to look even when they haven't got heads ..." She paused, took a sobbing breath, and concluded:

"Oh, Peter de—ah!" she said.

"A fat lot your ears were shut," said Peter.

"They were."

"Then how did you hear your precious Augustabel's name?"

"Only just at the end I did. Oh, Peter de—ah, only just at the very, very end of all."

Rose Ellen was a good deal like a doll herself. Her mouth closed more firmly than Augustabel's did, but she had the same biscuit-china complexion and the same close golden-brown curls. It was in the eyes that the greatest difference lay: the eyes of Augustabel were hard and blue; the eyes of Rose Ellen were very soft and brown.

"Come on, give her to me," said Peter, and then, in deep and awful tones, "Justice must be done."

At the last word he plunged forward, snatched at Augustabel, caught his foot in the gallows, and came down sideways on the top of the grandstand with a resounding crash.

Peter shouted, Rose Ellen shrieked, the head of the wax doll Maria rolled across the floor, and the door opened. An untidy maid stood on the threshold and surveyed the scene.

"Lor', you children!" she said in a good-natured drawling voice. "Who's going to pick all that up? Not me. Master Peter, you're wanted downstairs." Then she was gone again.

Peter made a hideous face, removed the scarlet dressing-gown, and went downstairs, his heart a little heavier at every step. He supposed one *had* to have relations. He supposed they had to come bothering. That was the sort of thing that was bound to happen when one's mother—Peter choked, jumped the last four steps, and burst rather vehemently into the dining-room.

Somebody said, "Good gracious!" Somebody else said, "Gently, gently, my boy." He caught a whisper of, "Boys have no feeling, absolutely none, my dear", and his Uncle Matthew said, "Shut the door, Peter."

Peter shut the door, came to a standstill about a yard away from it, and surveyed his relations. The room seemed to be quite full of them. He wondered whether other people had as many. The women had black dresses; the men wore black ties. They alluded to his mother as "Poor Olivia". One naturally hated people who did that.

Peter fished a bit of string out of his left-hand trouser pocket. It was rather sticky because there was an old peppermint bull's-eye, some greaseproof paper, a rabbit's tail, and a candle-end in the same pocket.

"Don't fidget, Peter," said Miss Charlotte Oakley, who was a second cousin.

But Peter took no notice. He looked frowningly at his bit of string, undid the knot that he had tied, and made another, a different sort of knot, very complicated.

If Peter had but known it, his relations were all suffering from the sort of embarrassment which makes the temper uncertain. Each of them was between two highly unpleasant alternatives. None of them wished to do anything for Peter, but each of them shrank from saying so. An almost penniless Peter; a great hulking boy clumping into one's house with muddy boots; that dreadfully mannerless boy of poor Olivia's; a creature that would simply eat you out of house and home—thoughts like these had reduced Peter's relatives to a condition in which everyone hoped that somebody else would speak first.

At the head of the table sat his father's surviving brother, Matthew Waring, a prosperous country solicitor. He had just undertaken to defray the cost of Peter's education, and felt that his conscience had no business to be troubling him with the suggestion that he might also make Peter's holidays his affair. "Plenty of room in the house, and it would liven things up," said his conscience unreasonably, but with some insistence. "Nice enough lad, don't like 'em namby-pamby myself, but of course Emily would never hear of it," was his reply. Emily sat next to him, a woman with a red face and a light, hard eye. Matthew Waring feared her a good deal more than he feared his conscience. From the moment that she had whispered, "Think of his boots on the carpets," the matter had been settled.

Emily Waring liked her brother Matthew, but she loved her own way, and regarded boys as a wholly unnecessary evil. Boys in general were bad enough, but this boy of poor Olivia's—well, look at him!

All the relations looked at Peter. A well-grown boy of twelve; of noticeably sturdy build; thick, colourless hair standing on end; a smudged and freckled face; dilapidated clothes; a stocking with a gaping tear, and shoes that were out at the toes; grimy hands that fiddled perpetually with a disreputable piece of string. There really was nothing very attractive about Peter.

"He certainly doesn't take after his father," said Emily Waring grimly. "Poor Henry was one of the handsomest young men I ever saw."

"He is not in the least like our family," said Miss Oakley. She tossed her head a little, and added, "Poor Olivia was considered a lovely girl."

"The question is, the holidays," said Matthew Waring; but his sister Emily interrupted him.

"Your Uncle Matthew has most kindly undertaken to send you to school, Peter," she said. "He was naturally under no obligation to do this, but out of respect for your poor father—"

"Now, Emily, now, Emily," said her brother.

He had seen a scowl pass over Peter's face, rendering it considerably less attractive than before, and he spoke uneasily.

"Allow me to finish what I was saying, Matthew. Your uncle, as I said, is going to educate you, and we think that some of your mother's relations may be able to offer you a home during the holidays."

Miss Charlotte Oakley flushed. Her married sister, Mrs. Spottiswoode, coughed and looked at her rings. They were very handsome rings, and she was a well-jointured widow, with a soft enough heart. She did not dislike Peter, not really; though, of course, he would be a great nuisance in the house, and Charlotte would be put about. She looked at her sister, and half opened her lips as if to say something.

"We are only cousins, Miss Waring," said Charlotte Oakley in a high, protesting voice.

"Though brought up with dear Olivia—and I'm sure I was always as fond of her as if she were my own sister, and fonder...." Mrs Spottiswoode began to dab her eyes with a very small handkerchief which diffused an almost suffocating odour of heliotrope.

Emily Waring sniffed disapprovingly.

A little dried-up man, who had not spoken before, leaned across the table and whispered to Matthew Waring. His name was Miles Banham, and he was Olivia Waring's stepbrother.

"The money's the difficulty, of course," he said. "I haven't got a sou myself, as you all know, and I'm off to Japan again next week. But somewhere ..." His voice sank lower. "It's just a chance—why not ask him?"

The scowl on Peter's face deepened. He had made six knots in his piece of string, and was beginning a seventh—one he had learnt from Jane's brother, who was a sailor; he was never quite sure of it. Suddenly he became aware that he was being addressed. His Uncle Matthew was leaning forward, looking at him intently. Everyone was looking at him.

Matthew Waring drummed on the table, and said in rather a loud voice:

"Peter, did your mother ever speak to you about the Annam Jewel?"

Peter stopped looking at his piece of string—he stopped in the very middle of a knot—and looked at his relations instead. His Cousin Charlotte had a very flushed face. She was saying:

"Poor Olivia had a secretive nature, she never would tell *me* a word about it, though we were like sisters. Not a word, I do assure you, Miss Waring, though I implored her to give me her confidence. I felt—Ruth and I both felt—that it was only right for someone on her own side of the family to know the *facts*, but not a word could I get out of her. Now I only ask you, is it likely that she would tell that boy what she wouldn't tell me?"

Miles Banham's eyes twinkled. Matthew Waring continued to drum on the table, and said dryly:

"I'm sure I don't know, Miss Oakley. Peter, however, can tell us Come, Peter, *did* your mother ever speak to you of the Annam Jewel?"

Peter frowned. His eyes went from one face to another. Cousin Ruth Spottiswoode was wiping her eyes. Uncle Matthew had a red face and grey hair. He didn't like Aunt Emily—he felt sure that he would never like Aunt Emily. Uncle Miles was the best of the lot; he didn't jaw, and he didn't say, "Poor Olivia!"

Miles Banham put out a sunburnt hand to him. "Come on, Peter," he said; "did you ever hear of the Annam Jewel?"

Uncle Miles had eyes like a monkey, little, and bright, and brown. Peter met them full, and said gruffly:

"Perhaps."

"No manners at all," said Charlotte Oakley quite audibly.

But with that one word Peter had gained the respect of his Uncle Matthew and the affection of his Uncle Miles.

Miles Banham laughed.

"Won't be pumped, eh? Quite right, too. Better take him into your business, Waring. Soul of discretion, eh? Well, look here, Peter, you won't be pumped, but will you do a swap? All on the level, and between gentlemen. You tell us what you know, and I'll tell you what I know. I do know something," he added, with a nod that included everyone at the table. "Well, is it a bargain?"

Peter had dropped his piece of string. He dived into his right-hand pocket, rejected a slate-pencil, a stick of sealing-wax, and an apple, and produced about a yard of crumpled pink ribbon. He nodded at Miles Banham and began to make knots in the ribbon.

"She did tell him something, then," said Emily Waring in a sharp whisper, every word of which reached Peter's ears.

"I was quite sure of it." Miles Banham's tone was curt. "Well now, Peter—"

"You first," said Peter, struggling with his knot.

"What nonsense!" said Emily Waring. "Peter, if your mother ever told you anything, it's your absolute duty to let us know what it was. It's most important. A little boy like you cannot possibly understand how important it is, but you *can* understand that it is your duty to tell us everything that you know at once. And do, for goodness' sake, stop fiddling with that horrible piece of pink ribbon," she ended sharply.

"Peter, come here," said Miles Banham. His voice sounded cool and easy after Emily Waring's rasp.

Peter came nearer warily. He hated being touched; but Miles Banham merely twinkled at him and said:

"So you want to hear me first? And after that you'll tell us what you know? Honour bright? All right. I don't mind."

He was sitting with one elbow on the table, leaning hard against the arm of his chair, which he had pushed askew. His little brown face was covered with fine lines. He was clean-shaven, and had lost two of his front teeth.

"Well, here's my yarn," he said.

Miss Oakley leaned forward. Mrs. Spottiswoode let her handkerchief fall into her lap. The scent of heliotrope hung in the air.

"The story begins with your Uncle James." He coughed slightly, threw a whimsical glance over his shoulder at Matthew and Emily, and again addressed Peter. "He—er, was what is called wild; rather like myself, in fact; didn't pass his exams; didn't get into a profession; didn't write home very regularly; in fact—er, all that sort of thing. Well, twelve years ago your Uncle James was in Annam—don't ask me how he got there, or what he was doing, because it's a case of least said soonest mended—but he was there, for some weeks at any rate. We know that for certain, and we also know, or I should say believe, that whilst he was there he came into possession of a very remarkable stone, known as the Annam Jewel. We don't know that for certain, but the evidence is tolerably convincing. We don't even know for a fact that there is or ever was, such a stone. I've heard rumours of it for twenty years; and I've met old men who had heard the same stories when they were young, but I've never met anyone who had actually seen it.

Peter had dropped the pink ribbon. His deep-set eyes were fixed on Miles Banham's face, his grubby hand pressed against Miles Banham's knee.

"What is it?" he said. "The Jewel?"

"No one knows," said Miles Banham in his quick, cool voice. "No one knows, because no one has seen it. They call it the Annam Jewel; and Annam means 'The Hidden Way'. It was a hidden thing, a sacred jewel, kept in a most secret place. I believe James Waring had it in his possession. He is known to have gone inland. He had two companions, a man called Henderson, and a man who went by the name of Dale—it wasn't his real name, I believe. They quarrelled and parted.

"Now we come to another part of the story. Your father, Henry Waring, was at that time a captain in the Gunners at Hong Kong. He and your mother had been married about six months. He had no idea of his brother James' whereabouts until he got a cable from him. It was in a cipher which they had made up and used when they were schoolboys. It told him to come at once to Tourane, which is one of the ports of Annam. It said that he had secured a great treasure, but had no money and could not get it away alone. It besought Henry to come without delay. Your mother didn't want him to go. She didn't want him to go at all, but he overbore her and went. They were very hard up, and he wanted to make money for her. She hated the East, and he wanted to get her out of it. He wanted to settle at home in the country with a bit of land, and horses, and dogs; and the idea of the treasure got hold of him.

"Well, he went off, and your mother had letters from him. I don't know what was in them, for she wouldn't tell me. You see, I'm being quite frank with you, Peter. From first to last she only told me two things. The first was that your Uncle James was dead or dying when Henry got there; and the other was that Henry had had an accident and was coming back. Well, he came back, and you were born; and he lived six months after that. He was utterly changed, and very bitter.

I saw him several times—I was coming and going round Hong Kong at the time—but he never told me anything, and Olivia never told me anything either. Once he said something about enemies following him, and several times he began talking as if he expected to be very rich. The last time I saw him he said: 'Peter will have it, but not till he's twenty-five. I'm done for.' That's all I know."

Peter drew a very long breath.

Ruth Spottiswoode took up her handkerchief again.

"Now, Peter, it's your turn," said Miles Banham. "You've had my yarn. Now let's have yours. What did your mother tell you about the Annam Jewel? Out with it!"

"She said—she said ..." Peter went back a pace, shoved both hands into his pockets, and faced his relations. "She only said never to have anything to do with it."

Chapter Two

THERE WAS a moment's silence. Then Miles Banham gave his knee a loud, resounding slap.

"Spoofed, by gum!" he said, and broke into his funny cackling laugh.

The other relations did not laugh. Charlotte Oakley exclaimed, "Nonsense!" Emily Waring coughed; and her brother Matthew said, frowning, "Tell us just exactly what she said."

"That's what she said," said Peter.

"Yes, yes, quite so. But how did she come to speak of it at all? What introduced the subject? I mean, how did it all begin?"

Peter went back another step.

"I was reading," he said. "She said, 'Put down your book.' I put it down. She said, 'The Annam Jewel,' and asked me if I could remember the name. I said I could. I asked her what it was. She said, 'Never mind, you'll know when you're twenty-five—you'll have to know then.' Then she said, 'Don't have anything to do with it ever.' She asked me to promise."

"And did you?" Miles Banham put in the question, speaking very quickly.

Peter shook his head. His thick, fair eyebrows drew together in a frown that was almost a scowl.

"Why not?"

Peter shook his head again. He had told what he had covenanted to tell. He had no intention of explaining to uncles, and cousins, and aunts that you couldn't promise things when you didn't know what you were promising. They wouldn't understand Even his mother hadn't understood quite. She had most dreadfully wanted him to promise, but of course he couldn't.

"Well well," said Miles Banham, "if you won't say, you won't. A close tongue's not a bad thing, when all's said and done." He looked at the watch on his bony wrist, and jumped up. "By gum it's late. I'll have to hurry for my train. I've a man to see at the other end. So long, everyone. Here, Peter, I never can keep these things, so you might as well have one of them."

He pressed a pound note into Peter's grubby hand, opened the door briskly, and turned on the threshold to say a last malicious word.

"About those holidays—why not share him between you? Turn and turn about, you know—and it's all fair play." He sang the last words in a cracked falsetto, slammed the door, and was gone.

"Of all the preposterous—" began Emily Waring, but Matthew was too quick for her.

"Well, that's reasonable enough," he said. "Half the time with us, and half with you. Shall we settle it that way, Mrs. Spottiswoode?"

Peter heard his Cousin Ruth say: "Yes, oh yes, I suppose so. Yes, indeed; I'm sure that's reasonable enough, isn't it, Charlotte?" to which Charlotte responded gloomily that she did not consider it in the least reasonable, but that she supposed it would have to be. And immediately upon that Emily Waring was telling him that they did not expect gratitude, but she considered that it was his duty at least to thank his uncle and his cousins for all their kindness.

Peter had turned very pale. The fact that his relations did not in the least desire his presence either in the holidays or at any other time was not hidden from him. His Aunt Emily had taken care of that. He disliked his Aunt Emily more than words could say. She had eyes like marbles and a mouth like a trap. She had called him a little boy. He disliked her dreadfully. He therefore said nothing at all, and, getting hold of the door handle, began to twist it backwards and forwards. His one overpowering desire was to get out of the room. And then suddenly a new idea tumbled helter-skelter into his mind. All this talk of school and holidays—it had all been about him, Peter. No one had so much as mentioned Rose Ellen. What about Rose Ellen? He turned from the door, and shot the question at the relations.

"What about Rose Ellen?"

Matthew Waring cleared his throat. His sister Emily leaned across him.

"That reminds me, Miss Oakley," she said, "the institution you wrote to me about. I have three votes, and my friend Lady Cracknell has four. The Vicar also has four, and really, with one thing and another, I think we may make sure of getting her in at the next election. A really admirable place—such good discipline and everything run on the most practical lines."

"What about Rose Ellen?" said Peter.

"Emily, this discussion—defer it, please." Matthew Waring's tone was curt. He turned to Peter:

"My boy—er, we are in a somewhat difficult position. You know, of course, that the little girl is not really related in any way to—er, any of us. Your mother—"

"Most injudiciously," said Emily Waring.

"I was going to say that your mother adopted her, but that does not exactly describe the position. There were no formalities of any kind. Your mother was very kind-hearted. I understand that the little girl had been deserted by her own parents, and your mother, I fear unwisely, allowed herself to be burdened with a charge which she could ill afford."

"What about Rose Ellen?" said Peter for the third time.

A little while ago he had been most dreadfully afraid that he might disgrace himself by bursting into angry tears, but now something stubborn in him was taking away the desire to cry. He was pleased to see how very uncomfortable all the relations looked. He meant to go on asking "What about Rose Ellen?" until he got an answer.

Miss Oakley supplied the answer. Her tone was rather defiant. Ruth was soft-hearted enough for anything, and she had to protect her, she really had to.

"Your Aunt Emily has found a very nice home for Rose Ellen," she said, "where she will be taught to read, and write, and sew, and—er, all sorts of things."

"Is it a school?" said Peter, fastening a direct and frowning gaze upon her face.

Charlotte Oakley hesitated, and was lost. For neither the first nor the last time in her dealings with Peter there came into her mind the sinful thought that life would be easier if one had not been brought up always to tell the truth.

Peter turned away from her.

"Is it a school, Aunt Emily?" he said.

Emily Waring had no hesitations.

"It's an orphanage," she said. "One of the best-managed institutions I know. Rose Ellen will receive a thorough training, and I hope she will be grateful to Miss Oakley and to myself for placing her there."

Peter dragged the door open violently, plunged blindly out, and slammed it to with a bang that made the windows rattle.

Upstairs in the nursery it was getting dark. The room was cold and untidily desolate. Amongst the strewn bricks and fallen books Rose Ellen sat rigidly still. She held the doll Augustabel very tightly in her arms; her chin rested upon its mop of gold-brown hair; and, very steadily, the tears kept running down her cheeks and dropping into her lap. She did not attempt to wipe them away. She heard the furious bang of the door downstairs and Peter's noisy, stumbling ascent, and still cried on, softly and steadily.

Then, with another wild bang, Peter was in the room, a Peter who neither looked at her nor saw her. He flung himself down on the old nursery sofa, and lay there, torn with dry sobs that were horrible to hear. Rose Ellen cried on. Her world had fallen into pieces, and Peter was in one of his rages. It was the worst rage ever, it was part of the dreadfulness of everything. She cried on. Augustabel's frock was quite wet. And then suddenly Peter's nearness and the sound of his sobbing were too much for her. She gave a little, terrified cry, and called his name. Peter stopped sobbing at once, propped himself on one elbow, and said very gruffly:

"What is it?"

She dropped Augustabel, scrambled up, and ran to him.

"Peter de—ah, oh, Peter de—ah."

Panic had her, and she clung to him, trembling so violently that he could scarcely hold her; but by and by he managed to lift her on to his knees, and sat rocking her to and fro until her sobs died down and she put up a timid hand and touched his cheek.

"You're crying, Peter."

"I'm not."

"Oh, Peter de—ah, why are you crying?"

"I tell you I'm not, Rose Ellen."

"Nor I wasn't, really," said Rose Ellen, trembling and sniffing. "'Cos only babies cry, and I'm half grown up. But 'Gustabel couldn't help crying, she couldn't really, Peter dear."

This was a convention to which Peter was accustomed. He asked:

"Why did Augustabel cry?"

With both arms clasped tightly round Peter's neck, Rose Ellen's sense of being lost in the dark had gone. She rubbed the top of her head against Peter's chin, and said:

"It was because of the dreadful thing that Jane said—Augustabel couldn't help crying when she heard it."

Peter continued to rock her. His rage was yet in him, but he held it back from touching Rose Ellen. He rocked gently.

"What did Jane say?" he inquired, and felt Rose Ellen's little body quiver in his arms.

"Peter de—ah, I can't say it—Augustabel would cry again if I did, I know she would."

"Not if I hold you tight, she won't. See, like this. Now whisper it."

Rose Ellen put soft little lips to Peter's ear. A belated tear went trickling down his neck.

"She said they were going to send you away—an' me away—an' you into a school—an' me into a home—an' she didn't hold with homes—she said they broke you in—an' she said they was cold like charity—an' she said we shouldn't see each other any more—an' she said it was a cruel shame." The words came in little gasps, and with the last one Rose Ellen began to shake again dreadfully. Peter spoke in a loud, commanding voice:

"Rose Ellen, you're to stop! You're not to cry another single tear, and Augustabel isn't to cry one either! There's nothing to cry about, and you're not to cry!"

"Isn't it true, Peter?" said Rose Ellen.

Peter hugged her very tight.

"Rose Ellen, you're a big girl," he said, still in that loud voice. "You've got to be sensible. I've got to go to school, and you've got to go to school."

"She said it wasn't a school. Oh, Peter de—ah, she said it."

"I don't care what she said. I've got to go to school, and you've got to go to school. No, listen, Rose Ellen, you're not to cry, you're to listen. We've both got to go to school, and at the end of the first term I shall come and see you, and, if you're not happy, I shall take you away."

Rose Ellen made a little joyful sound between a laugh and a sob.

"Peter, really?" She paused, sobbed again, and added, "Truly?"

"Word of honour," said Peter, "and really and truly. And, oh, Rose Ellen, what a silly little goose of a thing you are to cry yourself into a jelly about going to school! Everybody must go to school."

"Augustabel too?"

"Of course."

"And you'll come, you'll promise to come?"

"I swear it with a deadly oath," said Peter.

Chapter Three

THREE MONTHS LATER the second week of Peter's Easter holidays was drawing to a close. He had gone straight from school to Mrs.

Spottiswoode's house at Wimbledon, and after ten days there was about to depart on a visit to Matthew Waring at Ledlington.

He sat in the window seat of Ruth Spottiswoode's pleasant, conventional drawing-room, industriously whittling a penholder into a sharp-pointed dart—it was one of Ruth Spottiswoode's penholders. As he whittled he could hear his Cousin Charlotte speaking in her most decided manner. She and Cousin Ruth were in the hall, and the door into the drawing-room was open.

"My dear Ruth, you're like butter with him, *melted* butter. You make yourself absolutely ridiculous. It's a mercy that he goes tomorrow. Emily Waring'll wheel him into line."

"You're very unfair, Charlotte. I told you I'd speak to him, and I will. He—he probably forgot."

Charlotte laughed derisively.

"You can't forget what you never remember," she said, and went out, shutting the hall door sharply behind her.

Ruth Spottiswoode came back into the drawing-room. She straightened the sofa cushions, poked the fire which was burning brightly and needed no attention, and then, crossing over to a small ornamental writing-table, she began to fidget with the things upon it. Peter went on whittling. Ruth Spottiswoode picked up a stick of sky-blue sealing-wax, looked at it fixedly for a moment, and then laid it down again upon the little silver tray which it shared with three more sticks of ornamental wax and a rose-coloured candle.

"Peter," she said.

"'M," said Peter.

"Did you forget to wash your hands for lunch?"

Peter shook his head.

"Cousin Charlotte thought you did, dear. She—she noticed them. She said ... oh, Peter, you *must* have forgotten, for they're dreadfully black now."

Peter broke the point of his dart, and said, "Dash!" Frowning intently, he began on a new one.

Mrs. Spottiswoode came nearer, fluttering. She was plump, but she fluttered. She reminded Peter of a hen, partly because she fluttered, and partly because of the little clucking noises she made.

"You know, Peter, you *ought* to wash your hands."

"All right," said Peter, in a bored voice.

Then he stopped whittling and got up. He did this because he was afraid that Cousin Ruth was going to kiss him. He didn't mind presenting his cheek or a portion of his ear to her at breakfast and bedtime, but he had a strong objection to desultory embraces at odd moments.

"Oh, Peter!" said Ruth reproachfully. She sighed and added, "You're going away tomorrow, you know."

"What time?" asked Peter, with interest.

"Well, Cousin Charlotte wrote the letter, and she said you could be with them for lunch. Of course, I really think it would have suited them much better if you hadn't got there till teatime."

"'M," said Peter. Then, after a slight pause, "May I write a letter, Cousin Ruth?"

"Yes, of course. You can write at my table. Who do you want to write to?"

Peter gazed at her seriously.

"I want to write to Uncle Matthew."

"But, my dear boy, we've written to him—Charlotte wrote to him. You don't need to write."

"I think it would be better if I did," said Peter.

"Oh!" It was an exclamation of pure astonishment, checked almost at once and followed by, "Now that's really very nice and polite of you, Peter, and I'm sure your Uncle Matthew will be pleased, and—and your Aunt Emily. Of course, you really ought to write to your Aunt Emily, you know, Peter dear, and not to your Uncle Matthew, as she's the lady of the house, and—yes, I *think* you ought to write your Aunt Emily."

Peter shook his head.

"Uncle Matthew," he said laconically. "May I seal it with your sealing-wax, Cousin Ruth?"

"Of course you can, dear boy. Which stick would you like? Well, never mind; you can choose when you've written your letter. And I do think it was a very nice, polite thought—your writing to Uncle

Matthew, I mean, and I'm sure he'll be very much pleased. I must remember to tell Cousin Charlotte that it was your own idea."

"Yes," said Peter. "May I use the red ink, Cousin Ruth?"

"Anything you like, dear boy."

Peter, who had settled himself in the position which he affected for writing, received an unexpected kiss upon the top of his head. He scowled at the inkstand, and was much relieved when his Cousin Ruth, announcing that she would just go and lie down for an hour before tea, fluttered from the room. Peter sniffed the air, making deep wrinkles in his nose. Cousin Ruth used a lot of scent; he didn't like scent; he never meant to let Rose Ellen use it. With a little jerk he pulled a sheet of lilac-tinted paper towards him, and began to write:

Dear Uncle Matthew. He wrote the name with one "t" first; looked at it critically; added a second; looked at it again; and, in attempting to strike out the first "t", produced a very large red blot. He proceeded resolutely to the next line.

> *Cousin Charlotte has written to say I will come to lunch tomorrow. It will be more conveniant—convenniant—convienent if I do not come till Monday. I will send a wire.—*
>
> *Your affectionate nephew,*
>
> *Peter Waring.*

He made another large blot over his signature, and an attempt to sop it up with a piece of heliotrope blotting paper resulted in a further disaster. He folded the sheet, enclosed it in an envelope, addressed it, and proceeded to the really exhilarating business of sealing the envelope in three places. He used pink, purple, and green wax, and made patterns. He reduced the rose-coloured candle to a guttering wreck. He enjoyed himself very much. When he had quite finished he went to post his letter.

As he walked down the drive between the budding lilacs and horse-chestnut trees, he reviewed the situation. He had to see Rose Ellen. He had promised Rose Ellen that he would see her, and naturally he had to keep his promise. The relations hadn't seemed to understand this at all. It was very odd—but then relations *were* odd.

He had begun about Rose Ellen on the very first day of the holidays. Cousin Ruth had looked sorry, and Cousin Charlotte had looked cross. Neither of them seemed to think that it mattered about breaking his promise. They both said he couldn't possibly go and see Rose Ellen. Peter said, "Why?" and went on saying, "Why?" until they explained in alternate sentences, getting a little flustered and rather red, that it wouldn't do at all.

"Why?" said Peter.

"Because, my dear boy, little Rose Ellen—a nice little girl, I'm sure, and it's very natural for you to be concerned about her, and it does you credit, doesn't it, Charlotte?" That was Ruth Spottiswoode.

Then Cousin Charlotte, red and cross:

"Just put it out of your mind, like a sensible boy, Peter. Rose Ellen is being brought up in quite a different class to you, and it would be most unsuitable for you to go on being thrown with her."

"Why?" said Peter.

Then they both began again. Cousin Ruth said he was a dear boy and he must be guided by them; and Cousin Charlotte said that Institutions didn't allow visitors. Peter went on saying, "Why?" until Cousin Charlotte lost her temper and went out of the room, banging the door. This was injudicious, as it left Ruth Spottiswoode more or less at Peter's mercy. He took full advantage of the position, and obtained a good deal of useful information. Cousin Ruth had even shown him a picture of St. Gunburga's, under the impression that the imposing building with the group of uniformed staff and quaintly clad children in the foreground would satisfy Peter and make him drop the subject.

Peter scowled whenever he thought of that picture. He hated it quite frightfully. He hated the thought of Rose Ellen in those clothes. He didn't care what the relations said. He was going to see Rose Ellen. Today was Friday. Uncle Matthew would be expecting him in time for lunch tomorrow, but tomorrow morning Uncle Matthew would get his, Peter's, letter saying not to expect him until Monday.

He began to arrange his plans very carefully. Tomorrow he would go and see Rose Ellen. If she was quite well and happy, he would go on to Uncle Matthew's in the evening and explain that, after all, it was better for him to get there before Sunday. If Rose Ellen was unhappy—Peter stood quite still and kicked a large stone several times very hard with his left foot—if Rose Ellen was unhappy, there was only one thing to be done: he would have to take her away.

He stood by the letter-box with his letter in his hand, balanced it for a moment, and shot it through the slit with a jerk. If he had to run away with Rose Ellen, the letter would give them two days' clear start.

Chapter Four

PETER STARTED on his journey at eleven o'clock next morning. Charlotte Oakley said good-bye to him in the hall with a hard, brief kiss and a smile of relief, but Ruth Spottiswoode came with him to the station. She embarrassed Peter very much by giving him a hug and several real kisses under the very eyes of his fellow-travellers. At the last minute she gave him ten shillings. Peter saw her dabbing her eyes as the train glided out of the station.

At Waterloo he collected his luggage, had it put on a taxi, and drove to Victoria. By dint of asking questions, he discovered that Parberry, the station for St. Gunburga's, was on a branch line, and that there was no direct connection with Ledlington. There was a train for Parberry in half an hour; he would have to change twice. After some thought he deposited his boxes in the left-luggage office. There was a tin play-box and a worn leather trunk. At the last moment he opened the trunk, rummaged in it, and brought out a white sweater and a grey woollen scarf. At the third attempt he succeeded in cramming these into his bag, which bulged horribly. He then made his way to the platform and waited for his train.

Presently he was sitting in a corner seat, watching rows of little houses slide past. He felt very much pleased with himself. The plan had worked beautifully. There had, to be sure, been one terrible moment when Ruth Spottiswoode, fluttering, had murmured:

"He is rather *young* to go all across London by himself. Don't you *think*, Charlotte, that it would be better if I saw him off at Victoria? *Wouldn't* you like me to see you off at Victoria, Peter dear?"

Charlotte Oakley said, "Nonsense!" very sharply.

Peter said, "No, Cousin Ruth," in a tone so final that the threatened danger was averted.

As the train jerked onwards he reviewed his financial position. It had been immensely strengthened by Cousin Ruth's parting gift.

Peter had his own code, an odd one, but quite unbending. The journey money which was to take him to Ledlington was in a pocket by itself. Peter had drawn on it until he reached Victoria. He would draw on it again when he returned to Victoria, but the excursion to Parberry and all expenses incidental thereto were his own private affair, and must be paid for out of his own private money.

Miles Banham had given him a sovereign three months ago. Just how much resolution and self-denial it had taken to preserve that sovereign intact throughout the term, only Peter knew. He regretted that he had not been able to save any of his pocket-money to speak of. His assets, therefore, were one sovereign, one half-sovereign, a sixpence, a threepenny bit which he had forgotten to put into the plate on Sunday, and fourpence halfpenny in coppers. Peter segregated the entire amount in his safest pocket, and felt pleasantly affluent.

An hour later he alighted at Parberry station, where he purchased with his sixpence three ham sandwiches, all very dry, and with his threepenny bit of cup of strong and boiling tea. He felt annoyed about the tea; ginger-beer would have been nicer.

He gave up his ticket, left the station, and, wandering into a small and very dirty sweet-shop, inquired the way to St. Gunburga's. He also bought a pennyworth of acid drops—Rose Ellen liked acid drops.

He learnt that St. Gunburga's lay a mile out of Parberry.

"You can't miss it," said the sweet-shop woman. "'Orrid, great staring barrack of a place. Looks as if they scrubbed it hall over hevery day. Perreps they do," she added, patting a large flat fringe. She was a short, bulging young woman with an odd black eye, the sort that always seems to be looking round a corner at something which nobody else can see. Peter didn't like her very much, but he was out for information.

"Is it a nice place?" he asked, spinning his penny on the counter.

The woman sniffed.

"I don't 'old with hinstitutions myself," she said.

"Why?" asked Peter.

"None of your imperence."

A young man had come into the shop, and her manner to Peter suddenly became very short.

Peter emerged into the street, asked his way once or twice again, and presently found himself on a road that ran steadily uphill. At first there were houses on either side. They began as villas, and ended as straggly cottages with daffodils coming up between gooseberry and currant bushes in the front gardens. Peter noticed that the cottages seemed to have more flowers than the villas; he wondered why.

When he came to St. Gunburga's he agreed with the woman in the shop. You couldn't miss it, you couldn't possibly miss it. It was very large, very square, and it had a great many windows. None of the windows had any curtains, which gave them a hard staring look. The walls were built of the bright, yellowish red brick which always looks as if it had just been scraped. There was not the least scrap of ivy, or moss, or any growing thing upon the brick. The house was surrounded by about an acre of asphalt, and the acre of asphalt was bounded by a high, grey stone wall with plenty of broken glass on the top of it. In the middle of the wall facing the road there was a tall gate of wrought iron, with the words "St. Gunburga's" across the top of it in hard, gilt letters. There was no grass. There were no flowers. There were no trees.

Peter had a practical soul. He hated St. Gunburga's with a deep, cold hatred, but he did not waste any time in thinking about it. He walked on up the road, and presently climbed a fence, cut back across a field, and began to skirt the grey stone wall which lay between him and Rose Ellen.

St. Gunburga's had been planted on an upland slope amongst fields. They were perfectly good fields, with the normal amount of grass and hedgerows with ivy and docks and celandine growing in them. There were a few elm trees, quite green; willows with withered catkins; and some very prickly hawthorns, well on in leaf.

Peter made his way to the end of the wall. He could hear voices on the other side of it. He turned the corner and stood still, listening.

The wall rose on his right to a height of between seven and eight feet. On his left was a ditch, and beyond the ditch a hedgerow with a few trees standing up above it. Between the ditch and the wall there was a sort of alleyway, nine or ten feet across, where the grass grew rank.

Peter looked at the wall and then at the trees. The farther ones were scraggy wrecks pollarded almost out of recognition, but the one nearest to the corner of the wall was still recognizable as an elm. It ran up to a good height, the trunk densely wreathed with ivy. Some branches stretched backwards over a field beyond the hedgerow, but all the boughs on the side towards St. Gunburga's had been lopped. Some of them lay overgrown with moss in the alleyway and the ditch. Great pendant masses of ivy covered the shortened stumps which remained upon the tree.

Peter climbed over the hedge, got to the farther side of the trunk, and swarmed up it. About twelve feet up he worked his way round the trunk, and found the end of a branch upon which he could sit astride. The ivy from another branch immediately overhead hung down between him and St. Gunburga's like a curtain. He worked himself a little farther along, parted the ivy, and looked over on to the asphalt playground.

Some of the girls were playing tag, some of them walking about, some standing in groups. Two of the staff were walking up and down at the far end.

All the girls were dressed alike. They wore frocks of brown serge, made with straight, tight bodices, and full, bunchy skirts which came down to their ankles. They had grey lisle stockings, and clumping black shoes. On their heads they wore small sailor hats with a dull purple ribbon which had the words "St. Gunburga's" upon it in black letters.

The whole stretch of the playground lay between Peter and the building. The wall over which he looked ran parallel to the wall which bounded the high road.

Peter held the ivy apart, and searched the dreary waste of asphalt for Rose Ellen. She was not one of those playing tag. His eyes searched the groups without finding her. He saw her at last, standing close to the wall, on his side of the ground, it is true, but some fifty yards away.

She stood close to the wall, and at first he was not sure that it was she, for her head was turned away. Then she moved and began to walk slowly in his direction.

Peter's heart gave a leap. It was like a miracle. He had to see her, and she came. He did not know that every day Rose Ellen walked down the ground keeping close to the wall, with her eyes on the asphalt, until she came to a certain place. Every day she stood still when she got to this place, and looked up. She did this because she was playing that she was in a garden, and when she looked up she knew that she would see the trees that grew in the hedge beyond the wall. From her special place she could see how the new buds were coming on.

The other girls teased her about it. They did not call her Rose Ellen, but just Ellen. They had decided that Ellen was "a little bit off it". Some of them called her "Moony Loony". But Rose Ellen continued to walk daily to the bottom of the playground and to stare at the budding trees.

Peter watched her coming. She walked slowly, and as if she were tired. Her head was bent. When she looked up, and Peter saw her face, he knew straight away all the things which he had come here to find out. He knew at once that he would have to take Rose Ellen away. She was thin, and her pretty colour was gone. There were big black marks under her eyes like smudges. She looked like a doll that had been left out in the rain, but there was something more than that, something which made Peter feel as he had never felt in all his life before, something which he never forgot. It was the patient look in Rose Ellen's eyes as she lifted them to look at the trees. Peter often wished that he could forget it; but he never could.

Peter's feelings always translated themselves into action with the smallest possible delay. He took an acid drop out of his pocket and threw it deftly at Rose Ellen. It just grazed her cheek, and she put up a hand, touched the place, and then went on looking up with the same steady, unseeing gaze. Peter threw another acid drop. It hit her on the nose, and this time Rose Ellen looked down, stooped, picked up the sweet, and stood there staring at it.

Peter made a speaking-tube of his hands.

"Rose Ellen!" he said.

Rose Ellen tilted her head and looked straight up into the sky.

"Rose Ellen!"

She looked all round in a bewildered fashion. Peter stuck his head out through the ivy.

"Rose Ellen!" he said a little louder.

And then she saw him. Just for a moment every vestige of colour drained out of her little face. Then her hands went up under her chin, tightly clasped together. The colour came back with a rush, making her look like the old Rose Ellen, and she said in a little whispering voice with a deep sigh in it:

"Oh, Peter de—ah."

Peter could hardly hear the words, but he knew very well what they were. He nodded at Rose Ellen, and said in a terrific stage whisper:

"I've come to fetch you away."

Rose Ellen sighed again. She shook her head slowly.

"You can't," she said.

"Why?" said Peter.

Rose Ellen didn't know why. She only knew that dreadful, cold finality of unhappiness which paralyses hope and effort. She shook her head again. Peter frowned horribly at her.

"I'll get you away tonight," he said. "You've got to do what I tell you. Do you hear? You've got to do exactly what I tell you. You've got to get into the playground as soon as it's dark, and come down to this corner. I'll do the rest."

Peter's words were large, and his tone assured. He had, as a matter of fact, not the slightest idea of how he was going to get Rose Ellen over the wall. He only knew that he was going to get her over it. Rose Ellen shook her head once more.

"I can't," she said.

"If Peter had been upon solid earth he would have stamped his foot. As it was, he could only produce a murkier frown and a more aggressive whisper:

"You've got to! I shall be here. I shall be here all night until you come. You've *got* to come! Then I shall take you away, and you'll be ever so jolly."

He had time and only just time, to finish what he had to say. A bell began to ring with loud, clanging strokes.

Rose Ellen turned and ran back along the way by which she had come. The playground emptied. The bell stopped ringing.

Chapter Five

PETER CLIMBED DOWN into the field behind the hedgerow. He had no watch, but he guessed that it must be getting on for three o'clock. The sun would set at about half past six. It would be at least twenty minutes later before it would be safe for him to get Rose Ellen over the wall—no, twenty minutes wasn't enough. He looked at the sky. The day had been grey, and here on the upland the clouds hung low. There were more clouds, blacker ones, away on the horizon; that would help. It might be dark enough at seven. He would just have to wait and see.

He hoped Rose Ellen would not do anything stupid. That was the worst of girls, you never knew where you were with them dreadfully clever one minute, and simply too stupid for words the next.

He had four hours. He began to tick off on his fingers what he had to do. First—plans:

1. A plan to get over the wall himself.
2. A plan to get Rose Ellen over the wall.
3. A plan to get them both away from Parberry.
4. A plan of what to do with Rose Ellen when they had both got away.

Peter concentrated on the first plan. He climbed the hedgerow, and went and measured himself against the wall. He was five foot three and three-quarters, and the wall appeared to be eight feet high, leaving a balance of two feet eight and a quarter inches in favour of the wall. This required thought.

Peter backed away from the wall, frowned at it ferociously, and thought. Then he descended into the ditch at the foot of the hedgerow, and began to tug at the lopped boughs which lay half in, half out of it. Some were too heavy for him to move, others rotten and slimy; but after a while he pulled one or two quite useful ones clear of the rest. They were good, stout limbs with some side branches and knobby excrescences. Peter laid them handy, and considered that plans one and two were in good train. There was nothing more for him to do here until it began to get dusk. He therefore cut back across the fields, reached the high road, and walked down the hill into Parberry.

Rose Ellen sat on a hard wooden form, and sewed on a long, hard seam. The large classroom with its bare windows and stone floor was cold. Rose Ellen's hands were cold. If she lifted her head from her work she could see more forms and desks, rows and rows of them, stretching away in front of her, with a teacher's desk like a sort of watch-tower at the far end.

Miss Jones was the teacher. She was the sort of person who sees everything. She could see in an instant if you stopped sewing, or dropped you thimble, or knotted your thread. Then she would rap on the desk with a ruler and say, very loud and high, "Ellen Smith, attention!" Or it might be, "Gladys Clark!" or "Violet Brown!" But it was very often "Ellen Smith!"

Ellen Smith was Rose Ellen. She didn't know why she was Ellen Smith, and she hated being Ellen Smith; but that was the way it was. She went on sewing, with little cold fingers that made a great many mistakes. She always did make mistakes, but today she made more than usual because she was thinking about Peter. Every time she thought about him, something inside her said, "Oh, Peter de—ah," and a crying feeling came into her throat and eyes. She did not cry, because Ellen Smith had learnt not to cry. It seemed a long, long time since Peter had talked to her over the wall. Really it was only about three hours, but it seemed a long time. They had had afternoon lessons and tea, and now the sewing-class was nearly over. Some of the girls had finished already and were putting their work away in the desks which stood between the forms. Miss Jones had come down from her watchtower and was walking down the line, looking at the work before it was put away. She came to Rose Ellen and made a clicking sound with her tongue.

Rose Ellen stood up, her legs shaking a little, and saw Miss Jones mark her work in two places with a blue chalk cross.

"Carelessness and inattention," said Miss Jones. "You will stay behind and do this piece again." She passed on.

Rose Ellen took her seam and began to unpick it. All the piece between the blue crosses had to be unpicked and done again. It was heavy, unbleached stuff, very cold to handle.

The other girls got up and went out. Miss Jones returned to her watch-tower and sounded a bell. A monitress came in and lit the gas; then she, too, went out and shut the door.

There was half an hour allowed for recreation before bedtime. Rose Ellen very often missed it. She would miss it tonight. Every now and then she looked up at the darkening windows. Peter would be waiting out there. He had said that he would wait there all night. Rose Ellen thought and thought, and could see no possible way in which she could obey Peter and get out into the playground that night. It was just one of those things which could not be done. On the other hand, Peter said, "Do it!" When Peter said to do a thing, Rose Ellen always did it.

She went on sewing. Miss Jones had taken a novel out of her desk and was reading it. The classroom door opened so suddenly that she had not time to close the book before Ethel Dawkins, the monitress, came up to her, rather breathless.

"Please, Miss Jones, Miss Featherstone wants to speak to you immediate."

Miss Jones got up in a flurry. Miss Featherstone was the Principal, and no one ever kept her waiting.

"Put your work away, Ellen Smith," she said. "Put out the gas and lock up the classroom when she's finished, Ethel. The keys are on my desk." She spoke the last word at the door, and was gone.

Rose Ellen got up gratefully and stretched herself. Then she looked round with some apprehension. Ethel Dawkins was a bully, and Rose Ellen was afraid of her. To her surprise she was alone in the classroom. Ethel had followed Miss Jones down the passage.

Rose Ellen put her work into her desk, and walked up to the top of the room. It was nice to walk after sitting still for so long. She looked idly at the teacher's desk. And then the great idea came to her.

Miss Jones' novel still lay on the desk. The keys were lying there too; Ethel had not taken them with her. There were two keys on a big ring. One of them locked the door of the classroom and the inner door that led from the classroom to the cloakrooms beyond; and the other, the bigger key, locked the door which led from the cloakroom passage into the playground.

Rose Ellen took the keys. She was dreadfully, dreadfully frightened, because at any moment Ethel might come back. Peter had said, "Come!" and she always did what Peter said. She took the keys in a very cold hand that trembled, and ran to the cloakroom door. It was locked. She unlocked it, and passed into the dark passage beyond.

Rose Ellen was frightened of the dark. She ran down the passage, past the black cloakrooms which opened upon it, and came to the outer door. She unlocked it. Then she ran back again. If she could put the keys back on Miss Jones' desk, nobody would dream that she had gone outside. Ethel would only think that she had followed her along the passage.

She reached the desk, put down the keys, and then remained rooted to the ground with terror. Her hands clasped each other very tightly, her legs shook. Ethel was coming back, running! She came in rather flushed.

"Oh, lor', Moony Loony, what a time you've been!" she said. "It 'ud serve you right if I left you 'ere a bit longer. P'r'aps you'd 'urry up and get finished with your betters another time if I did."

She crossed to the desk, picked up the keys, and put out the nearest gas-light. A second light burned farther down the room over the place where Rose Ellen had been sitting. Ethel moved towards this, talking all the time and jangling the keys

"I've 'arf a mind to lock you in in the dark," she said. "'Ow'd you like that, Miss Loony Whiteface, eh?"

She turned, with the chain that controlled the gas-light in her hand, and fixed malicious eyes on Rose Ellen's rigid figure.

"Sulky, are you?" she said. "You just answer when your betters speak to you, or I'll put it across you, my lady. Wot, you won't? Obstinate, are you? All right, stay 'ere in the dark, and think it over!"

She gave the chain a vicious jerk as she spoke, and then made a dash with a view to intercepting any similar move on Rose Ellen's part. With her hand on the door, she spoke again.

"You 'aven't been a-learnin' of your catechism," she said. "Order meself lowly and reverently to all me betters—that's your motter, Loony, and don't you go fergettin' it again. You can say it over to yerself in the dark for a bit."

She slammed the door, only to open it again and say in sepulchral tones:

"Don't you ferget as this is the 'aunted classroom."

Then she shut the door again, and waited about a yard away from it, ready, if Rose Ellen cried out, to rush in and silence her, or, if one of the staff approached, to open the door quickly and appear to be ushering Rose Ellen out.

Rose Ellen stood in the pitch dark, the dark which she hated and feared. She kept on saying, "De—ah Peter. Oh, Peter de—ah," to herself. And when she heard Ethel move away from the door she made a most desperate effort and ran on tiptoe to that other door, the inner one which led to the cloakroom passage.

If you have to do things, you can do them. Peter always said that. Rose Ellen knew that she must go down the cloakroom passage. It didn't matter if she was afraid, she had to do it. It had been bad enough when she went to unlock the outer door, but then the light from the classroom had followed her, and now there was not one scrap of light anywhere.

She went very slowly, touching the wall. Three cloakrooms opened into the passage. She thought of them as black caves, empty and cold. She dared not run lest Something should come out of one of those empty places and catch her. She came to the outer door. Her little hands shook so much that she could scarcely open it. She had to strain and tug. Then it swung inwards, and she slipped through the opening and shut it behind her. The passage had been quite dark, black dark, but the playground was a grey dusk full of shadows: you couldn't see anything, but it was only grey, not black.

Rose Ellen crept towards the left-hand wall. She wanted to get close to something that she could touch. The curtainless windows of

St. Gunburga's stared at her. She reached the wall and leaned against it. All the windows were watching her. She could hear a rustling sound in the trees beyond the wall. She must go to Peter; she just had to. She went. It was at this moment that Ethel Dawkins opened the door of the classroom and, in a piercing whisper, called Rose Ellen's name. As there was no reply, she bounced into the room and struck a match. The empty room frightened her, but when the full gas-light failed to disclose Ellen Smith in a dead faint on the floor, she convinced herself that the dratted little Loony must have given her the slip either at the moment of her opening the door, or when she was putting out the lights. She put them out again now, grumbling to herself, locked up the classroom, and, meeting Miss Jones in the hall, handed her the keys. Subsequently she deposed with great fluency to having seen Ellen go upstairs.

Peter was waiting upon the top of the wall. He had spread a sweater over the broken glass, but the seat could not be described as a comfortable one. He hoped Rose Ellen would not be very long. When he heard her little, hesitating footsteps, he felt a certain glow of pride. He had told her to come and she came.

He said, "Hullo!" and heard her answer with a piteous catch of the breath:

"Peter?"

Peter had reached the top of the wall by dint of using a strong bough with cross-branches as a ladder.

He now hauled and tugged at this bough, got it on to the top of the wall and lowered it, butt-end first, until it rested in the angle formed by the corner. Next moment he had scrambled down into the playground, landing with a thud that drew a little gasp from Rose Ellen.

She did not speak when he got up, but clutched him very tight and trembled. Peter gave her a hug, told her she was a brick, and came at once to business.

"Now, Rose Ellen, I'm going to put you up on the top of the wall. You must climb on my back. I'll kneel down, and you must stand on my shoulders. Catch hold of this branch—feel, it's quite firm—and steady yourself whilst I get up. It won't be difficult, and you're not to be a little mug and get frightened. There's my coat and a sweater on the top of the wall, so you won't get cut. Now, come on!"

He got down on his knees, grasping the butt-end of the branch, and Rose Ellen climbed easily to a standing position on his shoulders. Then came the ticklish part of the job. Peter said, "Are you ready?" and began to get on to his feet, bearing down upon the branch and leaning forward so as to keep Rose Ellen well in the angle. There was one dizzy moment when he felt her swing backwards, but she caught at the wall and got her balance again. Now that Peter was standing, Rose Ellen could hold on to the coping, and her head was clear of the wall. Peter put his hands up.

"I'm going to push you on to the top of the wall with my hands under your feet. Right foot first. Feel for my hand and hold on all you can."

Rose Ellen had stopped shaking. She did exactly as she was told. She was light, and Peter was strong. Lifting and straining, he pushed her up high enough to get her knee on to the place where his coat covered the glass. The rest was easy.

Peter swarmed up the branch, dropped it down on the other side, lowered Rose Ellen, and followed her, bringing his coat with him. He had two surface cuts, and was very much out of breath; but the thing was done. He picked up the sweater from the grass where it had dropped with Rose Ellen, and entered upon the next stage of the proceedings.

"Take off that dress," he said, and Rose Ellen obeyed. "Now put this on."

He handed her the sweater.

"Am I going to be a boy?"

"I expect so."

"But my petticoat shows, Peter de—ah."

Peter felt in the dusk. The petticoat, of the same old-fashioned make as the discarded dress, stood out below the sweater in a deep, stiff frill.

Peter was in a dilemma. If she took the petticoat off, Rose Ellen would be cold. If she kept it on, she would certainly attract attention. It was at this moment that the rhyme of "The Little Old Woman" came to his assistance—the little old woman who went to sleep upon the King's highway, and

By there came a pedlar whose name was Stout,
He cut her petticoats all round about,
He cut her petticoats up to her knees ...

Peter extracted a clasp-knife from his pocket and began to cut Rose Ellen's petticoats all round about, only he went one better than the pedlar, and took them off, not up to her knees, but a good two inches above them. Then he groped in the grass, until he found a heavy fish-basket. He had purchased it in Parberry for threepence, and it contained a German sausage, a loaf of bread, half a pound of cheese, eight penny buns, six bananas, and two oranges. On the top of the bananas and oranges there was a cheap serge cap and a pair of dark-blue shorts.

Peter assisted Rose Ellen to stuff the remains of her petticoats into the shorts, and put the cap firmly on her head. They had cut her hair very short, but it still curled. The cap fitted very well. Peter then rolled the cut-off pieces of petticoat inside the coarse woollen dress, pushed the bundle well down between the ivy and the trunk of the nearest tree, put on his coat, picked up the fish-basket and his own handbag, and led the way back to the road.

Chapter Six

ROSE ELLEN followed him like a little dog. Peter's sweater felt warm and light. Every now and then she patted the new shorts approvingly. It was frightfully nice to be a boy. She came out on to the high road with the feeling of having come home. It was home because Peter was there, and because she was Rose Ellen again. She caught Peter up and nuzzled her head against his arm.

"Augustabel—" she said.

"What about Augustabel?"

"Oh, Peter de—ah, she's in a apple tree."

"Why on earth—"

"Because of not being allowed to take her *there*." Rose Ellen nodded mournfully in the direction of St. Gunburga's.

"Where is she?"

"In a apple tree—in a garden—belonging to a cottage."

"Where?" said Peter again.

"It's the third cottage," said Rose Ellen. "I always look at the tree when we go to church on Sunday."

"How did she get there?"

"I was in the cottage, waiting to go—there." Again the nod indicated St. Gunburga's. "There was a woman there and she was nice. She said she would like to keep me, and then I could have Augustabel, but she had a husband, and he said no. I don't like husbands very much, Peter de—ah."

"How did Augustabel get in the tree?"

"There's a hole. I put her in when no one wasn't looking. You'll get her out, won't you, Peter?"

Peter said he would. He hoped it wouldn't take very long, for at any moment there might be a hue and cry after Rose Ellen. It never entered his head, however, that they should abandon Augustabel. He knew Rose Ellen too well.

They stopped outside the wall of the cottage garden, and Peter climbed it, directed in breathless whispers by Rose Ellen, who remained in the road. The tree was the nearest tree but two; and it had a waggly branch that you could play see-saw on; and last year there was a nest in it; and the hole was a little way up, just about as high as Rose Ellen's shoulder; and would Peter mind telling Augustabel that it was only him, because she might think it was a robber and be most dreadfully frightened.

Peter kept saying "S-s-h" at intervals, but he found the tree and the hole, fished out Augustabel, and rejoined Rose Ellen without much difficulty. They walked on in silence. Rose Ellen had no words; her heart was much too full. She clasped a damp and draggled Augustabel tight, tight in her arms, and trotted beside Peter in a state of fervent happiness.

Peter had used his afternoon to some advantage. He did not take her through Parberry, but struck off to the left amongst the first scattered houses, coming at last by devious ways to the fence which guarded the railway embankment. They climbed over this, and proceeded along the bank until they came to the shunting-yard. Peter seemed to know his way. He dropped down upon the track, passing several vans, and finally came to a standstill beside a truck which was covered with a tarpaulin.

Earlier in the afternoon he had hung about the yard and asked a number of intelligent questions. The truck contained sacks of grain, and it would be attached to the goods train which left Parberry at ten-fifteen.

He loosened the tarpaulin and lifted Rose Ellen up. The sacks were standing in rows, and between the rows were valley-like depressions, not deep, but deep enough for Rose Ellen to lie full length in one, and Peter in another. The tarpaulin covered them. Peter stood his bag on end on the top of one of the sacks; this lifted the tarpaulin and let in some air. They lay in the dark, and ate German sausage and bananas.

Later on Rose Ellen's hand came feeling softly between the sacks until it touched Peter's shoulder.

"Peter de—ah," said a very small voice.

"S-s-h, you mustn't talk!" said Peter.

"I won't, if you hold my hand just for a little, Peter de—ah."

"All right," said Peter, in a gruff whisper.

He held the hand that first clung to his and presently relaxed; it was a very little hand. By and by they were both asleep.

It was many hours before Peter woke. He was one of those people who come broad awake at once. One minute he was sailing the Caribbean Sea in a pirate ship, and the next instant there he was, very stiff, lying between sacks of grain with a tarpaulin over his head, and realizing that what had waked him was a sharp jerk which meant that their truck was being shunted. The shunting went on for some time, and then ceased.

After listening for a while Peter very cautiously raised the tarpaulin at the end of the truck and looked out. It was light, but not very light. The sun had not risen. Everything looked odd and grey. There were trucks, and railway lines, and a fence. Peter slipped to the ground, extracted his bag and the fish-basket, and woke Rose Ellen.

It was getting lighter every minute. This was quite a strange place, flat and green, not a bit like Parberry. The name of the station was Hastney Mere. They left it behind them and took the road. The sun was rising as they crossed a little bridge and came to a path that led through water-meadows golden with kingcups. The sky looked very new and clean. They sat by the side of the path and ate bread and cheese and oranges. Then they walked on again.

"Where are we going?" said Rose Ellen.

Peter frowned at the sunrise. He had really no idea, but he wasn't going to tell Rose Ellen that. He said:

"You'll see," and then added grandly, "I'm going to find a home for you."

Rose Ellen repeated the information to Augustabel in a whisper. Presently she said:

"Peter de—ah."

Peter turned on her.

"Rose Ellen, you're saying Petah. You've been saying it every time."

"I haven't, Petah."

"You have. You're doing it now."

She nuzzled her head against him.

"I like doing it, Petah."

"You're a little mug, Rose Ellen. What is it?"

"I wanted to know—"

"What did you want to know?"

Rose Ellen stood quite still, and fixed serious brown eyes upon Peter's face. There was already a little more colour in her cheeks.

"I wanted to know what is my name."

"Rose Ellen Waring," said Peter stoutly. "What else should it be?"

Rose Ellen put a finger in her mouth. Her eyes were wet and round.

"They said it wasn't—they said it was Ellen Smiff—they said it wasn't never Waring at all—they said I wasn't your sister, Peter."

"What does it matter what they say? No, you're not to cry. Your name is Rose Ellen Waring. Have you got that?"

Rose Ellen nodded. They began to walk again.

"I didn't like Ellen Smiff. I hated Ellen Smiff."

"You're a first-class little mug," said Peter cheerfully.

"I don't want my name to be Smiff," said Rose Ellen. "Ethel Dawkins said it would have to be Smiff f'r ever and ever unless I got married, and she said nobody wouldn't ever want to marry me," She ended with a piteous little sniff, and Peter's heart was melted within him.

"I'll marry you," he declared in a spirit of true self-sacrifice. "That is, I'll marry you if you buck up and don't cry."

Rose Ellen winked very hard and turned her adoring gaze upon Peter.

"And then," she said, "would my name be really Waring? Truly, and really, and f'r ever and ever?"

"Of course it would."

The path wound among the water-meadows, and presently, finding a little valley, climbed with it to a wood where beeches spread their leafless branches over drifts of last year's leaves.

Rose Ellen had begun to flag. It came home to Peter that they could not go much farther.

"Are you tired?" he said.

Rose Ellen walked a little faster. She said, "No!" rather quickly, and then added in a very small voice, "Augustabel is a little bit tired."

"All right," said Peter, "so am I."

They struck off to the left and found a hollow full of dry leaves. A few very long-stalked primroses grew here and there. Rose Ellen sat down by a clump of primroses and rocked Augustabel. Every now and then she just touched one of the flowers with the tips of her fingers.

They spent the greater part of the day in the wood. The sun shone, and the air was mild. Not a soul came near them. Rose Ellen was very happy.

Chapter Seven

IT WAS MIDDAY on Monday when Mrs. Spottiswoode received a wire from Matthew Waring:

Little girl disappeared from orphanage. Is Peter with you? Please wire at once.

She was too much upset to do anything at once except sob, and gasp, and dab her eyes, and say over and over again: "I knew he was too young to travel alone. I told you so, and you wouldn't listen to me, Charlotte."

It was Charlotte who wrote the answer:

Peter left here Saturday morning to go to you.

By Monday evening a description of Peter and Rose Ellen had been telegraphed to police stations all over the country, and Matthew Waring's temper was hourly becoming worse.

Peter and Rose Ellen had spent the night in the beech wood to which they had returned after a pleasant afternoon excursion, in the course of which Peter obtained milk in a bottle and some hard-boiled eggs from a farm; he explained quite truthfully that he was camping out.

The night was fine and warm. Peter heaped beech leaves over them both, and they slept like birds in a nest. But the morning dawned red.

"Where are we going?" said Rose Ellen when they had breakfasted.

Peter didn't know; that was the trouble—he didn't know at all. He led the way back to the path, and they followed it until it came out upon a heathery upland covered with sheep tracks. It was a wide place, and empty. They walked on and saw no house.

They sat down amongst the heather, ate their midday meal, and afterwards Rose Ellen fell asleep, curled up like a kitten, with Augustabel in her arms. Peter did not mean to sleep, but a drowsiness came over him. When at last he woke the sunshine was gone. He waked Rose Ellen, and they took the road again. The sky was all clouds, and a small, cold wind blew across their path. The way seemed very long.

"Are you cold, Rose Ellen?" said Peter.

Rose Ellen shivered, and shook her head.

"Honest injun?"

Rose Ellen hesitated, and looked away.

"Augustabel is just a teeny bit cold," she said.

Peter put his coat on her. The wind grew colder. He looked about and found a hollow, where they rested for a while. The sky began to darken and the clouds to hang down. There was not a house in sight.

Peter put down his bag and the now empty basket and walked a little way. About a quarter of a mile farther on the ground began to slope downwards. He could see trees in the distance.

Peter stood still and looked at the trees. There was a dreadful heaviness upon him. He had brought Rose Ellen here, and he must find shelter for her. The wind promised a stormy night, and Rose Ellen was too little to be out all night in the rain. Peter stood there, frowning dreadfully; and, still frowning, he put up the first real prayer that he had ever prayed.

"I don't know what to do," he said. "I don't know where there's a place for Rose Ellen. I expect You know. I expect You are bound to know. There must be a place for her, and a proper home, not an institution one like that beastly St. Gunburga's, because she's too little not to have a proper home and someone to take care of her. And please let us find it quickly, because it's going to rain like anything, and Rose Ellen isn't old enough to be out all night in the ram, she really isn't."

Peter concluded this very unorthodox prayer in the orthodox manner, and went back to Rose Ellen. He found her shivering in spite of his coat. They went on, following the downward slope and making for the trees. Long before they reached them, rain had begun to fall in torrents, soaking them to the skin. Rose Ellen walked more and more slowly. Then, with the coming of darkness, the rain ceased and the wind drove a track through the clouds, leaving a clear space from which a cold, white moon looked out.

They came through the trees, black trees dripping mournfully, and found themselves on the edge of a metalled road. A few hundred yards down this road a village church stood, ivy-covered. The ivy dripped too. The road took a sharp turn just here and ran between high stone walls.

Peter's spirits rose. A church was no good; churches were always shut. But opposite the church, behind the other wall, was a house, and it seemed inconceivable to him that any house should not mean at least temporary shelter for Rose Ellen. As the thought went through his mind, a door in the right-hand wall opened suddenly, and a maid-servant came running out. She had a cloak over her head, and she seemed to be in a hurry. Peter heard a man whistle a few yards down the road. The girl ran to meet him.

Without an instant's hesitation Peter took Rose Ellen by the hand and went through the door in the wall. They found themselves in a funny, narrow alleyway with flagstones underfoot and very high brick walls on either hand; it was almost like a tunnel. At the far end of it light streamed from an open door—light and warmth. Peter looked in, and saw a large scullery opening into the kitchen beyond. He knocked and waited. Rose Ellen pressed against him, trembling with cold. No one came. He knocked again. And then Rose Ellen did a surprising thing. Quite suddenly she pulled her hand out of Peter's and ran into the house. Peter followed.

The kitchen was empty. Peter looked longingly at the generous fire, but Rose Ellen had already run out into the passage beyond. There was nobody in the passage, but a sound of voices and cheerful laughter came from a room on their left.

Rose Ellen ran along the passage until she came to the back stairs. She was on the tenth step when Peter's whisper reached her, "Rose Ellen, come down!" but Rose Ellen never turned her head. Peter caught her up as she opened the door which led on to the first-floor landing. Her little, drenched feet had left wet marks on every step.

"Come back, Rose Ellen!" said Peter.

Rose Ellen shook her head.

"Augustabel won't go back," she said. "Augustabel likes this house. Oh, Peter de—ah, she likes it very much indeed."

The landing had a soft, rich carpet on the floor. The light was soft and rich. A long corridor stretched in front of them, with a shaded light burning at the far end. On their right there was another passage, unlighted except by the moon which shone in through live long windows. The windows had arched tops like church windows. The moonlight lay in five broad bars upon the polished floor.

"Come back, Rose Ellen! You must!" said Peter, in a dreadfully piercing whisper; but Rose Ellen only shook her head again, and darted down the moonlit passage.

Opposite the windows there were doors. One door was a little open. Peter stopped to look in, but the room was dark. As he stopped, he put out his hand and touched something hot. A large radiator filled the space between this door and the next. Peter's heart leapt for joy. They could hide in one of the rooms and dry all their clothes! It was really a surprising bit of luck.

Meanwhile Rose Ellen had opened the door at the end of the corridor and come, still running, into a large room which was quite light because the moon shone straight in through two tall windows. Peter followed, and Rose Ellen clutched at him.

"Oh, Peter, Peter de—ah," she said, "Oh, Augustabel *does* like this house, she *does*."

The room was a nursery. There were bars to the tall windows, and a high wire guard about the empty fireplace. The mild head of a rocking-horse looked out of one corner at them. There was cork carpeting on the floor. There were soft woolly rugs.

"Take off your wet things, Rose Ellen," said Peter, severely practical.

Rose Ellen sat down on a woolly mat and took off her wet shoes and stockings, the drenched serge shorts, and Peter's sweater.

"My petticoat isn't so dreadfully wet," she said.

Peter felt it, and frowned. Then he took one of the woolly mats and wrapped it round Rose Ellen and Augustabel.

"There's a hot place for these to dry. I won't be a minute," he said, and went out.

He had reached the radiator when he heard the sound. It was like someone moving softly. In an instant he had slipped through the half-open door, and stood on the threshold of the dark room, holding his breath and listening. The sound was coming nearer. Peter leaned forward very cautiously, and saw that someone was coming along the corridor, a lady in a dark, traily dress. She stood still in one of the moonlight patches. She looked very sad, very sad indeed, and sort of hungry. She was looking at the wet footmarks on the passage floor. And then, all of a sudden, a really dreadful thing happened. Rose Ellen opened the nursery door. Peter couldn't stop her; he couldn't do anything.

She opened the door and came running out, a queer, pathetic little figure with bare arms and legs, and a draggly, wet petticoat cut off above the knees.

The lady looked up at the sound of the opening door. She saw Rose Ellen in the moonlight, and, for a moment, she thought—who knows what she thought? She stood leaning against the wall, and then with a little gasping, sobbing breath she slipped into a half-sitting, half-kneeling position.

"I thought," she whispered, "I thought ..." and then, "No, no."

Rose Ellen stood and looked at her. They looked at each other. Rose Ellen's eyes began to fill with tears; they brimmed over. The lady put out both her arms, and Rose Ellen ran straight into them.

Peter came out into the passage. He was clasping Rose Ellen's wet clothes. He heard the lady say:

"You little, little thing, you're wet." And then she looked up and saw Peter, and made a sound like a very faint scream.

Rose Ellen was hugging the lady. She looked over her shoulder, and said:

"It's only Peter de—ah."

Peter told his story in Mrs. Mortimer's little grey sitting-room. It was all grey and soft, and there were bowls of violets everywhere. There was a door which led into Mrs. Mortimer's bedroom, and every now and then she got up and looked in to see if Rose Ellen, warmed, fed, and comforted, was really asleep in the small blue bed which had once belonged to another little girl.

Peter didn't make a long story of it. He sat on the hearthrug, and explained in jerky sentences that Rose Ellen wasn't really his sister; that she had no relations; that St. Gunburga's was a beastly place, and naturally he, Peter, *had* to take her away and find her a home.

Mrs. Mortimer sat with her elbow on her knee and her chin in her hand. She didn't look at Peter. She looked into the heart of the wood fire and saw pictures there. When Peter had finished she nodded and said:

"Will you give her to me, Peter?"

Peter got up.

"I don't know," he said. "May I go to bed now, please?"

Chapter Eight

ROSE ELLEN CAME dancing into the breakfast-room next morning. It was a very nice room. Two long windows opened upon a garden of lawns set with cedar trees, and of borders all golden with daffodils.

Rose Ellen had a pink colour in her cheeks. Her brown eyes shone. Her short curls had been brushed until they looked like dark gold. She wore a brown linen overall with buttercups and daisies worked on it, and in her arms she held Augustabel, rather pale from a drastic washing.

"Oh, Peter de—ah," she said, and then stopped because she saw the daffodils.

Mrs. Mortimer came into the room behind her and asked Peter if he had slept well. After that she looked at Rose Ellen all the time.

"I'm going to make clothes for Augustabel, Peter," said Rose Ellen. She nodded at Peter over her bread and milk.

Augustabel had a chair of her own and a little bowl from which she too might eat bread and milk if she chose.

"I'm going to make a velvet frock, a blue velvet frock, Peter, an' a satin frock, an' a white woolly frock. Dearest says she will help me."

Peter frowned at Mrs. Mortimer, and went on eating his breakfast. After breakfast he talked to Rose Ellen; and after he had talked to Rose Ellen, Mrs. Mortimer asked him for the second time.

"Well, Peter, will you give me Rose Ellen?" She smiled sweetly, but there was something in her eyes that made Peter feel angry. It was something that looked as if Rose Ellen was hers already, and as if she dared Peter to take her away.

They were in the little grey sitting-room. The mantelpiece had china figures on it, frail and delicately coloured. Peter picked one up and began to fidget with it. It was a shepherdess with a garland of roses and a rose-wreathed crook.

"Will you, Peter?" said Mrs. Mortimer.

Peter had turned away, but now he looked at her. There was something defiant in his look. His fingers had closed hard upon the Dresden shepherdess.

"I can look after her and make her happy," said Mrs. Mortimer. "I want her very much, Peter."

Peter nodded.

"You wouldn't let them get her again?" he said. "They mustn't get her again. She wants someone to be fond of her. I expect it's just because she's a girl and rather little for her age. They weren't fond of her at that beastly place."

"I won't let them get her back," said Mrs. Mortimer quickly. "You'll have to give me your uncle's address, Peter, and then my solicitor will arrange it all with him. There won't be any difficulty about it, but if there were, I'd run away with her like you did. Will you give her to me, Peter?"

"All right," said Peter gruffly.

The Dresden figure snapped suddenly in two. Peter let the pieces fall on the hearth. Neither he nor Mrs. Mortimer looked at them.

"Thank you, Peter," she said, and shook his rather unwilling hand.

Peter went away an hour later. He left Rose Ellen making the blue velvet dress for Augustabel.

The station was only half a mile away. He set out for it, bag in hand. He had accomplished his object; he had found a home for Rose Ellen. He must now get back to Victoria, retrieve his luggage, and join his Uncle Matthew at Ledlington, twenty-four hours later than the time he had fixed in his letter. Fortunately, he still had Miles Banham's sovereign; that would take him to Victoria, and he could then begin to use his journey money again.

Just outside the station he put down his bag in order to get the money out of his waistcoat pocket. The waistcoat pocket was empty. He felt in every pocket, but the sovereign was gone. He had twopence in coppers, and his official journey money which he could not use until he reached Victoria. Peter never thought of using it, nor did it occur to him to return and tell Mrs. Mortimer what had happened. Instead, he inquired the way to the nearest large station, and set out to walk the eight miles which lay between him and it.

As he walked he thought. He thought about the Annam Jewel. He never spoke of it, but he thought of it very often; and in his thoughts it was a living splendour. If the actual Jewel had been torn from its shrine all those years ago by covetous, blood-stained hands, the vision of the Jewel had come into a new resting-place, secret and silent. It lay in a very sacred shrine in the heart of Peter's dream. When he was twenty-five he would behold the Jewel. It would be his. It is impossible to explain what the Jewel meant to Peter. Peter never spoke of it to anyone. It was all the dreams come true; it was Romance; it was Adventure; it was Deadly Peril and Achievement.

He tramped the eight miles, and did not know the way was long, or trouble because he had a hundred miles to cover and only twopence to spend. In the land of Romance and High Adventure no road is weary.

Twenty-four hours later he reached Ledlington. He had stolen a ride on a train, only to be discovered and thrown roughly off. After a second tramp he had been more fortunate, and had reached Victoria very hungry, very dirty, and very footsore. From there all was plain sailing. His journey money now came into legitimate use, and he bought his ticket with the pride of a millionaire.

He did not ring the front door bell, but went round by the garden, and walked in at Matthew Waring's study window.

His uncle sat at the table, writing. At the sound of Peter's entry he turned, upset the ink, and uttered an odd, wordless exclamation. His eyes were hard from want of sleep.

"Good God, boy, where have you been? Where's the little girl?"

The door opened as he spoke. Emily Waring stood on the threshold. For the first time in their joint lives Matthew turned on her in a fury.

"Go away!" he said, not loudly, but with a cold anger which was more cutting.

"Go away! You've done harm enough, Emily. *Will* you go away?"

Emily went. One can be sorry for her. She did not think of herself as a hard or an unjust woman. She thought that Rose Ellen must be dead. No, she did not put it like that. She thought that something must have happened to Rose Ellen, something dreadful. Suddenly she saw herself, hard and cold, Matthew hating her, telling her to go away.

Matthew Waring turned again to Peter.

"For God's sake, boy, where's the little girl?"

"I've found a home for her," said Peter.

"You—"

"I said I'd take her away if she wasn't happy," said Peter doggedly.

"Oh, you did, did you?" said Mr, Waring, with the sudden anger of relief. "You took her away, and none of us knowing where you were, whether you were alive or dead! A pretty business, I must say, a pretty disgraceful business."

He banged on the table with his fist, and glared at Peter, who had dropped his bag and stood with his hands in his pockets, wondering why grown-up people lost their tempers so easily. It bored him frightfully. He wanted something to eat and a wash, but Uncle Matthew kept on talking at the top of his voice.

"And you think it honest, *honest* to use your journey money for such a purpose?"

Peter's hand came out of his pocket with a handful of change in it. He put the little pile of silver and coppers on the edge of the table, and glared back at Matthew Waring.

"I didn't!" he said furiously.

"You didn't what? What's this? God bless my soul, what's this?"

Peter explained, shortly, gruffly, angrily.

Matthew Waring looked at him for a moment in silence. Then he said:

"Well, well ..." And after a pause, "You say you found the little girl a home?"

Peter nodded. His hands were in his pockets again. There was another pause. Peter was so frightfully empty that he couldn't remember what it felt like not to be empty. Then Matthew Waring said suddenly:

"When did you last have something to eat?"

"I'm not sure," said Peter. "There was a banana this morning, but I don't know if you count a banana."

"Oh, go away and get some food!" said Mr. Waring loudly and explosively.

Chapter Nine

DURING THE NEXT five years Peter saw very little of Rose Ellen. Mrs. Mortimer adopted her formally, and she had no wish to encourage too much intimacy with a boy whose ultimate career in life was likely to be bounded by the walls of a country solicitor's office; Rose Ellen would be her heiress; also she was jealous of Peter's place in Rose Ellen's affections. Rose Ellen did not speak of Peter. She loved Mrs. Mortimer, and throve like a plant in a sunny place, but she never forgot. She had one of those rare natures which have no capacity for forgetting. Once in each holidays Peter came, stayed a day and a night, and was gone again. As the children began to grow up, Mrs. Mortimer regarded even this limited intercourse with disfavour. She made plans for taking Rose Ellen abroad: Switzerland at Christmas; the Riviera in spring; Norway in summer. She thought it would be quite possible to be out of Peter's reach during the holidays.

When Peter was seventeen he went to spend a fortnight of the summer holidays with the Coverdales. He met Sylvia Coverdale in Ledlington, where she was staying with an elderly cousin. He met her in very romantic circumstances which combined a bicycle accident, a car which was grossly exceeding the speed limit, a scream from Sylvia who thought her last hour had come, and a really good exhibition of presence of mind and dexterity on the part of Peter.

Sylvia was eighteen, distractingly pretty, and an arrant flirt. She told Peter he had saved her life. She said saving a person's life was a Link, wasn't it? Didn't Peter think it was a Link? Peter thought a good deal, but he didn't say very much. Sylvia rather threw him off his balance. He escorted her to the cousin's door, and went for a ten-mile walk, in the course of which he decided that he would become a millionaire as rapidly as possible, marry Sylvia, and give her the Annam Jewel on their wedding day.

Sylvia sat down and wrote a romantic and illegible account of the adventure to her father. The result (i) of the romance, and (ii) of the illegibility, was that Peter was invited to stay at Sunnings. This, perhaps, needs explanation.

The romance affected the matter because Sylvia had recently become engaged to a most undesirable and impecunious young poet of the name of Cyril Marling, and her parent, who detested poets in general, and Cyril in particular, entertained a hope that peter might distract his daughter's mind.

The illegibility had this bearing upon the situation, that Mr. Coverdale received the impression that Peter's surname was Wareham. A Waring would never have been invited to Sunnings. The name had associations too dark and dangerous, and Coverdale had grown cautious, as befitted a landed proprietor and a Justice of the Peace.

Miss Coverdale, who kept house for her brother, was frankly horrified at the idea of entertaining a schoolboy.

"My dear, think of his boots," she said to Sylvia, "and his voice! You know how sensitive your father is to noise, and nobody ever knows what a boy of that age will do next."

Sylvia kissed her aunt very prettily.

"Now, Jane Ann, don't fuss," she said. "He'll be as good as gold, and you won't have to bother with him at all. He's my property."

"Oh, my dear, I don't approve of your engagement, as you know—and indeed, Sylvia darling, I don't think you are really steady enough to be engaged to anyone—and, as you know, marriage is a terrible responsibility—and people who write poetry never seem to have any money or a settled home, or—or a stake in the county—and very often, my dear, their religious and moral principles are not at all what one would wish for in a husband. Where was I, Sylvia dear? I know I meant to say something, and I think that I haven't said it. No, I'm sure I haven't. Now what was it?"

Sylvia giggled.

"Darling, I don't know," she said.

"I know what it was. I don't approve of your engagement, as you know; but when you speak of this Mr. Waring being your property—well, what will Mr. Marling say?"

"Cyril's coming for the week-end," said Sylvia. She stuck her chin in the air and made limpid eyes at Miss Coverdale. "You can ask him when he comes."

Peter arrived next day. Miss Coverdale looked at him helplessly. He was very large, and very awkward, and he stooped. He was extraordinarily untidy even for a schoolboy. He had the largest, reddest hands, the largest, worst-shod feet, and the boniest wrists and ankles which she had ever beheld. He had the kind of thick, fair hair which stands on end and looks dusty. At first he appeared to have no conversation. When addressed he would blush crimson and mutter unintelligibly. When not addressed he would sit sprawling in a chair and fiddle with something—a book, a box, a trinket, or a bit of string.

When Sylvia kissed her aunt good night, she remarked cheerfully:

"You see, Jane Ann, he's *perfectly* quiet," to which Miss Coverdale's only response was a very deep sigh.

Peter arrived on the Saturday afternoon. On Sunday he was quiescent. On Monday he sent the cat and the cook into convulsions by the very simple expedient of tying the cat up in alternate festoons of red and white crinkled paper. The cat's name was Penelope, and she was of a highly nervous and excitable disposition. When Peter had finished with her, he roared with laughter and held her up in front of a looking-glass. Penelope uttered one piercing shriek of outraged vanity, tore a hole in Peter's cheek, and rushed like a streak of red-and-white lightning down the stairs, through the hall, and into the kitchen. There was a large piece of raw turbot lying on the kitchen table. Penelope sprang upon the turbot and began to dance up and down, clawing pieces out of the fish and emitting satanic screams. The cook was bending over the fire. When she turned round to see what was happening, Penelope sprang right at her face.

"Such a valuable cook," said Miss Coverdale tearfully. "Such a quiet cat, and a most excellent mouser. And, Sylvia darling, if your father hadn't gone away this morning, where on earth should we have got any fish for dinner?"

"As a matter of fact, I don't know where we shall get it now," said Sylvia.

"We shan't," said Miss Coverdale simply. "But of course it doesn't matter about us. Do you know, darling, that I feel it is quite a providence that your dear father should be called away on business at this juncture."

They talked to Peter next day after the cook had given notice. Sylvia talked to him, and Miss Coverdale talked to him. Peter stood with his back to the fireplace and blushed. He also shuffled continuously from one foot to another and fiddled with a bit of string.

About half-way through the proceedings Sylvia stamped her foot and snatched the string. Peter made not the slightest attempt to retain it, but immediately produced another piece from his waistcoat pocket and began to fiddle with that. Sylvia got up and ran out of the room, banging the door behind her.

Romance, it will be seen, was rather under a cloud.

On Tuesday Peter took the hall clock to pieces. He said he had noticed that it gained three minutes every day, so he concluded that it required regulating. He said he had often taken clocks to pieces. The trouble was that, owing to some peculiarity of this particular clock, it remained in pieces. Peter's efforts to put it together again being quite unsuccessful. Miss Coverdale became terribly agitated, but Sylvia, still on the cold side of Romance, contented herself with observing that the nearest reliable watchmaker lived five miles away. Peter immediately swept the fragments of the clock into a very dirty cotton bandanna, and vanished from the scene. He was away about four hours, returning very late for dinner. The clock was going. He explained that he had put it together himself. Wilkins, it appeared, was a jolly good sort. Wilkins had given him some jolly good tips, but he had put the clock together himself.

On Wednesday Peter was discovered taking pot shots at Sylvia's pet robin with an air-gun. The robin sat on the topmost branch of a tree, and regarded Peter with a good deal of interest. Sylvia behaved rather like Penelope. She rushed at Peter, snatched away the gun, and boxed his ears.

On Thursday Cyril Marling arrived. He was a slim young man with a long nose and a high brow. His other features were negligible. He wore his hair about twelve inches long and brushed smoothly back from the brow to the nape of the neck.

"I thought he was coming for the week-end," said Miss Coverdale fretfully.

"Well, darling, so he is," said Sylvia.

"Your father won't like it."

"My father isn't here, Jane Ann. Do stop fussing."

Peter did not like it either. He loathed Cyril Marling at sight, and after Cyril and Sylvia had spent nearly the whole of Friday together on the river, he loathed Cyril a good deal more.

"What on earth were you doing all day?" he said gloomily to Sylvia after dinner.

They were having coffee outside on the terrace. Cyril Marling had just risen to get the sugar, and Peter had taken his chair.

"What on earth were you doing?"

Sylvia in the moonlight made a very pretty picture. She gazed ecstatically at Peter, and said:

"We had a lovely time. Cyril read poetry to me."

"Poetry!" said Peter, in disgusted tones.

"Yes, poetry. Lovely, lovely verses written specially for me."

"Good lord! You don't mean to say he writes it?"

"Of course he does; he's a poet."

"How rotten!"

There was real conviction in Peter's tones. He seemed to be oblivious of the fact that Cyril Marling had returned. He continued to sprawl in the chair which he had annexed.

Sylvia laughed.

"Oh, Peter, how rude! I love poetry. Cyril, why on earth don't you find yourself a chair?"

"*That's* my chair," said Cyril rather peevishly.

Peter merely hunched himself and said nothing. He looked very large and heavy. After a moment's indecision Cyril sat down on Sylvia's other side.

"Poetry is rotten stuff," said Peter. "It's dead easy, too. I know a chap at school who does it. He's a bit of a rotter, no good at games, and all that sort of thing. He says writing poetry's as easy as falling out of bed."

"Is it, Cyril?" said Sylvia wickedly.

"It depends on what you call poetry," said Cyril loftily.

Sylvia giggled. She was enjoying herself very much.

"Oh!" she said, clapping her hands. "I've got the loveliest idea. It really is simply the loveliest. You shall both write some poetry for me. It will be too exciting. You know I simply adore poetry. I suppose it's because I was born in the East, and I always think the East is so frightfully romantic and poetic."

Peter had been fidgeting with a loose piece of cane on the arm of his chair. Suddenly his fingers were still, and he said slowly:

"I was born in the East, too."

Sylvia clapped her hands again.

"That's another Link," she said. "I mean a Link between us— between Peter and me."

She nodded at Cyril Marling, who seemed far from pleased.

"Peter's saving my life was the first Link; and our both being born in the East is the second. I do wonder what the third will be. Of course there'll have to be a third. Things always go in threes, you know."

"Where were you born?" said Peter in a slow, deep voice.

"I was born in Annam," said Sylvia Coverdale.

Peter got up with a jerk that upset his chair. Without a word he strode across the terrace and went stumbling down the steps that led into the garden.

Sylvia and the Jewel; the Jewel and Sylvia. That was the third Link. Peter felt the wonder and the glory of it as an overwhelming wave. Practically it stunned him. He did not know where his feet had carried him until he found himself on the river's brink. His feet were almost in the water. Dark willows swept down into the stream, the moonlight lay upon it like light upon a looking-glass. Peter saw nothing but Sylvia's face and Sylvia's eyes, more beautiful than any jewel in the world.

Chapter Ten

NEXT DAY Sylvia smiled sweetly upon Peter, and asked him if he would take her on the river. She was out with him all the morning. In the afternoon she and Cyril detached themselves from the rest of the party and were seen no more.

Peter penetrated into the library, discovered and took down Beeton's *Great Book of Poetry*, and sat for two hours, alternately glaring at the printed page and tapping out metres upon the library table. At the end of the time he compiled what he thought would be a useful list of rhymes, and plunged into verse.

Miss Coverdale came into Sylvia's room that evening and found her in a state of high amusement and delight.

"Oh, Sylvia, you'll be late for dinner," said Miss Coverdale.

Sylvia shook her head. She was seated before her looking-glass attired in a very flimsy white slip. She had just finished doing her hair, and was engaged in improving the arch of her eyebrows with a soft pencil. She giggled and looked over her shoulder at Miss Coverdale.

"Guess what's happened, Jane Anne," she said. "A perfectly priceless thing."

Her cheeks were very pink, and her eyes very blue.

"Oh, my dear, nothing dreadful, I hope."

"Now, Jane Ann—dreadful? No, it's Peter."

"What about him?" Miss Coverdale's tone was anxious.

Sylvia jumped up and began to dance round the room, holding up her short skirts and singing in her pretty, clear voice:

"Peter's fallen in love with me,
Peter's fallen in love with me;
With me, with capital M, E, Me.
Jane Ann, he's fallen in love with me."

"Nonsense, Sylvia."

"Oh, people do, you know."

Sylvia stopped dancing and picked up a frightfully crumpled sheet of paper from among the odds and ends which littered her dressing-table.

"Read this," she said. "No, I'll read it out to you, or you'll miss the full beauty of it."

She struck an attitude and declaimed:

"TO SYLVIA

"You are the fairest star that ever shone,
Bar none.

I really think you are
Quite like a star,
Because a star looks bright
At night,
And you
Look stunning in the evening too.
So, Sylvia, marry me and be a darling,
Don't marry Marling.

"You see, Jane Ann, it's a proposal. That's my sixth, if I count Jimmy Brown when I was thirteen, which, I suppose, isn't really fair."

"Sylvia darling," said Miss Coverdale, "you know I don't like finding fault with you, but I don't really—no, I mean, do you really—no, I don't seem to be able to express just what I do mean—but is it, is it really quite delicate to talk like that?"

Sylvia had taken up her hand-glass and was deepening the red of her mouth a little. She looked up, brilliant with mischief.

"My blessed Jane Ann, when I'm married I shall furnish a darling little ark for you to live in, and then you'll feel really at home. I simply love people falling in love with me," she added, "and I do call it a triumph to have got a poem out of Peter."

On Sunday, Peter suffered the pangs of neglect. Sylvia and Cyril had had a *rapprochement* following upon a violent scene. They wandered about together, looking sentimental and making other people feel *de trop*.

Peter sat on the terrace all the afternoon. When Sylvia and Cyril were in sight he stared at them. When they were not in sight he stared into vacancy. After tea he went for a walk. On the way he passed Sylvia and Cyril in a boat, and received the impression that Cyril was reciting an ardent love poem. Sylvia was actually blushing. On the way home he walked into Sylvia and Cyril at a stile. They were leaning against it, very close together, and, just as Peter came up, Cyril kissed Sylvia, and Sylvia let him do it. Peter crashed past them, and went home with all the demons of jealousy tearing him.

That evening things came to a head. Afterwards Miss Coverdale was never quite sure what had happened. It was a most lovely evening, and Sylvia said that she wanted to walk in the rose garden and feel romantic. She invited Peter to escort her there, and Peter, who had not uttered a single word for at least two hours, got up and stalked away beside her in total silence.

About half an hour later Sylvia came back to the house alone. She looked very white, and said she was going to bed. Peter did not return. When the dinner bell rang he was still absent. Miss Coverdale and Cyril Marling dined *tête-à-tête*, and both seemed to be relieved when the meal was over. Cyril vanished almost immediately, and at ten Miss Coverdale was just thinking of going to her room when the door was violently wrenched open, and in rushed Sylvia in her dressing-gown. Her face was ashy, and in her hands she grasped a crumpled paper.

"Jane Ann," she cried, "Oh, Jane Ann!" and dropped on her knees at Miss Coverdale's side. "What shall I do, what shall I do, what shall I *do?*"

She thrust the paper into the old lady's trembling hands and began to sob miserably. Miss Coverdale straightened the paper out and read, in Peter's untidy hand, his second and last effort at Poetry:

> "I cannot bear it when you smile
> At other people on a stile.
> I cannot bear it when you float
> With other people in a boat.
> The pains of love have riven me,
> The pains of love have driven me
> To do what many a broken-hearted
> Lover has done when he is parted
> From the being he adores in vain
> And fears he'll never see again.
> My love for you is past all bearing.
> Perhaps you'll sometimes think of Peter Waring."

"No!" said Miss Coverdale, in a sharp, high voice that was not quite a scream. "Oh no, no! It's not *possible!*"

Sylvia's teeth were chattering.

"We quarrelled," she whispered. "I said dreadful things. I said ..." She broke off, shuddering. "He didn't say anything after that. He didn't speak, he only looked. Oh, Jane Ann, I can see him looking at me." She sobbed and clung to the trembling Miss Coverdale. "The river!" she said, only just above her breath.

This time Miss Coverdale really screamed.

"No, no!" she cried. "Oh, Sylvia, my darling, no!"

There was a dreadful silence. Sylvia's face was hidden, her whole body shook. Suddenly she flung up her head and looked about her wildly.

"I'm a wicked girl," she said. "Oh, Jane Ann, I'm wicked all through. Oh, don't let me be punished like this, and I promise, I *promise*, I'll never flirt again."

Mr. Coverdale, who had opened the door quietly a moment before, now closed it behind him and crossed the room.

"My child, what an admirable resolution!" he said.

Both women screamed. His tone changed, taking on a slight shade of impatience.

"Jane, what's the matter? Has anything happened?"

"Yes—yes—dreadful!" gasped Miss Coverdale.

"Well, in heaven's name, what? If it's Sylvia's ridiculous engagement that has gone smash, I may as well tell you that I can support the blow."

"Not Cyril—Peter!" said Sylvia, with white lips.

"Peter? Oh yes, the Link, the romantic cub. So you've been devastating him? Well, my dear, he'll get over it—we do, you know."

"No—not if he's drowned," sobbed Sylvia.

"Drowned? Rubbish!" said Mr. Coverdale. "What's this?"

He took the paper which Sylvia pushed into his hand, turned so as to get a good light upon it, and read Peter's horrible composition aloud in a voice tinged with sarcastic amusement.

"My *dear* Sylvia," he said, half-way through—and then suddenly, on the last words, his tone altered and hardened. He said, "Peter Waring?" And then very sharply, "Wareham—you told me his name was Wareham."

"No, no," said Sylvia, "it's Waring—it always was."

She was still on her knees, clutching Miss Coverdale's chair with one hand. With the other she put back her disordered fair hair. She stared at her father and saw in his face something that she did not understand. He folded up the paper and put it in his pocket before he spoke. Then he turned to his sister.

"My dear Jane, you've distressed yourself quite unnecessarily. I met young Waring on his way to the junction, and offered him a lift which he refused. Now, perhaps, you will leave us, as I wish to speak to Sylvia."

When the door had closed upon Miss Coverdale's good nights, he laid his hand on Sylvia's shoulder, pulled her to her feet, and turned her so that she faced the light.

"Now," he said, "why did you lie to me about the boy's name?"

"I didn't, I didn't."

"You wrote Wareham to me."

"N—never. It's m—my wr—writing. Jane Ann knew his name was Waring. Everybody kn—knew it."

The colour was beginning to come back into Sylvia's face. Peter wasn't drowned. She had nothing to reproach herself with. Fear, going out, left room for curiosity.

"Why shouldn't his name be Waring?" she asked.

"What's his father's name? Do you know?"

He had never heard that James Waring had a son. Perhaps the whole thing was a false alarm. But there was the young brother who came over to Tourane afterwards—the soldier. What was his name? He looked back into memory, and saw again the lifted blind, the native servant standing there with a visiting-card, and the name on it, clear black on white: "Captain Henry Waring, R.A."

"What was his father's name? Who was he?" He thought his voice sounded as if it came from a great distance, and, as if from a distance, he heard Sylvia reply:

"His father was a soldier, a gunner. His name was Henry. And when I told him where I was born—"

Coverdale became aware that his hand still lay on Sylvia's shoulder. She cried out under the sudden pressure, and he said harshly:

"You told him where you were born! And, pray, who told *you* where you were born?"

Sylvia's breath came fast.

"It was in the old desk, my mother's desk—you gave it me. There was a little diary stuck at the back of one of the drawers, with all the leaves torn out but one. It had the date and the place where I was born in Annam. It had—"

Coverdale uttered an impatient exclamation, pushed his daughter away from him, and, turning, walked the length of the room and back. Sylvia stood still and watched him, curious, fascinated, afraid. He returned, came to a standstill before her, looked her steadily in the face, and said:

"I'm going to speak very seriously to you. I want you to give me your whole attention." He paused for a moment, his eyes bitter, his lips just touched with sarcasm. "Sylvia," he said, "you have a very pretty face and, as I believe, a nature light enough. I have seen these things in you, but I see something else besides, something that you have from me, an instinct of self-interest—or shall we say self-protection?—it sounds prettier and comes to much the same thing. Call it what you like, it's to that instinct that I'm talking now. If it hasn't sufficient strength to curb your chattering tongue, then I tell you this quite seriously—you will suffer a great deal more than I shall."

He spoke quickly, his eyes downcast; but every now and then he lifted them and looked full at Sylvia for an instant. He saw her face change and harden. What he saw pleased him. He went on, speaking a little more slowly:

"All men play the fool sometimes. Eighteen years ago I played the fool in Annam. I got mixed up with a very serious affair. I was not there under my own name. Practically no one knows that I was ever in Annam at all. If the affair became public now—well ..." He shrugged his shoulders slightly. "Well, I don't pretend that it would be pleasant for me, but for you, Sylvia, it would be social ruin."

He looked at her keenly and laid one hand upon her shoulder again.

"Now, my child, somehow I do not associate you with social ruin. I think you'd do your best to avoid it. A brilliant social success is rather more in your line, I imagine. I never opposed this ridiculous engagement of yours because—well, I knew that it was not worth bothering about. Quite frankly, I did not see you settling down in the suburbs as Mrs. Marling. No, you'll make a brilliant marriage some day, if you can hold your tongue. If you can't—well, I'm afraid even the suburbs will pass you by upon the other side."

"Oh!" said Sylvia on a shuddering breath. She drew back a pace and put her hands before her eyes.

"Oh!" she said again. A long shiver went over her.

Her father's manner changed.

"Now," he said, "when you mentioned Annam, what did this boy say?"

"He didn't say anything."

"Did he seem to take any notice? How did he look?"

"He didn't," said Sylvia. "I mean he didn't speak, or look, or do anything. He just got up and pushed past us all and went off."

"When you mentioned Annam?"

"Yes, when I said Annam, he just pushed his chair over and went off."

Coverdale beat with his closed fist upon the open palm of his other hand. Every muscle in his thin, smooth face had tightened. He looked old. There was a silence before he said:

"Did he speak of it again? Tell me exactly."

"No, no, he didn't."

"Sylvia, tell me. Did he speak of—of a jewel? If you can recall the slightest reference, you must tell me."

"No—yes, he didn't until this evening. I don't know what he meant."

He took both her hands in his.

"Don't be frightened. Try and get it clear. Tell me just what he said—the exact words."

Sylvia's wide blue eyes met his.

"Oh, I don't know," she said. "I don't think he meant anything. We were in the rose garden, and—and he ..."

"He was making love to you, I suppose?"

Sylvia flushed.

"Yes, he was. And—and all of a sudden he went down on his knees, and—and he was kissing my hand—and he said: 'You're the only jewel I want, but I'll give you the other one to wear.' That's what he said."

"That was all?"

"Yes. I laughed at him. We quarrelled. He frightened me, and I ran away."

There was a long silence. Coverdale let go of his daughter's hands.

"Very well," he said, "that ends it. Do you hear, Sylvia, the thing's done. You've quarrelled—you drop his acquaintance, and you hold your tongue—if you don't, I'm afraid, my child, that you'll pay a heavier penalty than you've any idea of. That's all. We won't speak about it again."

Sylvia lay awake a long time that night. When she slept, it was to dream that she was being married to Peter Waring in Westminster Abbey. Her shoes were sewn with diamonds, and Peter gave her a small gladstone bag which burst open in the nave and poured forth a flood of precious stones. Then someone called out in a loud ringing voice, "I forbid the banns," and she woke up.

Chapter Eleven

PETER WENT DOWN to Merton Clevery. Mrs. Mortimer, who was not expecting him for another week, showed no particular enthusiasm when he arrived. This did not worry him. He knew very well that he came to Merton Clevery on sufferance. He came because it was his business to come. He did not like coming; but it was his business to see Rose Ellen; so he came.

They went into the orchard, and sat under the crab-apple tree. Its branches, heavy with tiny rose-flushed apples, hung down over Rose Ellen's head. She leaned against the tree, and Peter lay full length on the grass beside her and talked. He always talked to Rose Ellen, and Rose Ellen always listened. She wore a brown linen dress, and her thick, curly plait of hair hung over one shoulder. She still had the rose-leaf complexion of her babyhood. Her brown eyes were like pools.

Peter told her all about Sylvia, speaking in the rapt whisper of the devotee, and Rose Ellen listened, not looking at him. She was plaiting a yellow grass stalk into a ring.

"She must be lovely," she said when Peter paused for breath.

"She's frightfully lovely," said Peter. "She is ... Rose Ellen, if you could see her, you'd know that you'd never seen a really lovely person before. That's how I felt the very first minute."

"Oh, Peter de—ah," said Rose Ellen.

She said "Petah" as she had always said it. Sometimes Peter teased her about it, but she went on doing it. Rose Ellen could be very determined and she liked saying "Petah"—that was the way she always thought of him.

"She's like—I'll tell you what she's like," said Peter in gruff, impassioned tones. "You know what a stained-glass window looks like when you see it from outside all rough and dull. That's what most people are like. Then you go inside, and you see the light coming through the window, all the colours frightfully bright and shining like—like jewels. That's what she's like. She's like a jewel herself. She's like the most wonderful jewel in the world."

His voice dropped to a whisper, and he looked past Rose Ellen without seeing her. He was seeing Sylvia and the Jewel, the Jewel and Sylvia; each the only one in the world, the heart's desire of men.

Rose Ellen looked at him with troubled eyes. She said at last in a small, low voice:

"Is she fond of you, Peter?"

Peter exclaimed and flung out an impatient hand.

"You don't understand a bit," he said. "You talk as if she was just an ordinary sort of girl. I don't expect her to be *fond* of me. I don't expect her to be fond of anyone. You wouldn't talk about a queen being fond of the people who—who think it an honour to serve her, would you? She's like that."

"Isn't she fond of people, then?" said Rose Ellen.

"I tell you she's like a queen or a princess. People ought to wait on her, and do things because of her, and—and love her frightfully, of course."

"She isn't fond of people, then?" said Rose Ellen, still with those troubled eyes.

"She's like a jewel," said Peter; "she's like a beautiful, shining jewel."

Rose Ellen was silent. She slipped the plaited ring on to one of her fingers, and then, very slowly, she pulled it off again. She looked at Peter, and saw his eyes full of something which hurt.

She said, "Oh, Peter, is she?" and then, "Peter, I don't like jewels much."

Peter stared at her, all angry scorn.

"You little mug, you don't know what you're talking about!"

Rose Ellen nodded wisely. Her hands clasped one another very tight.

"I do. I do," she said. "Dearest has lots, and, indeed, I don't like them—not very much, Peter de—ah. They're hard, and they're cold, and the colour in them doesn't change. They're not like flowers."

"Of course they're not," said Peter. "Who wants them to be?"

"I do," said Rose Ellen. "I would like them much better if they were flowers. I like things to be soft, and to smell sweet like flowers do. I think I don't really like jewels at all, Peter de—ah."

Peter laughed rather angrily.

"You're just a little, stupid thing that doesn't know what she's talking about," he said. "But then you haven't seen Sylvia. If you did see her, you'd simply adore her."

Rose Ellen did not speak, she played with her plaited ring. After a long pause Peter said under his breath:

"Rose Ellen, can you keep a secret?"

Rose Ellen nodded.

"Sure? Girls are such awful blabs."

"I'm not," she said.

"You'd tell your Mrs. Mortimer."

She shook her head again.

"Promise, then."

She frowned.

"I won't promise. I said I wouldn't tell."

"Better promise, to make sure."

She shook her head.

"Little mug!"

He caught her hand and squeezed it teasingly. For a moment he was the old Peter again, her Peter.

"Little obstinate mug. Won't promise, won't tell?"

"I won't tell, Peter de—ah," said Rose Ellen very seriously.

He told her all he knew about the Annam Jewel.

Rose Ellen listened, looking down at him as he lay propped on his elbows, his chin resting between two large fists, his eyes looking past Rose Ellen and the orchard, on through the years.

"When I am twenty-five …" he said, and broke off.

"Yes, Peter?"

He started, threw a fleeting glance at her, hesitated, and said, frowning:

"When I am twenty-five I shall marry Sylvia, and give her the Jewel to wear."

It was out of his inmost heart that he spoke. Rose Ellen knew that. She said:

"It's a long time till you're twenty-five, Peter de—ah."

Peter said nothing. After a long minute he made a sudden movement and buried his face in Rose Ellen's lap.

"I love her so frightfully," he whispered.

Rose Ellen saw his shoulders heave. Her soft mouth trembled a little, but she did not speak. After a minute or two she dropped her little ring of plaited grass and laid a small brown hand on Peter's head.

Chapter Twelve

IN 1914, Peter was twenty and Rose Ellen sixteen. Peter was in the Argentine on a horse ranch, and Rose Ellen was at a finishing school—a most expensive finishing school.

Mrs. Mortimer was a good deal relieved when she heard that Peter had left the country after a flaring row with his uncle.

The cause of the row was Peter's unqualified refusal to enter his uncle's office. Matthew Waring behaved as many another man has behaved in like circumstances. His own disappointment blinded him; he became incapable of seeing anything else. He accused Peter of ingratitude, and paraded his hurt feelings, his loneliness, and his affection for Peter, and ended with an unconditional surrender, an introduction to people of repute in the Argentine, and some really generous financial backing.

Peter's twenty-first birthday found him in France.

At twenty-five the war was behind him, and he had inherited eight hundred a year from Matthew Waring.

The years had brought odd changes. Mrs. Mortimer had turned Merton Clevery into a convalescent home. In the second year of the war she married one of her patients, an excellent, dull, jocose man of the name of Gaisford. Rose Ellen, thrilled to the depths of an unselfish heart, had shared in Dearest's happiness. It was only when she discovered that it was going to be impossible to break Major Gaisford of his habit of calling her Rosie that her romantic feelings received a slight chill.

Mrs. Gaisford continued to love Rose Ellen, but Rose Ellen was no longer the one supreme object of her existence. In 1917 her cup of happiness overflowed; she became the proud mother of a remarkably fine little boy—a healthy, red-faced, jolly infant, whom everyone pronounced to be the living image of his father. Rose Ellen adored the baby. The news, broken to her with much tact, that she must no longer consider herself the heiress of Merton Clevery left her quite unruffled. Only, after four years, instead of being at the centre of the family, she found herself, as it were, upon its edge.

During the years of the war she only saw Peter four times. At twenty she was a little lonely, without knowing it.

A week before his twenty-fifth birthday Peter went down to Merton Clevery for a few days. His affairs had kept him busy during the month that had elapsed since he had been demobilized, but he responded now to quite a gracious invitation from Mrs. Gaisford. The situation had changed: she was no longer jealous; Rose Ellen was no longer an heiress; and Peter was no longer quite ineligible.

Peter took the train, not to Merton, but to Hastney Mere. It was a fine spring day, and he had a fancy to cross the water-meadows and climb up through the beech woods to the heathery upland beyond, as he had done thirteen years before with little Rose Ellen.

The road that had seemed so long then was nothing of a tramp to Peter now. He came out on the heath in full sunshine, and walked along the grassy track until he came to the hollow where he had left Rose Ellen in the wind and the rain whilst he went forward to spy out the land. He hesitated a moment, and then turned off the path and went down into the hollow.

Rose Ellen was sitting there—not the little Rose Ellen of whom he had been thinking, with her cropped head and drenched sweater, but a quite grown up Rose Ellen in a green linen dress and a wide rush hat. She was singing under her breath.

Peter stood and looked at her. She was nice to look at. He decided approvingly that Rose Ellen grown up was a very pretty girl. He called out to her, and she jumped up and came to meet him.

For the first time, Peter did not kiss her. He had always kissed Rose Ellen. He had certainly meant to kiss her now, but somehow he didn't do it. He had not the slightest idea that it was Rose Ellen who had stopped him. She gave him both her hands and a lovely smile, and she said:

"Oh, Petah de—ah!" And quite suddenly Peter was as unable to kiss her as if they had never met before.

They sat on the grass and talked, falling quickly and easily into the old intimacy; and, as usual, it was Peter who talked and Rose Ellen who listened. He was full of his plans and at a word they came pouring out.

"You're not going back to the Argentine, are you, Peter?"

Rose Ellen's voice shook just a very little as she put the question. The Argentine was a long way off. After the war she didn't feel as if she could bear Peter to go right away to the other side of the map.

Peter shook his head.

"No, I'm not going back. I'm a bit fed up. I want to be in England; and Uncle Matthew's money makes it possible. It was frightfully decent of him to leave it to me, wasn't it?"

Rose Ellen nodded. Little warm waves of thankfulness were beating upon her. She felt so dreadfully glad that she couldn't speak, so she nodded, and her delicate pink colour rose a little.

"There's a friend of mine, a fellow called Tressilian—you'd like him awfully, he's a most amusing chap—we're going into partnership. We're going to breed horses. He's got family acres in Devonshire and no money; and I've got Uncle Matthew's money and no acres. I think we ought to make quite a good thing of it. He's down there now, and I'm seeing to things in town. There's a good deal of business connected with Uncle Matthew's estate that had to stand over till I got back."

"It sounds lovely," said Rose Ellen.

They walked home slowly, Peter still discoursing.

It was next day when they were in the orchard that Rose Ellen asked him about Sylvia Coverdale. They were sitting under the very tree where they had sat when Rose Ellen made her little plaited ring, and Peter told her that when he was twenty-five he was going to marry Sylvia and give her the Annam Jewel. From that day to this he had never mentioned Sylvia again. In a week Peter would be twenty-five. Rose Ellen could keep the question back no longer. The apple tree was full of pink-and-white blossom. Rose Ellen filled her hands with the fallen petals and made a little pile of them on the lap of her rose-coloured gown. She looked down at the pink and white, and she said:

"Do you ever see Sylvia Coverdale, Peter?"

"Oh, she's married," said Peter carelessly. "Yes, I see her sometimes. She's is a widow now. Her name's Moreland, Lady Moreland."

"Is she as pretty as ever?" said Rose Ellen.

She didn't look at Peter.

"Oh, prettier, much prettier," said Peter.

Rose Ellen laughed.

"Oh, Peter!" she said. "How could she be?"

"Why?"

"Because she was so very lovely then. I didn't think anyone could be prettier than that."

"I was fearfully keen on her when I was seventeen," said Peter.

"And not now?"

This time Rose Ellen did look. She had to see Peter's face, because she simply had to know what perhaps he would not tell her in words. She kept her soft voice steady.

"Oh, lord, no—not like that. She's frightfully pretty and—and an awfully good sort, and we're great friends."

"Have you seen much of her?"

"Well, I always seemed to run across her if I was ever on leave. I'd like you to meet her. You'd like her immensely. She's very sympathetic and feminine, you know—not a bit like most of the girls one comes across. You'd like her no end."

"Should I?" said Rose Ellen. Then her colour rose, and she said with a sudden smile. "Are you still going to give her the Annam Jewel, Peter?"

"Not much!" said Peter cheerfully.

The day he went away was the last of the hot spring days. Clouds were already piling up from the south-west when Rose Ellen walked with him across the fields to Merton. She was happy because Dearest had been very kind indeed and Peter was coming down again quite soon.

Peter talked about his horse farm. He was very keen about it. When they reached the station there was not too much time. Peter took his ticket, got into an empty third-class carriage, and went on talking about horses, and Devonshire, and Jim Tressilian.

"You'll have to come and keep house for us," he said cheerfully as the train began to move. "Mrs. Mortimer doesn't want you now. She's got old Gaisford and the baby, and can very well spare you."

Rose Ellen walked back with a scarlet colour in her cheeks and two wounds in her heart. One of the wounds was just a surface one, because, although it was true in a sense that Dearest could do without her, she had accustomed herself to the thought. The other wound was a very deep one; Rose Ellen's happiness was draining away through it. She had thought, yes, she had really thought—the scarlet burned her cheeks—but Peter would never have said that about coming to keep house unless he was just thinking of her as his sister.

"And I'm not, I'm not! I won't be, and I'm not."

She stood quite still in the middle of a field, and remembered how Peter had said, "When we're grown up I'll marry you, and then your name will really be Waring." That was years and years before he had said that he would marry Sylvia when he was twenty-five. Now he was going back to London. Something in Rose Ellen said that he was going back to Sylvia.

She walked home very slowly.

Chapter Thirteen

AT TWELVE O'CLOCK on the morning of his twenty-fifth birthday Peter Waring emerged from the offices of Messrs. Wadsgrove, Wadsgrove, Spenlow & Walton, with a dispatch case in his hand. He called a taxi, and drove straight to his rooms in Bury Street.

Twenty minutes later he was breaking the seals which had guarded his father's papers for twenty-five years. The seals bore the Waring crest—a clenched fist and the words "Be Ware". The ring which had made the impression was on the little finger of Peter's left hand. He unlocked the box and threw back the lid. His hand did not shake, but it was a tremendous moment. He had the feeling that here, at this instant, he was leaving the land of everyday behind, and passing into some place of adventurous dreams beyond. He was about to possess the Annam Jewel, to see and handle the Annam Jewel; and always the Annam Jewel had meant for him romance, the something beyond. Once it had meant Sylvia Coverdale to him. When he was twenty-five he would receive the Annam Jewel and he would marry Sylvia.

He paused for a moment, with his hand on the papers under the lid, and thought about Sylvia.

She had married well, if not brilliantly. She was Lady Moreland when Peter went to the Argentine. Now she was a widow of three years' standing. Peter had met her only the day before. He was dining with her tonight.

Peter thought of her with an admiration untinged by romance. It was no longer Sylvia and the Jewel, the Jewel and Sylvia. The Jewel reigned alone.

He lifted a sheet of foolscap and saw, written across it in pencil, "For my son Peter when he is twenty-five", and a scrawled "Henry Waring". Under the sheet of paper was an exercise-book with a black cover. Peter laid it aside, and saw in the bottom of the case a small, square cardboard box. He took it up, opened it, pulled back a layer of discoloured cotton wool, and saw the Jewel. It was a little smaller than his thumb nail. It was not like any jewel that he had ever seen. There was red in it, but it was not a ruby; there was blue in it, and green, but it was neither a sapphire nor an emerald; there were all these colours, but it was not an opal.

Peter set down the box, picked up the Jewel between his finger and thumb, and walked with it to the window, frowning. The day was dull; that was why the Jewel had no fire. It was May, but the sky was leaden. The colours in the Jewel seemed dull. He pulled down the blind with a jerk, switched on the centre drop light, and held the Jewel right under it, turning it this way and that. It was dull and cold.

Peter knew very little about precious stones, but it seemed to him that the thing was too light by half. He went back to the window and tried the edge of the Jewel on the glass. After a moment's puzzled scrutiny he sat down at the table, dropped the Jewel back upon the stained cotton wool, and took up the black exercise-book. He turned the leaves and saw that they were closely written on, partly in ink and partly in pencil.

He left the light burning, and settled himself to read. The entries began abruptly, at the top of a left-hand page, with part of an old letter attached by its corners. There was no beginning to the first sentence:

> ... found James pretty far gone, but able to dictate and sign a will. He couldn't speak much, but he told me he had got the Jewel. He said the old priest gave it to him. Then he had a row with his partners. One of them got the Jewel away from him—a man called Henderson—Dutch-American. The other man is called Dale, but that's not his name. James did not know his real name, but said he found by accident that his Christian name was Roden—an unusual name—might be a clue.
>
> Henderson got away with the Jewel. James fell sick, and couldn't follow at once. When we found him there was a fight. I don't know if Dale was there or not. James wandered rather. James was hurt, but he got away with the Jewel. He left it to me in his will, and he gave it to me last night before he died. I shall take the next boat back...

Here the fragment of the letter ended.

The next entry was long, and had evidently been written bit by bit. It began in ink. As it proceeded, the writer had had recourse oftener and oftener to pencil. Some of the sentences were hardly legible. It ran:

"Half an hour after posting my letter to Olivia I discovered that the Jewel was false, a bad fake clumsily made. I had hardly looked at it before. The room was dark and my mind fully taken up with James' state. I sat down and thought, and became convinced, first, that there was a real Jewel, and second, that James had had it in his possession. It seemed certain that Henderson had somehow managed to get the Jewel copied and, on being tracked down, had let James get away with the fake. I began to make inquiries. I found that Dale had a wife and child up country and was supposed to be visiting them. I discovered that Henderson was lodging in the bazaar, in the house of a native jeweller.

"I made my plans, put on native dress, and went to see Henderson. There was a way up the back of the house from a veranda roof which an active man could climb. I was active enough then. I climbed to the window and looked in. There was a lamp burning on a table. Henderson sat with his back to me, bending forward, working at something. He is a heavy, square-built man, quite young, light-haired, and very strong. He has a round, white scar the size of a threepenny-bit on the back of his right hand. It looks like a burn—some acid, I should judge. I was very quiet, and he didn't hear me. He went on working. All at once he picked something up and held it to the light. I saw it over his shoulder. It was the Jewel. The sight of it took away my breath. I've never seen anything like it in my life, nor has anyone else. There isn't anything like it. There is only one Annam Jewel.

"I'm writing this quite soberly. You'll see the fake, and I want you to remember, when you see it, that it gives you no idea of what the living Jewel is. To compare the fake with the Jewel is like comparing a photograph with a beautiful woman. The life isn't there. The Jewel is like a breathing thing. It's the way the colours come and go, and mix and blend—red, blue, green, and gold. It's not an opal. I don't know what it is. It's just the Jewel.

"I'm writing this to make you feel that no risk, no labour will be too great if you can only get the Jewel in the end. And whilst I can write it, remember the Jewel is yours. The old priest gave it to James, James left it by will to me, and I have left it by will to you. Neither Dale nor Henderson have a shadow of a claim. The Jewel is yours, my son. Now I must get on.

"Henderson and I both looked at the Jewel, then he said with a Dutch oath, 'I'll beat you. I'll beat you yet. You're hard to beat, but I'll make a jewel yet that will cheat all the world except me.' He said it in a whisper, but I heard the words just as I've set them down.

"I have found out since that Henderson was apprenticed to a man called Michel, who made copies of famous jewels for people who didn't want to risk their real ones, or who wanted to pawn them, perhaps. He was a well-known man in Paris, and came smash over some big fraudulent deal. Henderson disappeared. His real name is Henders— I'm sure from what I have found out that it is the same man.

"He leant back in his chair and held the Jewel to the light. I got my knee on to the window-sill, and then I saw that he heard something. He turned, and I sprang at the same time. He was much stronger than I, but I tripped him, and we went down together. His head struck against a copper water-vessel. The Jewel rolled across the floor. I was up first. I snatched it and made for the window. As I dropped to the veranda roof I heard him stumble across the room. He fired through the window, and I knew that I was hit, but I didn't think very much of it. I got back to my place, took James' papers, and went over to the hotel.

"There was a boat leaving next day. I meant to take it. I was a fool. I ought to have sat up all night with a revolver, but I didn't. I had a bullet through my shoulder, and I went to bed. I didn't mean to sleep, but the next thing I knew was waking in the pitch dark to feel the muzzle of a revolver tight against my temple. There was a hand over my mouth, a very strong, thin hand—not Henderson's—and a voice— not Henderson's voice—whispered in my ear, 'You won't move, will you? It's quite useless, and I'd really hate to shoot you.' It was a gentleman's voice, not like Henderson's. I knew it must be Dale. Then a match was struck in the middle of the room, and I saw Henderson there. He'd a little bit of candle about two inches high in his hand. He lit it and put it on the table. I saw Dale's face close to mine, thin, dark, clean-shaven—a smallish man, probably a wastrel of good family. He said, 'Quick now, Waring, where's the Jewel?' Then with sudden ferocity, 'Quick, or I'll let Henderson smash you! It'll make less noise than shooting.' There was just one slender chance. I took it.

"I had put the real Jewel in my tobacco-pouch. The fake was in a little pill-box on the washstand. I pointed. Henderson opened the box and flung the fake at me with an oath, asking me if I thought he was the sort of fool who didn't know his own work. Dale was feeling under the pillow. He found my pouch there, tossed it to Henderson, and Henderson fished out the Jewel. He laughed, and put it in his pocket. Dale got up, still keeping me covered. I think I must have been light-headed, because as soon as Dale moved, I jumped at him, and he fired. He didn't hit me. I rushed at Henderson, and saw him pull out his revolver. Dale said, 'No, no!' but Henderson fired. I went down, and that's all I know about it.

"It was a month before I could be moved. Dale and Henderson got away. I came back to Hong Kong as soon as they'd let me travel...."

The writing broke off. Peter turned the page. There were only two or three more entries, short passages rather faintly scrawled in pencil. The first ran:

"James talked a good deal when he was light-headed. He said some things over and over. I think they were things that the priest had said to him. They weren't things he would have thought of for himself."

Two lines were left blank. Then followed a single sentence:

"The blue is the Celestial Heaven; the red is the Elemental fire; the Green is the Living Earth; and the Gold is the Ray of Wisdom in the heart of man."

And below:

"He said this over and over; I'm sure I've got it correctly. I don't know what he meant by it."

Farther down was another very illegible scrawl. Peter held the book to the light, and made it out with difficulty:

"'Can these things be taken by violence?' He said this three times. Twice he said, 'Violence follows the violent man.' I feel sure the old priest must have said this to him."

The last entry was at the very bottom of the page, quite neatly written:

"*N.B.*—To find out the real name of the man who calls himself Roden Dale...."

Peter turned the leaf. The rest of the book was blank.

Chapter Fourteen

PETER DINED that night with Sylvia Moreland.

"The Merritts have failed me," she said when he arrived. "They're the most unreliable creatures on earth. You remember Jane Ann, of course."

Peter shook hands with Miss Coverdale, who looked up at him with a puzzled air.

"I'm sure I shouldn't have known you," she said.

"That was a compliment, Peter," said Sylvia, as they went in to dinner.

Peter was, indeed, no longer the gawky boy who had spent an adventurous week at Sunnings. He was still plain, but after a sufficiently pleasant fashion. He was tall, and powerfully built without being clumsy. His clothes were like other people's clothes.

Miss Coverdale vanished when Sylvia led the way back to the drawing-room after dinner.

"D'you like my room, Peter?" she said. "Look at it whilst I read a letter, and tell me after due reflection."

Sylvia's room was unlike any other that Peter had seen. The carpet was black, and so were the curtains and the covers of the big easy-chairs. The walls were white. Brilliant cushions of Chinese blue and Imperial yellow glowed against the black of the chairs, and a long divan at one end of the room was heaped with them. The only flowers were a dozen white orchids in a bowl of pale-green jade.

Sylvia stood beside the hearth, warming a very pretty foot and reading her letter. She was dressed as if she was sixteen instead of twenty-six, in a slender white frock with a pale blue sash. The contrast between this simplicity and the careful art of complexion and hair was startling. At eighteen, Sylvia had darkened her eyebrows and reddened her lips. At twenty-six, she was a very delicate and exquisite work of art, as carefully tinted as a miniature. Her hair was the brightest gold of which her taste would approve. The effect was, as has been said, startling but very pretty.

She opened her hand, and allowed the letter which she had been reading to flutter down into the fire. It lay for a moment on a bed of glowing coal, then shrivelled and went up in flame.

Sylvia laughed, sighed and looked at Peter.

"Why are men's hearts so brittle?" she said.

"I don't know," said Peter. "Are they?"

She nodded.

"If you were me, you'd know. Yours, of course, is made of some patent unbreakable stuff, so you're safe—you don't know how nice that is. Of course, really," said Sylvia, looking down into the fire, "really you know, Peter, you're one of my very oldest friends. When everybody's frightfully tiresome ..." She laughed and flashed a look at him. "That's one of your words, 'frightfully'. May I borrow it? Well, when everyone's frightfully tiresome, and things go wrong, and people _will_ make love to me, and the world's a hollow mockery—you know the sort of thing—I just say to myself, 'There's always Peter. Peter's _safe_.'"

Peter felt vaguely annoyed. It sounded as if he were the cat, or Miss Coverdale. He said rather shortly:

"I thought you liked being made love to!"

"Is that why you never do it?" said Sylvia.

"I don't know," said Peter.

Sylvia laughed again.

"We've got right away from the subject," she said. "We were considering how safe you are. You weren't always, you know. You nearly frightened me out of my life once. Do you remember, in the rose garden at Sunnings?"

"Was it in the rose garden?"

She looked reproachful.

"Oh, Peter, it was, and *most* romantic—all the proper things; the most heavenly warm evening; and moonlight; and the last rose of summer; and—you really were in love with me then."

Peter did not speak. He felt disturbed, and wondered vaguely what Sylvia was driving at.

"You frightened me dreadfully," said Sylvia. "I ran all the way back to the house."

Peter continued to say nothing. There didn't really seem to be anything to say. He thought Sylvia was looking very pretty, but he wished she would talk about something else.

"My father was furious," said Sylvia.

"Did you always tell him when people made love to you?" asked Peter. He smiled as he spoke, but he was getting rather angry.

"Oh, well, no. But he asked endless questions."

Sylvia left the fire, and balanced herself on the arm of one of the big black chairs.

"Peter, do sit. I simply hate you towering over me and being superior."

"I like standing," said Peter.

Sylvia looked up at him, her hands clasped about her knees.

"Peter, I do want to ask you something," she said. "Will you tell me?"

"I don't know," said Peter. "What is it?"

"Well, when you—you know, in the rose garden ..."

There was a pause. Peter just let it be a pause, and presently Sylvia broke it.

"You made love awfully well, you know, Peter," she said. "And you did say some thrilling things. I always wished that I hadn't got frightened and run away, because I did so want to know some more about the Jewel."

"What Jewel?"

"You said you were going to have one when you were twenty-five. It sounded most mysterious and romantic. And you said you were going to give it to me, Peter." Sylvia's pretty voice sank low.

"What would you have done with it?" Peter had taken a mandarin's button off the mantelshelf and was shifting it absently from one hand to the other. It was of a bright pale blue finished with golden filigree.

"I? What's the use of asking me that? I haven't got it. But what I'm dying to know is, have you got it, Peter? You're twenty-five. You must be. You look more."

Peter laughed.

"I can answer one of the questions. I am twenty-five today."

Sylvia drew a long breath. Her blue eyes shone.

"And you've got the Jewel? Oh, Peter!"

Peter set the mandarin's button back upon the mantelpiece, frowned at it, and shifted it half an inch to the right.

"That's a jolly colour," he said. "It matches your eyes awfully well—I noticed it when you looked at me just now. It's odd, because I don't think I've ever seen anything that matched them before."

He gazed artlessly at her for a moment, then sat down, pushing a chair back a little so as to get farther from the fire. This brought him within reach of a small table with a lamp upon it. The lamplight shone down upon two brilliantly coloured objects—a little tray of Canton enamel, and a book exquisitely bound in leather of the same Imperial yellow.

Sylvia swung her foot to and fro, watching the sparkle of the old paste buckle on her shoe. "Was that intentional? I mustn't startle him," were the thoughts that passed swiftly through her mind. Aloud she said:

"Talking of jewels, Peter—of course you've been to The Luxe to see the latest sensation?"

Peter shook his head lazily.

"I didn't know there was a latest sensation."

"Ignorant savage! Do you mean to tell me that you haven't heard about Mrs. Hendebakker, and her amazing jewel? Why, everybody's talking about it. You can't get a table at The Luxe for love or money, because everyone goes there to see Mrs. Hendebakker and the jewel come down to dinner."

"And who is Mrs. Hendebakker?"

Peter had picked up the little enamelled tray, and was turning it so as to see the colours on its border. It looked small in his big brown hands. He was only mildly interested in what Sylvia was saying.

"Mrs. Hendebakker," said Sylvia impressively, "is the wife of Virgil P. Hendebakker; and Virgil P. Hendebakker is *the* very latest American millionaire. They've got a magnificent private suite at The Luxe, but they always dine in the public dining-room. It's a most thrilling performance, I do assure you, Peter—exactly like Royalty coming in, which, I suppose, is why they do it. She comes in alone, with Virgil P. walking a yard behind her. She always wears dead black *and* the jewel, and everyone stops eating and turns round to look at her."

"At her or at the jewel?" said Peter.

Sylvia laughed.

"Well, they're both worth looking at," she said. "Some people admire her quite enormously. She's the South American type—very magnificent, you know—but the jewel is really 'It'."

"What is it?" said Peter.

He had stopped turning the little Canton tray, and was just staring at it. He had the oddest feeling that something was going to happen. He heard Sylvia say:

"That's just what everybody wants to know. No one has seen anything like it before, and nobody, *nobody* knows what it is."

Peter spoke stiffly without looking up. He said:

"What is it like?"

"I've seen it, but I can't describe it. It isn't like anything but itself—that's what's so exciting. It's green, and blue, and red, and yellow; but it isn't an opal—everybody's quite sure of that. It's just itself, and perfectly, perfectly lovely."

Something said, "The Annam Jewel". The words seemed to come like a thunder-clap out of a clear sky. It was a moment before Peter realized that they had only sounded in his own mind. Sylvia was spreading her fingers to the fire, and saying lightly:

"By hook or by crook you must manage to see it, Peter. It's worth it."

She got up as she spoke, and changed her position, coming nearer to Peter and sinking down in a graceful attitude on a bright-blue and gold pouffe.

"I don't know why we began to talk about jewels," she said. "I know they don't interest men a bit; and, really and truly, I wanted to talk to you about something quite different." She propped her chin on her hands, and looked at him appealingly. "You know, Peter, I really meant it when I said you were my oldest friend. I want to ask your advice. I—I'm in an awful hole."

Peter came to himself with a little start. The enamel tray dropped on the floor. He bent to pick it up, and said, not quite in his natural voice, "What have you been doing, Sylvia?" after which he achieved quite a creditable smile.

Sylvia continued to gaze.

"You see, I feel I can tell you about it because—well, you haven't any money yourself, so you won't think I'm trying to borrow." She paused, and added, "Will you?"

"Of course not," said Peter warmly.

Sylvia repressed a desire to frown. Her manner became a shade more pathetic.

"It's really a dreadful hole. If—if I can't get out of it, I'm done."

"How done?"

"Smashed," said Sylvia. "Broke. Done in. Before the war I should have had to run away from my creditors and live in third-rate foreign hotels, but now I don't know what one does."

Peter was frowning.

"Good lord, Sylvia, you don't mean it! You're not serious?"

"Peter!" Sylvia put out one hand and just touched his knee with it. "Of *course* I'm serious." Her voice began to tremble a little. "I hate being serious, but one has to be when one's ruined, and—and—it comes to that."

"I thought Moreland left you quite well off."

"Everything's so dreadfully expensive," sighed Sylvia.

"Even orchids," said Peter rather grimly.

Sylvia's eyes did not fall.

"Yes, even orchids," she said.

There was a silence—of consternation on Peter's part.

He got up, and stood leaning against the mantelpiece, frowning heavily.

"Look here, Sylvia," he said, "what do you want me to do?"

"I don't know," said Sylvia. "I just wanted to talk. It's—it's so lonely with no one to talk to."

Her eyes filled with tears, but Peter was not looking at her.

"What's the good of talking?" he said. "Do you know what your assets are? Do you know what you owe?"

Sylvia shook her head.

"Then, my dear girl, the first thing to do is to find out. I can't be any earthly use to you unless you can give me some facts. But, look here, if you're in a mess, why don't you go to your father? Where is he?"

"He's at Sunnings," said Sylvia, "up to his eyes in his old books and manuscripts and things. He doesn't care; and, besides, he's awfully hard up himself. The war hit him pretty hard, and he talks of selling Sunnings and going off to the East again—China, you know."

"Not Annam?" said Peter.

He heard his own voice say the words, but he did not know why he said them. He looked full at Sylvia as he spoke, and saw her shiver as if a cold wind had blown between them.

"Why did you say that?" she asked.

"I don't know," said Peter slowly. "You were born there, weren't you?"

Sylvia shook her head.

"No, in China; I was born in China. What in the world made you think of such an out-of-the-way place as Annam?"

A dark look fell upon Peter's face. Across eight years he could hear her voice saying, "I was born in Annam." Why was she lying about it now?

Sylvia reached out her hand and took up the book that lay under the lamp, the book with the brilliant yellow cover.

"Father's a tremendous Chinese scholar," she said. "He lived in China for years. My mother was a missionary's daughter, and I was born there. He's *the* authority on old Chinese manuscripts. This is his last book."

She held it out as she spoke. Peter took it mechanically. On the yellow suède cover he read in gold lettering, *Two Old Chinese Manuscripts*. He opened the book and saw the title-page. The author's name stood out very black on the white paper—Roden Coverdale.

Chapter Fifteen

PETER WALKED ACROSS to the little table and laid the yellow book down upon it. Then he took up the enamel tray, which was rather precariously balanced on the arm of the chair, and put it carefully back in its place. The two yellow things lay in the lamplight. Peter looked fixedly at them for a moment, moved the tray just a little, and sat down.

"About your affairs ..." he said, frowning. He talked of them for about a quarter of an hour or twenty minutes, and finished by saying:

"Get the figures, the exact sums, as far as you can; and if you really want me to, I'll go through them with you and see what can be done to straighten things out."

"Oh, you *are* good," said Sylvia.

Peter got up and said good night. When he got back to his rooms he took out the exercise-book with the black cover which contained his father's notes. He turned the pages until he came to the place where Henry Waring had written:

The other man is called Dale, but that's not his real name. James did not know his real name, but said he found by accident that his Christian name was Roden—an unusual name—might be a clue.

Then he turned to the last entry in the book. It stood out boldly in strong contrast to the illegible scrawl which preceded it:

"*N.B.*—To find out the real name of the man who calls himself Roden Dale ..."

Roden Dale—Roden Coverdale! It was beyond a coincidence. And Sylvia, who had told him eight years ago that Annam was her birthplace, and tonight had lied to him ... His face darkened, his eyes became intent.

Dale had had a wife and child up country. The child must have been Sylvia. She said her father had asked so many questions. Questions? Questions, of course, about him, Peter, and what he had said to her, and what she had said to him. Roden Dale—Roden Coverdale would be concerned to know what Sylvia had said to Peter, and what Peter had said to Sylvia on the subject of Annam. As a sequel, the Sylvia who had prattled about her birthplace had become the Sylvia who had lied about it carefully and with circumstance.

Certainly Roden Dale was Roden Coverdale.

Peter closed the book and locked it away in his father's dispatch box.

Roden Dale was Roden Coverdale. What next? How did this fact affect Sylvia and himself?

He thought about it for a long time. James and Henry Waring had undoubtedly lost their lives in a struggle to gain or retain the Annam Jewel. They were on one side of the struggle, and on the other were Roden Coverdale and the man Henderson. James Waring was Peter's uncle, and Henry his father. In some sort Roden Coverdale was guilty of their deaths. The narrative, however, exonerated Coverdale from actual violence: it was Henderson who had fired.

Peter shook himself impatiently, and began to walk up and down. It all seemed to him a very long time ago. These old feuds were rotten things—one wasn't in the Middle Ages any longer. What on earth had this violence and bloodshed of twenty-five years ago to do with Sylvia and himself? Sylvia was a pal, and she was up against it; she wanted helping; she wanted someone to look after her— women did—and he was going to help her if she were fifty times the daughter of Roden Dale.

That something in Peter which at twelve had made him set out with thirty shillings in his pocket to rescue Rose Ellen and find her a home was in the ascendant. Sylvia was up against it, and she had appealed to him. Something much stronger than family feuds urged him to her assistance.

As soon as Peter left her, Sylvia Moreland changed her white shoes for black ones, covered her dress with a long, dark coat, and pulled a small, black velvet cap down over her fair hair. She then called a taxi, and drove to a well-known restaurant. She paid the man, and went through the swing doors into the vestibule. After waiting for, perhaps, half a minute, she passed out again into the street and, turning to the left, began to walk slowly along the pavement. She had not gone fifty yards before a man came up from behind and joined her. Sylvia glanced up at him and recognized the massive build and heavy, clean-shaven face of Mr. Virgil P. Hendebakker. She nodded, and they walked on together.

"You've seen him?" said Mr. Hendebakker.

Sylvia nodded again.

"Well, that being so, I should be glad if you would hand over any impressions that you have managed to collect."

He spoke like an American, but beneath his accent was a suggestion of something guttural. One would have said that the United States had not had the privilege of giving him birth.

"Oh, impressions?" Sylvia's tone was impatient. "What's the use of talking about Peter and impressions in the same breath? He's about as impressionable as a paving-stone."

"Maybe, but it's your impressions I'm after, not his. What did you get out of him?"

"Nothing, absolutely nothing."

"Did you ask him point-blank if he had the Jewel?"

"I did. I did really."

"And ...?"

"I don't know if he even heard me. He was fidgeting with something on the mantelpiece in the exasperating way he has, and he just made a remark about its colour as if he hadn't taken in what I was saying. I didn't like to ask again, but later I talked about you and Anita, and described the Jewel to him. He hardly seemed interested at all."

They walked in silence for a minute or two. Then Hendebakker said:

"It doesn't matter. It's your father's copy that matters. If this young Waring has one at all, it's just a rough thing that wouldn't take in the lowest sneak-thief. You're sure he showed no interest?"

He put the question sharply, turning so that he could see Sylvia's face in the glare of a street lamp.

"I couldn't see that he did. I thought he was bored."

"Well," said Hendebakker, "if that's so, he's out of it. The game's between me and Dale, as it's been these twenty-five years. Your father," he added, "he passed as Dale for short. It's him and me and the Jewel. And I calculate that this is the last hand and that I hold some real good cards—you, for instance, my dear. You make a pretty queen of diamonds, I reckon—queen of diamonds or queen of trumps, and I rather think it's queen of trumps."

Sylvia flashed an angry look at him, but did not speak.

"Now," he said, "this is where we are. I've got the Jewel, and Dale's got the copy I made after we got to New York. And I want that copy, never you mind why I want it, and you're going to get it for me."

"Am I?" Sylvia's defiant eyes met Hendebakker's cold, light stare, and could not sustain it. "How dare you?" she said.

"Oh, come, Lady Moreland."

She stood still, quivering.

"If you speak my name, I go home at once, or, better still, I'll say yours so loud that everyone hears it."

"Now, now, that was just a slip of mine," he said. "You listen to me, and stop being angry. There's no business in getting angry, and what you've got to bear in mind is that we're in a business deal together. You can't afford to get angry in a business deal. You take that from me—you can't afford it."

"I hate the whole thing," said Sylvia.

"That's not business either," said Mr. Hendebakker reprovingly. "You just set to work and think about how you'd hate to have all your creditors sue you, and what a mighty thin time you'd have on what was left when they were through with you. I'm giving you a pretty good price that'll clear you and make you real comfortable. You keep right on thinking on those lines and you'll pretty soon quit making fool objections to what's just a matter of business. Now, you listen to me. Your father's got a copy of the Jewel that it don't suit me for him to have. I'm having paragraphs from the Press mailed to him every day. You know the sort of thing—'What Is It?' 'The Great Hendebakker Jewel Mystery'; 'The Beautiful Mrs. Hendebakker and Her Jewel'. Well, there'll come a point when Dale will want to have a look at his copy. He doesn't keep it in his house, or I shouldn't be bothering you; I'd have had it long ago. I guess it's in a safe at his London bank, and by and by he'll come running up to town to take a look at it. Maybe he'll ask you some questions. Maybe he'll tell you that what he's got is the real Jewel, and not a copy at all."

Hendebakker looked closely at Sylvia's profile as he spoke.

"It doesn't much matter what he says, but what you say matters a lot. You've got to ask to see the Jewel. You've got to get round him so that he doesn't just go to the bank and look at it there, and come away again. He's got to bring it away with him and you've got to get it for me."

"I can't," said Sylvia. "I won't."

"You won't?" Hendebakker laughed. "Think that over."

His smooth manner suddenly dropped from him. Sylvia's glance showed her the man beneath the manner—cold, brutal, ferocious. She trembled from head to foot, and closed her eyes. Hendebakker slipped his hand inside her arm.

"I reckon you're not such a fool as to think you can say 'I won't' to me. You'll do as you're told. And, by gum, if you don't, I'll smash you! Now, listen. If Dale sends for you to Sunnings, you'll wire to me, 'Shares keeping steady'. If you have word of his coming to town, you'll wire, 'Shares rising'. If he gets the Jewel out of the bank, wire me, 'Sell at once'. And when you get the Jewel, come straight to The Luxe with it, and don't delay an instant. Now, repeat what I've said."

Sylvia obeyed.

Chapter Sixteen

NEXT MORNING, Peter received a letter which surprised him a good deal. It was from his uncle, Miles Banham, whom he had neither seen nor heard from for thirteen years, and it was written on the paper of The Luxe hotel. To anyone who knew Miles Banham this last circumstance was sufficiently startling.

The letter ran as follows:

Dear Peter,

(1) I dug your address out of Ruth and Charlotte. They seem to love you a good deal nowadays. It was not ever thus. Temp. mut.!

(2) I'm rich. This is so improbable that I'm still educating myself to believe it—you needn't.

(3) I want you to dine with me tonight at this pothouse. If already engaged, chuck the engagement and come. Seven forty-five in the lounge.

(4) I really mean it about chucking the engagement.

Yours,

Miles Banham.

Peter had no engagement, and was delighted at the prospect of meeting Miles again. He had never forgotten the sovereign which had been the one bright spot in what he recollected as one of the beastliest days of his whole life. This thought came first, and was immediately followed by another. He was going to dine at The Luxe. With any luck he would see the entry of Mrs. Hendebakker as described by Sylvia; he would see the Jewel.

At seven forty-five that evening he was shaking hands with Miles Banham and finding that he remembered him very well. Miles had not changed at all. He was brown, wiry, and rather shrivelled-looking. His malicious, bright eyes sparkled with vigour. His high, cracked voice was very cordial, as he greeted Peter and introduced him to "my friend, Mr. Cowan".

Mr. Cowan was a thin, middle-aged Jew, with melancholy eyes and the most charming smile.

They went in to dinner, Miles Banham talking all the time and gesturing with his hands in an odd, foreign way. He was obviously in a state of pleased excitement.

"Have you ever dined at The Luxe before, Peter?" he inquired. "If you have, I disown you."

"I haven't," said Peter.

"Good, good! No, don't take that place; I want you to face the door. There, like that. As the rich uncle, you observe that I grow tyrannical."

He gave his funny, cackling laugh. "It's dashed amusing, isn't it? All these years the ne'er-do-well, the pauper, the wastrel—and then, all of a sudden, rich! Me, Miles Banham, rich! Oh, lord, it makes me laugh."

Mr. Cowan smiled his charming smile, but he did not look at his host; he looked towards the doorway on his right. Without quite knowing why, Peter also looked in that direction. Miles Banham looked at Peter.

The Gold Room of The Luxe was full to overflowing. The hum of voices rose and fell. Quite suddenly there was a hush. The voices ceased. Here and there a chair scraped on the polished floor. With a rustling sound, like the sound of a low wind amongst leaves, all the people at all the tables turned to look in the direction in which Mr. Cowan was looking.

A man was standing just inside the door of which Miles Banham had spoken. He was big and clumsily built; his head almost bald; his face clean-shaven, with a heavy jowl; his eyes light, and as hard as pebbles. He stood for a moment as if waiting, and then moved to one side. A woman came through the doorway and began to walk slowly down the crowded room, with the man a yard behind her.

Peter put his elbow on the table, rested his chin on his hand, and looked.

Anita Hendebakker was worth looking at—a magnificent creature with a skin of warm whiteness, eyes like dark flowers, and lips and cheeks of a vivid carnation. A great deal of the warm whiteness was visible. Every other woman in the room wore a dress at least ten inches off the ground, but Mrs. Hendebakker's sheath-like garment of black velvet touched the floor as she walked. It was cut extravagantly low, and right across the breast of it there stretched two exquisitely wrought diamond wings. Where the wings met the Jewel flamed.

Miles Banham was the only person in the room whose eyes were not fastened upon the Jewel. He looked at Peter and saw him flush to the very roots of his hair, and saw how he clenched the hand on which his chin was resting. He watched till the flush faded and a deep frown succeeded it.

Peter was conscious of nothing but the Jewel. Here was the Annam Jewel, and it was his by right. He saw it resting between the diamond wings, and he saw nothing else.

Anita Hendebakker came slowly towards them, walking with an indolent grace and ease. She seemed unconscious that all those people were staring at her. She held her head high; it was a small head, smoothly banded with sleek, black hair. Her colour did not vary, but with each step she took, the colours in the Jewel changed, melted, rushed into one another—the red, the blue, the burning emerald, and the inmost, mysterious golden ray. She passed, reached her table and sat down. Virgil Hendebakker also took his seat. All over the room the hum of conversation broke out again.

As Anita Hendebakker passed their table, Miles Banham shifted his gaze, and for a moment looked keenly at Mr. Cowan. Mr. Cowan, like everyone else in the room, was looking at the Jewel. Miles Banham saw his eyes very intent. Then, as Anita was at her nearest, an odd smile just touched Mr. Cowan's lips. He tapped the table lightly with his fingers, and looked away. He began to talk of plays, music, politics. He talked extremely well. The talk became general. No one mentioned Mrs. Hendebakker, and no one mentioned the Jewel.

It was just as coffee was being brought to them that Peter saw Lady Moreland. She was coming towards them alone. Her white dress glittered in the Gold Room. It was no longer the white of the *ingénue*. The filmy material which draped her was entirely covered with a delicate diamond tracery of spiders' webs. In the centre of each web lurked a black jet spider. A good many people looked at Sylvia as she crossed the room and stopped at Miles Banham's table.

Peter sprang up to meet her, and she touched him familiarly on the arm.

"Come and be introduced to some friends of mine," she said: and, as Peter murmured an introduction, she smiled and added, "Will you spare him just for a minute, Mr. Banham?"

"Do you like my frock, Peter?" she said in a confidential voice as they moved away together.

"I think the spiders are perfectly beastly," said Peter. "I like the glittery white part. What on earth made you have black spiders?"

"They're symbolic," said Sylvia with a funny, light laugh. "I'm in the web, and the spiders will have me unless—unless, oh, well, here we are."

Peter had been looking at her. He now saw that they had come to a standstill by the Hendebakkers' table. Before he realized what was happening, Sylvia was introducing him to Anita, and Virgil Hendebakker had risen to his feet with a smooth, "Very pleased to meet you, Mr. Waring."

Peter was experiencing sensations which he had never known before. Anita was wearing the Annam Jewel. She was Hendebakker's wife. Who and what was Hendebakker? How had he come by the Jewel? *Was he Henderson?* These thoughts had been battering themselves against Peter's consciousness during all the time that he had been eating, drinking, and talking. The force of their impact now became terrific. Hendebakker might be Henderson! The heavy build was there. The light eyes suggested that his hair had once been fair. The hand—that was the only certain thing, the scar on the back of the hand! The thought came like a flash.

As Hendebakker rose, his right hand rested on the table; he leaned upon it as he made his polite speech. Peter looked at the hand and saw what Henry Waring had seen and described twenty-five years before—a round white scar, the size of a threepenny-bit, half-way between the wrist and the middle knuckle. The hand was plump and smooth-skinned. The mark showed up distinctly.

"It's Henderson!" said Peter to himself. "It's Henderson!" And, as he said it, Hendebakker swung round and held out the hand with the scar.

"Very pleased to meet you, Mr. Waring," he repeated. His light eyes looked hard at Peter's face.

Peter had grown so pale that Anita, glancing at him lazily over her white shoulder, wondered what was the matter. Peter looked for a moment at Hendebakker, but made no movement to take his hand. The one thought which at that moment filled his mind was that this very hand had done murder upon his uncle and his father. He knew that he must say or do something; but he did not know what he would say or do. He heard Sylvia say, "Peter", and then he heard himself speak in a voice that was not at all like his ordinary voice, but sharper and colder. He heard himself say:

"Mr. Henderson, I believe—or is it Henders?"

Hendebakker raised his eyebrows, dropped his hand, stepped back half a pace.

"My name, sir, is Hendebakker—Virgil P. Hendebakker at your service—tolerably well known, too."

"Perhaps," said Peter, "there is a mistake somewhere."

Anita's lazy stare had become tinged with boredom.

"Sylvia, Mr. Waring, why do you not sit down?" she said. "They will take coffee with us, will they not, Virgilio?"

"I'm afraid," said Peter, "that I must be getting back to my party." He spoke gravely and quietly now; his self-control had returned to him.

He bowed and walked away. Mr. Hendebakker resumed his seat.

"And now," he said, speaking genially, "now I think we know where we are. Sit down, Lady Moreland, and have some coffee. Anita's been wild to see you all day."

Peter found his uncle and Mr. Cowan on their feet.

"Come up to my room," said Miles as he joined them. "Can't talk here—too many people."

They went up to the second floor where Mr. Banham had a private suite, no less. When the door of the sitting-room was closed, all three men remained standing. Miles was the first to speak.

"Now, Cowan," he said, "let's have it. That was one of the best dinners I've ever sat down to, and it was absolutely clean wasted on me. Out with it, man, out with it!"

Mr. Cowan seemed amused.

"What am I to come out with, my friend?"

Miles shook his fist at him.

"I saw it in your face," he said, "and I've been on thorns ever since." He turned to Peter. "Cowan knows more about precious stones than any man between this and China. That's why I asked him here tonight. That's why I asked you. Come to think of it, you'd better own up first, Peter. The thing that lovely lady had got stuck on the front of her frock—well, in one word, is it the Annam Jewel, or isn't it?"

"How should I know?" said Peter. He laid his arm along the mantelshelf as he spoke, and leaned on it. The room seemed to be quivering about him. He did not know that his face was ghastly.

"My good man, if it isn't, what's making you look as if you'd seen a ghost? You needn't be shy in front of Cowan or in front of me. I know a little more about the Jewel than most people do, though that's not saying much; and, as for Cowan, he's all solid moral worth, and probity, and cast-iron trustworthiness."

Mr. Cowan interposed.

"I think Mr. Waring has had a shock," he said. "It will be better if he says nothing until he is sure that he wishes to do so. As for what I have to say, it is very simple. I am, as my friend Banham says, an expert, or, as I prefer to put it, a specialist in precious stones."

He addressed himself to Peter.

"I am really a consultant. If it is a question of just how much cutting a great stone will bear, they do me the honour to send for me. Now, Mr. Waring, for years—yes, perhaps for thirty years—I have heard of a stone that is not like any other stone at all. The first I heard of it was in China when I was a youth. I was told there was mention of it in a very ancient Chinese manuscript. Since then I have heard, here and there, of this stone. I have never seen it. I have never met anyone who has seen it, or who has ever known a person who has seen it. I am interested; but I put it down, you understand, as one of those myths or legends which pass from one to another in the East and are as insubstantial as a mist. Then my friend Banham tells me a little more. He tells me, to be quite frank, the history of your family connection with the Jewel. You need not be troubled, Mr. Waring. I do not, perhaps, deserve all the pleasant things which my friend has said of me, but I certainly do not betray a confidence. Well, Banham tells me that; and then he tells me two other things. He says it is his belief that you will receive the Jewel when you are twenty-five, and he says the Jewel has appeared in London in possession of an American millionaire. I am naturally interested. He asked us both to dinner, and there enters a very beautiful woman, wearing something that I do not quite know how to describe."

Peter had been recovering himself. The room had become solid again. He looked at Mr. Cowan, frowned deeply, and said:

"She was wearing the Annam Jewel."

Miles Banham gave his knee a resounding slap. "Of course she was," he said triumphantly. "But how did she get it? That's the rub, how did she get it? And what did you get, Peter my boy?"

"I got a bit of glass," said Peter, "a fake—this."

He held out his hand with the sham Jewel in its palm.

Mr. Cowan nodded gravely.

"That was left you by your father?"

"That was left me by my father."

"Yes, that's very interesting," said Mr. Cowan, "very interesting indeed, because—and now I'm going to surprise you—the Jewel which Mrs. Hendebakker was wearing tonight—" he paused, and made a very slight gesture with his right hand—"that also is a fake."

Peter stood upright with a jerk. Miles Banham leaned forward, a hand on either knee, his withered brown face a-quiver with excitement, his eyes as bright and restless as a monkey's.

"What's that? What's that?" he said; and then, "By gum! By gum!"

"A fake?" said Peter. He lifted his arm from the mantelpiece and leaned back. "How could it be a fake? How could you tell?"

Mr. Cowan smiled.

"Ah, Mr. Waring," he said, "if I could tell you that—" he paused, and again made that slight gesture—"it is my *métier*, you see."

"But are you sure, Cowan, sure?" said Miles quickly.

Mr. Cowan nodded.

"I am sure," he said.

"Without handling it? Without any test?"

"Why, yes. I cannot explain—at least I think I cannot explain; but I will try. In all the great jewels there is something, something beyond the colour, the water, the fire—whatever you like to call it; I do not wish to be technical. This something, it is not life as we understand life, and yet it is the life of the stone. When Mrs. Hendebakker passed us, I looked for this something, and I did not find it. It is not there. No, I cannot explain; it will not go into words; but I am sure."

"If it's a fake, who made it?" said Miles quickly.

"That is it," said Mr. Cowan. "I know all the men who make such things, and I know of no one who could have made the stone we saw tonight." He nodded at Peter. "It *is* a stone, you know—a stone that has been made, not glass, or paste. Michel, now, he might have done it—"

Peter stood upright, his shoulders clear of the mantelpiece.

"Oh, Hendebakker made it," he said.

"Impossible!"

"No, sir, not impossible. You mentioned Michel. Now, I can't prove this, but Hendebakker's name used to be Henderson, and my father believed that it was Henders before that, and that he was Michel's assistant before the smash came."

"Ah," said Mr. Cowan gently. "Yes, that is very interesting; it would account for a great deal."

Miles Banham flung himself into a chair.

"By gum, what a mix-up!" he said. "Interesting evening we're having, aren't we? But what I want to know, my dear Cowan, and my excellent Peter, is—where is the real Jewel?"

Peter said nothing. Mr. Cowan pulled a chair into a comfortable position and seated himself.

"I wonder now," he said quietly, "whether there ever was a real Jewel!"

Chapter Seventeen

ROSE ELLEN CAME UP to town next day. Peter got her letter at breakfast.

Dearest wants me to look at coats for Jimmy, and I want hats and frocks. I'm sure you'd love to shop with me; and, anyhow, I thought we might have lunch somewhere. Would you like to meet my train?

Peter met the train. He was uncommonly pleased to see Rose Ellen. He didn't want to think about the Jewel, or Roden Coverdale, or Sylvia's money matters, or Virgil P. Hendebakker; most particularly he did not want to think about Virgil P. Hendebakker. It was extraordinarily pleasant to see Rose Ellen get out of the train. He thought she looked so cool, and fresh, and pretty.

They shopped coats for Jimmy—Jimmy being, of course, the Gaisford baby—and Rose Ellen bought two hats and three frocks, after which severe exercise they had lunch.

It was at lunch-time that the day began to cloud a little. It clouded for Rose Ellen when Peter started talking about Sylvia Moreland.

"I do want you to meet her," he said earnestly. "I've told her about you, of course; and I'm frightfully keen on your meeting. You don't really want to shop any more, do you? Because I thought that I could ring Sylvia up just to find out if she's going to be in, and we could go round there after we've had coffee."

"I've got lots more to do, Peter," said Rose Ellen.

"Not really? You can't have. You'll be stony-broke if you buy anything more. Look here. I'll telephone now and find out."

Peter came back triumphant.

"We're to go right along," he announced. "It's a bit of luck her being in—she has a frightful lot of engagements. I say, I'm most awfully glad you're going to meet her. You'll—you'll admire her frightfully."

"Shall I?" said Rose Ellen. A little sparkle came into her brown eyes. "And do you think, Peter dear, that she'll admire *me* frightfully, too?"

"You're getting vain," said Peter. "I shan't encourage you."

"Oh, Peter, but I want encouraging—I want it dreadfully, Peter de—ah." The sparkle died. Rose Ellen smiled her lovely smile.

Something warm and soft swept over Peter.

"You said 'Petah'," he said; "you said it worse than ever. Say it again. Say 'Petah de—ah'."

"I won't," said Rose Ellen. "I don't—I never do."

"And you never did? Oh, Rose Ellen, what a frightful story! You used to be truthful—but, removed from my moral influence—"

"Petah de—ah!" said Rose Ellen.

The sunshine lasted until they reached Sylvia's flat, when the day became so overcast that even Peter could not fail to be aware of it.

Sylvia was exquisite in black—the thinnest, latest, smartest black. Rose Ellen immediately realized that her coat and skirt were just a shade out of date. Sylvia greeted her graciously.

"Peter hasn't said your name," she said, "and it's so stupid of me, but I'm a little mixed—you don't call yourself Waring now, do you?"

"No," said Rose Ellen. "I took Mrs. Mortimer's name when she adopted me."

"Yes, of course. I suppose Peter told me, but changes of name are so difficult. Don't you find it rather confusing yourself? First your own name—I don't think Peter ever told me what it was—and then Waring, and then Mortimer, and—isn't she Mrs. Gaisford now? Shall you change again, or just stay as you are until you marry?"

The sparkle had returned to Rose Ellen's eyes. She met Sylvia's appraising glance, and said:

"I don't know, Lady Moreland. I haven't thought about it."

Just for a moment they looked at each other. In that moment Sylvia thought:

"Peter never told me how pretty she was. I wonder if he knows."

Rose Ellen's thought was sharper, thrusting deeper into the tender places of her heart:

"She hates me because she wants Peter. She's the sort that gets what she wants. She doesn't love him, but she wants him."

Sylvia turned to Peter.

"Oh, I met the Merritts this morning," she said. "They want you for their dance next week."

"I don't think I can go," said Peter.

"Oh yes, you can—with me. I told them you would, and they're counting on you."

Her manner was coolly possessive. She ignored Peter's frown, and explained to Rose Ellen.

"He's really getting fearfully dissipated, and I take great credit to myself for his dancing."

Then she began to talk to Peter about a play which they had seen together; a book she had lent him; a proposed expedition on the river with the Merritts. Every now and then she half turned to Rose Ellen with a casual, "I expect you're rather out of the way for theatres," or, "It's so difficult to keep up one's reading in the country, don't you think?"

After about a quarter of an hour of this sort of thing Rose Ellen got up.

"I'm so sorry," she said, "but my train won't wait for me, and I've left some of my shopping rather late."

Peter got up too. He was looking cross, and had been replying to Sylvia's flow of conversation with monosyllables.

"Oh, you mustn't go yet," said Sylvia. "Why, you must have quite a budget of country news to give Peter, and I'm sure he's dying to hear it—how the hens are laying, and all that sort of thing." Sylvia's tone was lightly impertinent. She smiled charmingly as she spoke.

Rose Ellen's colour deepened. She looked at Sylvia with a gentle dignity which seemed to set a distance between them. Sylvia read the look easily enough. It said, "Use your weapons; they are not mine."

Rose Ellen held out her hand.

"My news must keep," she said; "or I can give it to Peter next time he comes to Merton Clevery. Good-bye, Lady Moreland."

Peter followed her from the room. Neither of them spoke until they reached the street. Then Rose Ellen said:

"You needn't come to the station, Peter."

"I needn't, but I'm going to," said Peter gloomily. Then, after a pause: "I thought you'd have hit it off so well. Why on earth can't women get on together?"

"I don't know, Peter," said Rose Ellen.

They walked on in silence. At the corner of the street Rose Ellen turned on Peter.

"I hate hens, I simply *hate* them!" she said with vehemence.

"So do I," said Peter. "I should think everyone does."

He looked at Rose Ellen and saw that her eyes were bright with tears. He gave her arm a little squeeze.

"I say, Rose Ellen, don't. I'm a cross beast. Don't let's quarrel. But I did think you'd like her, because—well, she's a great friend of mine, and I like you to like my friends."

"She's most awfully pretty, Peter de—ah," said Ellen.

They finished the shopping, and Rose Ellen caught her train. Peter found her a corner seat in a carriage which contained two old ladies and an immense number of parcels. Just at the last moment, when Rose Ellen gave him both her hands, Peter felt that same sense of something soft and warm; it swept over him and filled him with a desire to go on holding Rose Ellen's hands. Then the train began to move. The warm moment was gone.

Chapter Eighteen

The library at Sunnings was a very pleasant room; from its window you could see how the lawns ran down to the river. The grass was not as carefully tended as it had been, and the shrubberies were overgrown, but a hundred different shades of spring green made the prospect a pleasing one.

Roden Coverdale sat at a table which faced the windows. Sometimes he sat quite still, watching the sunlight flicker on the distant water; sometimes he looked down, frowning at the newspaper cuttings which were spread on the table before him. There were a good many cuttings, mostly from the Society papers. He began to pick them up and make a little pile of them. Occasionally he read a few words. To the last one he gave a more careful scrutiny. It had only reached him that morning. He read it right through before he laid it down. It was an extract from one of those letters which have become a weekly feature in certain papers:

> Guess whom I saw last night—but you'll never! A real close-up, and with my very own *beaux yeux*. I give you three guesses. You don't know? You can't say. Then I s'pose I must tell you—why, the lovely, the beautiful, the *only* Mrs. Virgil P. with the lovely, the beautiful, the *only* Jewel pinned on the front of her frock as usual. My dearest, it's a Dream, a *Scream*. I've been seeing blue, and green, and red, and yellow lights ever since. And Reggie says that a friend of his who's a *great* friend of Marshall Simpkinson—*the* Marshall— says that it's simply *the* only one in the world, and that even *he* doesn't know what it is.

He got up and rang the bell.

"I'm going to town," he said to the maid who answered it. "The car for the four-fifteen, and have my bag packed—things for a couple of days. Ring up Lady Moreland and tell her I'm coming. Say, if it's at all inconvenient, I'll go on to an hotel. I don't want any letters forwarded."

Sylvia got her father's message at four. It was the day after Rose Ellen's visit to town. She hung up the receiver, and went to her room, where she dressed for the street.

Ten minutes later she was handing in a telegram addressed to Virgil P. Hendebakker at The Luxe hotel. It ran, "Shares rising", and was signed "Moreland".

Roden Coverdale dined alone with his daughter. It was not until after dinner that he gave any reason for his sudden visit to town. Then he leaned back in one of the large, black chairs and said, breaking in suddenly upon some triviality of Sylvia's:

"By the way, have you heard of or come across this Hendebakker man that the papers are so full of?"

"Are they full of him?" said Sylvia innocently.

"They seem to be. I'm getting rather tired of his name. Have you come across him at all?"

"Oh yes." Sylvia took up *Punch* and began to turn the leaves. "This is a frightfully good cartoon. Have you seen it? What were you saying? The Hendebakkers? Oh yes, I've seen quite a lot of them—Anita's a great friend of mine."

"Anita?"

"Mrs. Virgil P."

"Ah yes."

There was a pause. Sylvia began to feel nervous. Which would be most natural—for her to speak, or remain silent? Should she ask why he was interested in the Hendebakkers, or just leave it to him? But supposing he didn't say anything more! Oh, how she hated it all! And what an utter, utter fool she had been to let a man like Hendebakker get such a hold over her that she must do his bidding or say good-bye to all the things which made life tolerable!

The silence lasted until she could have screamed. Then Coverdale said:

"You are intimate with these people? What is he like?"

Sylvia described Hendebakker: the strength; the heavy build; the light, cold eyes.

"And the wife?" asked Coverdale.

"Oh, quite beautiful—young, you know; much too young for him, but they seem quite happy."

"And the Jewel that all the papers make such a fuss about?"

Sylvia's nervousness merged into triumph.

"It's the most extraordinary thing," she said; "it really is. You've never seen anything like it."

Coverdale got up.

"Haven't I, Sylvia my dear? Well, just between you and me, I rather think I have."

"Oh!" said Sylvia. She leaned forward, clasping her hands, her eyes shining, her face flushed. "I remember years ago you told me something about a jewel—that time Peter Waring stayed with us. Do you remember? I've never said a word to anyone, but you can't think how much I've wanted to know. You're going to tell me, aren't you? Oh, you must!"

He looked at her, his thin, dark face very grave, his eyes full of melancholy.

"Yes, I'm going to tell you, Sylvia," he said.

There was a pause. He stood with his back to the fireplace. A tiny fire burned there, just a handful of clear red embers. There were white lilies in the far corner of the room, a great sheaf of them in a rare porcelain jar of the Ming period; the scent hung heavy on the air. Coverdale began to speak, looking sometimes all the flowers, sometimes at his daughter's face:

"You're my only child, Sylvia. I'm going to tell you about the Jewel. I don't know if women ever reach the age of discretion; but most of them are strongly alive to the claims of self-interest. In any case—" he smiled slightly and watched the lamplight fall golden on a lily bud—"in any case, it really matters very little—to me."

Sylvia's breath came fast.

"Why do you talk like that?" she said. "I never know what you mean. What are you going to tell me? What about the Jewel?"

"Well," said Coverdale, "just this." He put his hand into his waistcoat pocket and took out a small silver matchbox. He pressed the spring. The lid flew back, and he shook into the palm of his left hand what appeared to be a screw of tissue paper.

"There," he said, holding it out to Sylvia, "take the paper off and look at it. At least, if you do talk, you'll be able to say truthfully that you've had the Annam Jewel in your hand."

Sylvia did not rise or change her position. Her fingers shook as she felt something hard between the folds of paper. Very slowly she undid the wrappings. Three folds—and then, there on the white paper, the Jewel. She looked at it, and could not speak.

"Well?" said Mr. Coverdale. "Ever seen anything like it before, Sylvia?"

"Yes," said Sylvia in a whisper. "Yes. I don't understand. I saw Anita wear it last night. Are there two?"

Coverdale picked up the Jewel, and held it under the light.

"Two like this?" he said.

Sylvia stared at it. Even to her untrained eyes the thing had a warmth and a glory which staggered her. The golden ray in the heart of it seemed to beat with a living pulse. The red, and the green, and the blue were like a rainbow come alive.

"Well, Sylvia?" said Roden Coverdale.

"Anita has one," she said, still in that whisper.

He laughed, reached for the tissue paper, and wrapped the Jewel in it carefully.

"There's only one Jewel," he said. "But I shall be interested to see Mrs. Hendebakker's copy."

He put the matchbox into his pocket.

"And now, my dear, I have to write a letter. May I use your table?"

Sylvia stood beside him at the little escritoire until she was sure that he had all he needed; then she slipped out of the room. When she returned she had a filmy scrap of a handkerchief in her hand. Inside the handkerchief there was a twist of tissue paper; and inside the tissue paper a coat button of a suitable size and shape.

Presently, when her father had finished his letter and had come back to the fire, she said:

"Let me see it again. You simply snatched it away, you know; and it's much, much too beautiful to take in all in a moment. Do let me have another look at it."

He dropped the matchbox into her outstretched hand, and watched her with a rather sardonic smile as she unwrapped the Jewel.

"Where have you had it put away all this time?" she said. "Was it at Sunnings, or have you had it stuck away in the bank? It's a perfectly frightful waste, anyhow."

Coverdale laughed a little.

"It wasn't at Sunnings," he said, "and it wasn't at the bank. I think, on the whole, that I won't tell you where it was. But this is the first time it has seen the light for twenty years; and tomorrow it goes back again."

"*What* a waste!" said Sylvia, sighing. "Why don't you give it to me, Father?" She spoke very lightly.

"You're a great deal better off without it, my dear," he said. "Don't look at it too long, or you won't be able to give it up; and, as I said, you're really better without it. Come, let me have it back."

Sylvia smoothed out the little square of paper, laid the Jewel in the middle of it, and slowly, regretfully, folded the paper over the stone, and twisted up the ends. Just as she finished doing so, the twist slipped down into her lap and was hidden for a moment under her handkerchief. The next instant she was pressing a little white screw into the silver matchbox, and was handing back the matchbox with a "There, take it whilst I can give it up."

Coverdale fished a thin steel chain out of his pocket, and snapped it on to the box with a spring catch. Then he began to talk of other things.

Sylvia sat with the Annam Jewel in her lap, listening to his voice as one listens to a distant sound like the hum of traffic. She was in a state between terror and triumph.

Coverdale talked of Sunnings, and his financial position. He spoke of selling the property and going East again. Sylvia said sometimes, "Yes," and sometimes, "No." Her colour, which had been bright, died slowly. The evening dragged like a dull play. Coverdale had had enough of it by half past ten. He remarked that Sylvia looked as if she had been having too many late nights, and they said good night.

In her room Sylvia stood listening, her handkerchief clasped tightly in her left hand. When the hand trembled she could feel a little rustling movement from within the handkerchief. She kept saying to herself, "It's the Annam Jewel. I've got the Annam Jewel." She heard Coverdale's door close, heard him moving in his room, and waited until the sounds of movement ceased. Then she slipped a warm wrap over her thin black dress, and let herself noiselessly out of the flat.

Chapter Nineteen

SYLVIA MORELAND paid off her taxi at the door of The Luxe hotel, and passed into the brilliantly lighted lounge.

In answer to her inquiry, the hall porter asserted that Mr. and Mrs. Hendebakker had not yet returned.

"I'll wait," said Sylvia. "Tell them as soon as they come in, please— Lady Moreland."

She sat down on a sofa which commanded a good view of the entrance. The golden lights in the roof shone upon a moving crowd of people; but all this outside world of colour, gaiety, and movement became to Sylvia something at which she looked from a great way off. She had a sense of separation, of distance, of the irrevocable. Her triumph was cold. A realization that she had taken a step of which she could not measure the consequences swept over her, and chilled her to the very bone. What had she done? What had she done? What would happen next? She began to be very much afraid. She had stolen the Jewel at Hendebakker's bidding. She had stolen it because she was so much afraid of Hendebakker; but now, with this new chill upon her, she began to be afraid of Roden Coverdale. If he knew—*when* he knew! Her heart began to beat heavily. She leaned back against the sapphire velvet of the settee and closed her eyes.

When he knew, *if* he knew! She clenched her hand. Why should he know? He had not looked at the Jewel for twenty years. Why should he look at it again before it went back to its hiding-place? And in that hiding-place it might lie unseen for another twenty years. What a fool she was! She had done brilliantly. Hendebakker would pay all her debts. She would be free; and it was safe, quite safe; her father would never know.

She lifted her head, opened her eyes, and saw Roden Coverdale come into the lounge.

Peter had dined with Miles Banham, done a theatre, and walked back to The Luxe with him. Once there, he declined supper, but stood by the lift for ten minutes or so talking. He had just turned away, and was crossing the lounge, when a gap in the moving stream of people gave him a glimpse of Sylvia Moreland that brought him to a standstill. It was Sylvia, but Sylvia as he had never seen her. He moved out of the crowd, and took a step or two towards her. She was leaning back, her black dress almost hidden by a long wrap of white fur. Her face was white too, and her eyes were closed.

Just for a moment Peter wondered if she had fainted. As the thought crossed his mind, she sat up and looked, not at him, but at the entrance. Instantly an extraordinary change came over her. She sprang to her feet, and then stood rigid, her eyes wide, her face so expressionless as to have lost all impress of thought or personality. Peter knew that look for what it was—terror, sheer, mindless terror. But Sylvia—what in the world could bring that look to Sylvia's face? He swung about and turned towards the entrance.

Anita Hendebakker had just come in. One hand held her lace mantilla together at the breast. All eyes rested upon her.

As Peter turned, Virgil Hendebakker came through the door and joined her. But Sylvia—Sylvia was not looking at the Hendebakkers. Peter, glancing over his shoulder at her, was aware of this. She wasn't looking at the Hendebakkers, but at a man who was standing by himself away on the right, a slight, dark man with an air of distinguished melancholy. Peter recognized him at once. It was Roden Coverdale.

He looked back at Sylvia and saw that she had begun to move. Very slowly she was edging towards one of the fluted gilt pillars which supported the roof. There was a bank of flame-coloured azaleas at its foot. Sylvia kept her face towards the entrance, and moved slowly,

slowly. What in the world ...? He crossed the floor quickly, and spoke her name:

"Sylvia, what on earth's the matter?" he said. "Are you ill?"

When Sylvia opened her eyes and saw her father come into the lounge she ceased to see anything else; there were a lot of lights; there was a room full of mist; there was her father's face. She couldn't see anything else. In an extremity of terror she began to move without any idea of where she was going. Under her fur wrap her stiffened fingers still clutched the handkerchief which held the Jewel. She took a few uncertain steps, and the mist grew thicker. She no longer saw anything at all. She did not know that her father had seen her and was beginning to move in her direction, or that the Hendebakkers were also coming towards her. She saw nothing till Peter touched her arm and she heard his voice, full of concern, asking if she were ill. And then the mist lifted, and she saw his face. It was Peter, kind, safe Peter—the relief, the blessed relief!

On the impulse her hand went out to him, the hand that held the Jewel. At her touch Peter looked down. Sylvia was pushing a handkerchief into his hand, a handkerchief that held something hard. And then, before he could speak, she had turned her back on him and was moving through the crowd. He heard Anita's voice say, "Ah, Sylvia, you will have supper with us. Will she not, Virgilio?" And then, as he himself moved forward, he saw Coverdale come up to his daughter and put a hand on her arm.

He had no wish to become any further involved with the Hendebakkers. From where he stood he could see the flash of the diamond wings on Anita's breast, and, between the wings, the glow of the Jewel. Cowan said it was a fake. If Cowan was right, what must the real Jewel be like? No, he must avoid the Hendebakkers. Sylvia was all right, since she was with her father. He put the handkerchief which she had given him into his pocket, and walked out of the hotel.

It was a fine, starry night. He speculated for a moment as to what had frightened Sylvia, and then, looking up at the sky, hoped that the day would be fair after such a fine night. Miles Banham, who had just bought a car, was going to drive him down to lunch at Wimbledon with Ruth Spottiswoode and her sister Charlotte. It would be a pity if it rained.

He let himself into his rooms, switched on the light, and fished out the handkerchief which Sylvia had given him, his thought casual and just tinged with amusement. "Wonder what she was playing at!" was the nearest it came to being formulated.

The handkerchief was crumpled up round something hard. Peter spread it out, wondering how anything so flimsy and so small could be of the slightest use. And then he burst out laughing. Sylvia must have been playing him a practical joke. He did not know what he had expected the handkerchief to contain, but he had certainly not guessed that it would be a sweet—one of those peppermints or caramels which are sold done up in a screw of paper. It was rather a stupid joke, anyhow—not much point in it.

He took up the screw of paper and untwisted it. Three twists— and something hard fell out upon the table and lay there under the unshaded light. It was the Jewel!

Peter felt exactly as if he had been hit. It was the Annam Jewel! But how? How on earth? Why, he had seen it blazing between the diamond wings on Anita Hendebakker's breast not a quarter of an hour ago. He put out his hand and touched it gingerly, moving it a little, and the four great colours leaped in it like flames—leaped, rushed together, melted, burned.

Peter turned from it with a jerk and walked to the window. Cowan—Cowan had said that the Hendebakker Jewel was a fake; and Cowan had said, "I wonder if there is a real Jewel at all."

Peter laughed. He heard his own laugh, and it startled him; it was so harsh and strained. "I wonder if there is a real Jewel at all." Good old Cowan, he wouldn't say that now—unless, unless all this was a dream. He walked back to the table and looked soberly and long at the Jewel. It was real. It was the Annam Jewel; the only one in the world. He looked at it, frowning. It was the Annam Jewel; and Sylvia Moreland had pushed it into his hand in the lounge at The Luxe hotel. How? Why? What had Sylvia to do with it at all?

Again Peter saw himself with a book in his hand, a book bound in Imperial Chinese yellow. Again he read the author's name, Roden

Coverdale. And then the book was another book, a shabby old exercise-book; and he was looking at what were probably the last words that his father had ever written:

"*N.B.*—To find out the real name of the man who calls himself Roden Dale ..."

Peter stood for a long time, frowning at the Jewel. As the tide of confused thoughts and fancies ebbed, it left bare these main facts. The Jewel before him was not the Hendebakker Jewel. Sylvia had pushed it into his hand; and from whom would Sylvia have got it except from her father—from Roden Dale? Sylvia had stolen it! The blank terror on her face was explained; she had taken the Jewel, and then suddenly, in the lounge at The Luxe, she had seen the man from whom she had stolen it—she had seen her father.

Peter's frown became a scowl. It was pretty beastly when you came to think of it, a girl robbing her father; but that, undoubtedly, was what Sylvia had been doing—how or why Peter had no idea; he merely came gloomily to the conclusion that it was a pretty rotten sort of show.

He stared at the Jewel with something like aversion. For years and years it had been at the very centre of his dream; and now here it was under his hand, beautiful beyond all his thought of it. The glory of the dream was gone, the glamour and the romance. He was conscious of a cold distaste. He put out his hand and touched it again, pushing it away with a little jerk of the finger. Once more the colours leapt and mingled, fused and dissolved. It was like watching the flow of light. He saw the blue burn to a deep blood-red, and the emerald flame into gold. His thought became more definite. There was the Jewel People had done some pretty beastly things because of it—battle, and murder, and sudden death. Peter had had enough of that sort of thing. It was beastly; he hated it. And now Sylvia—Sylvia with the look of panic on her face—why had she pushed the Jewel into his hand? What on earth did she expect him to do with it? Of one thing he felt quite sure—he wasn't going to be mixed up in any rotten sort of business like a girl stealing from her own father. The Jewel should go back to Coverdale in the morning. He wasn't sure whether the Jewel really belonged to Coverdale or not. If it belonged to him, let him keep it. If it was his,

Peter's, he might try to get it away from Coverdale, or he might not. He would have to think that out. But, in any case, Sylvia mustn't be mixed up in the affair. It was between him and Coverdale. Sylvia had nothing whatever to do with it.

Having arrived at this conclusion, Peter felt much lightened in spirit. He left Sylvia's handkerchief lying on the table, swept the Jewel off into the palm of his hand, and went into his bedroom, where he dropped it casually into the box which held his studs. Then he went to bed and slept the sleep of the single-minded.

Chapter Twenty

RODEN COVERDALE touched his daughter on the arm.

"Are you ready, my dear?" he said pleasantly.

He felt her quiver. Then Anita's voice broke in, "But you stay—you sup with us, Sylvia, do you not—and perhaps your friend also?"

Coverdale looked at her, smiled charmingly, and bowed as Sylvia murmured what might pass for an introduction. Then he turned a little, coming face to face with Hendebakker, and stopped smiling.

"Hullo, Dale!" said Hendebakker. "Quite a while since we met, isn't it?"

Coverdale's face was a blank.

"Why, yes," he said with a slight drawl, "so it is, Henders—quite a while."

It was a mutual declaration of war.

Anita's dark eyes looked with a puzzled expression from one to the other. She came a little closer to her husband.

"Virgilio ..." she began timidly.

And then Coverdale had drawn Sylvia's hand within his arm, and was bowing to her again.

"I fear I must take my daughter home," he said, speaking easily.

Neither he nor Sylvia spoke until they reached the flat. Then, as he pushed open the drawing-room door and switched on the lights, Sylvia hung back.

"I—I don't think I'll sit up tonight," she said, in a tone which hardly rose above a whisper. "It's pretty late, isn't it?"

She leaned against the jamb of the door. Coverdale drew her into the room.

"I won't keep you very long," he said. "You'd better sit down. You look tired."

"Yes, I am—tired." She was still whispering, but suddenly her voice broke into a sob. "Let me go, *please* let me go."

Coverdale looked at her curiously. What odd things women were!

"Come, Sylvia," he said, "pull yourself together. You really needn't look so scared. You know, you women are the most unaccountable creatures on earth. Men have a conscience or they don't have a conscience—or for conscience substitute moral sense. But women have something that they take off and on, as if it were a hat or a frock. It's not there one moment, and they'll lie and steal as cheerfully as the most hardened criminal; and then, half an hour later, on goes the conscience again—and pretty cowards it makes of them. As an affectionate parent, I would advise you, Sylvia my dear, either to wear your conscience always, or to get rid of it altogether."

"I don't know what you mean," said Sylvia pettishly.

"Oh yes, you do. You know very well."

He held out the silver matchbox, open, and shook the twisted screw on to her lap.

"Open it!" he said, in a tone which contrasted sharply with the very quiet one which he had been using.

Sylvia's fingers trembled. The paper rustled. A black satin button fell out upon the carpet and rolled a little way. Coverdale picked it up and balanced it on his forefinger.

"Quite a nice thing in its way, but not the Annam Jewel," he remarked. Then, still more gently, "And now, perhaps, you will give it back to me."

He flicked the button into the fire and held out his hand. Sylvia stared at the carpet.

"I don't know what you mean," she said.

"Don't you? Come, Sylvia, it's no good. Give it back."

"I haven't got it," said Sylvia.

He took both her hands, and lifted her to her feet.

"Now, Sylvia!"

"I haven't got it, I tell you."

"Then what have you done with it? You had it, and you went to The Luxe with it. Henders has a finger in the pie, I suppose. You were going to sell it to him?"

"Oh, you're hurting my hands! I didn't—I didn't give it to him."

"Simply because you hadn't the chance!" His tone was cool and contemptuous. "But you were going to. Come, Sylvia, the truth! You went to The Luxe to give the Jewel to Henders."

"I didn't want to. I hated it. He made me." The words came trembling from Sylvia's lips. "I didn't give it to him—I didn't."

"Then where is it? What have you done with it?"

"I couldn't help it, I really couldn't—you frightened me so dreadfully—and I thought I was going to faint."

"What couldn't you help? What did you do?"

Sylvia pulled her hands away. Her white fur wrap fell to the ground.

"I saw him," she said, "quite suddenly—and it seemed the only thing to do. It was wrapped up in my handkerchief, and I just pushed it into his hand in the crowd."

"The Jewel? You pushed the Jewel into his hand? Whose hand? What are you talking about?"

"It was Peter—it was Peter Waring," said Sylvia, with a sob.

Coverdale spread out his hands with a curious gesture. He stood silent for a full minute. Then he said, speaking softly as if to himself:

"So the wheel has come full circle again."

Peter arose next morning in good spirits. When he had had his breakfast he packed the Annam Jewel up carefully, using a small yellow cardboard box which had contained visiting-cards—he left the cards lying in a heap on his chest of drawers. Then he walked to the Regent Street post office, entered a telephone box, and called up Sylvia's flat. It was a maid who answered.

"Is Mr. Coverdale there?" Peter asked. "He's left? Can you give me his address? Oh, he's gone back to Sunnings? You're sure? Thank you. No, my name doesn't matter."

He rang off, and went to the counter, where he bought a registered envelope. Into this he pushed the yellow cardboard box, fastened the flap, and addressed the package to Roden Coverdale, Esquire. He walked away from the post office without a regret. The Annam Jewel was out of his hands. With Sylvia and her affairs he would deal presently. Meanwhile it was a most uncommonly jolly day; Peter was pleased with it and with the world in general.

He met Miles Banham by appointment at the garage where the car was housed. Miles was bursting with pride in his new possession, and mad keen to be off. Peter gathered that he had had three lessons in driving, and was prepared to go anywhere and do anything.

They set off at what seemed to Peter a rather heroic speed. Miles had a way of cutting corners which promised adventure. The rare and belated sounding of his horn suggested triumph over other vehicles successfully left behind, rather than a warning to those which still blocked his way.

"Slow movers some of these people, what? And as for these blighted pedestrians ..."

He shaved an errand boy on a bicycle, swerved in the direction of two stout ladies with shopping-baskets, and proceeded swiftly along the King's Road, talking all the time.

"I made my will yesterday," he remarked conversationally. "Thought I'd let you know that I'd left my bit to you."

"Good lord, Uncle Miles, don't talk about wills whilst you're driving like this!" said Peter, grinning.

"What? Why not? Rattling good mover, isn't she? I say, that was a near thing, wasn't it? Yes, I've left it all to you."

"It's frightfully good of you," said Peter. "I really think you'd better go a bit slower, or we shall be run in. You touched fifty that last spasm—it's a bit steep for the King's Road."

"What's fifty?" said Miles, with contempt. "All right, I'll go a bit easy; but just you wait till I get a chance to let her rip. Yes, as I say, you'll be a rich man."

"Oh no, I shan't," said Peter. "Look here, that's Putney Bridge, and you really must slow down. You'll get married, you see if you don't."

Miles Banham slowed down with extreme reluctance.

"Well, I don't know about that," he said. "Of course, I've thought about it; but it's a risk, my boy, a big risk; and I don't like taking risks."

"Oh, lord, Uncle, mind that perambulator!" said Peter. Miles avoided it by a frantic swerve and continued to talk.

"No, I don't like risks; and it's a big one, as I said. You see, the bother about marriage is that you never know where you are. Women—oh, damn this traffic! By Jove, we nearly took the wheel off that baker's van, didn't we? Women now—the bother about women is that the good ones are too good for any man living, and the bad ones are a damned sight too bad. What I would like is someone I'd been married to for ten years or so and got used to. I don't see starting in at my time of life. By gum, that dog nearly caught it! Sporting little beast, did you see how he jumped clear?"

"Look here, Uncle, you come down to twenty and stay there till we've passed all these shops," said Peter firmly.

"All right, all right. Now I've sometimes thought that Ruth Spottiswoode and I might hit it off. She's a nice woman, Ruth, and what I call comfortable. But then there's Charlotte—I couldn't live with Charlotte, I'm hanged if I could. Not but what she's a good woman and all that, but … no, I'm hanged if I could live with Charlotte."

"Perhaps you wouldn't have to," said Peter cheerfully. "She could live somewhere near, and just come in and out."

"Ah, but that's the question—could I stand it? Charlotte coming in and out, I mean. I've thought of that, you know; and then I've wondered whether I wouldn't rather have her in the house and be done with it. You see, it would be a bit awkward for me to go to Ruth and say, 'Look here, will you marry me? But I can't stick Charlotte at any price.' What are you grinning at? I tell you it's dam' serious—getting married's no joke, as you'll find when your turn comes."

Lunch was a highly successful meal: Ruth Spottiswoode, beaming and expansive in lavender silk and a new and most poignant kind of scent; Charlotte, grimly genial in a best dress that clinked with jet; and Miles, very much the returned hero. Peter felt himself a little boy again when the cousins addressed him. Charlotte's tone in particular, with its hint of "we mustn't spoil the child", took him back to the time when he was twelve years old.

When they were going away, Mrs. Spottiswoode drew him aside.

"Peter my dear, your Uncle Miles—does he wrap up sufficiently when driving in that open car?"

"I don't know," said Peter. "Shall I ask him?"

"No, no, my dearest boy. No, of course not. He might think it strange. But, of course, we are cousins, though not first cousins—and second half-cousin is not really a very *close* relation—only, of course, I've known Miles all my life, and that does seem to make a difference, doesn't it?"

"I should think it would," said Peter, putting his arm round her waist. He was very fond of his Cousin Ruth.

"You really think so? Of course, what he wants is someone to look after him, which is a thing no man ever learns to do for himself. No, my dearest boy, you may laugh as much as you like, but I've never yet met a man who could look after himself. You're all alike. It's no good saying you're not. For instance, tell me, Peter, do you ever remember to change your socks when they're damp, or to see that your vests and things are aired when they come home from the wash?"

Peter gave her a squeeze and a kiss.

"I air them with my own hands in front of my landlady's kitchen fire every Saturday night," he declared. "As for Uncle Miles, you'd better take him on yourself."

Ruth fluttered, and blushed to the roots of her hair.

Later on, as they drove off, Peter said:

"Cousin Ruth thinks you want someone to look after you. She thinks we both do. She's afraid we don't air our socks before we put them on."

"What? *Does* she now? *Does* she? Now, Ruth's what I call a real, old-fashioned, womanly woman—and you needn't laugh, my boy, about her wanting things to be aired, because I can remember my dear mother being just the same." He skidded round a corner in meditative silence, just missed a tradesman's delivery van, and added in a tone of triumph, "I told you Ruth was a nice woman; but then there's Charlotte—there's always Charlotte. I'm pretty sure I couldn't stick Charlotte. Hullo, here's a good stretch of road. Now you just see what she can do."

They crossed Wimbledon Common at a speed which appeared to gratify Miles a good deal, and then came down to what he called a crawl until they had passed Surbiton.

"We'll run into Guildford for tea," said Miles. "Splendid road, and I might look up a fellow I used to know in Hong Kong."

They never reached Guildford. Half a mile out of Cobham they collided with a farm wagon and came off second best. Miles was very much annoyed. He took the simple view that horse vehicles had really no right to the use of the roads; but that, pending their total supersession by something less archaic, it became them to order themselves lowly and reverently to all their betters, as he himself had been taught in his catechism. That one of these anachronisms should have done in his new thirty-horse-power car was an insult which elicited from him an astonishing flow of Anglo-Oriental language.

In the upshot they were towed ignominiously into Cobham, where they kicked their heels for four or five hours. Peter would not abandon Miles, and nothing would induce Miles to abandon his car.

It was past ten o'clock when Peter reached his rooms. He let himself in. In the passage he encountered his landlady; she wore an air of subdued importance.

"Jones 'as just stepped out," she explained, "and, 'earing your key, sir, I thought I'd just let you know as your sister's been here waiting for you for quite a while."

"My sister?" said Peter, in tones of stupefaction.

"Called at three o'clock, she did," said Mrs. Jones, with a slight sniff. "Jones opened the door, and she asked for you, and when he said you was out, she asked when you would be back. She went away, and come back again, and since six o'clock she's been a-sittin' and a-waitin' for you."

"My sister?" repeated Peter. He found himself very angry. What on earth could have brought Rose Ellen to town like this, and to his rooms?

"So she said, sir. Miss Waring, sir, she said." Mrs. Jones sniffed again; this time it was undoubtedly the sniff of feminine virtue.

Peter stiffened.

"Will you call a taxi, please?" he said. "I shall be seeing my sister home. I've been delayed."

He was not at all pleased with Rose Ellen. She ought to have known better. He would tell her so in no measured terms.

He opened the door of his sitting-room and went in. A woman in black with a long veil was sitting in one of his arm-chairs. She jumped up as he came in. It was not Rose Ellen. It was Sylvia Moreland.

"What on earth ...?" said Peter.

Sylvia stamped her foot, and said:

"Oh, Peter, you've come at last. I thought you were *never* coming. Give it to me, give it to me—quick!"

"Give you what?" said Peter.

She flung back her veil with an impatient gesture.

"The Jewel—the Jewel! Give me the Jewel—give it me at once!"

"I haven't got it," said Peter.

Sylvia caught his arm.

"You must have it, you must have it; I gave it you. What are you talking about? I gave it you last night at The Luxe—it was wrapped up in my handkerchief—I pushed it into your hand, and you took it. Give it back to me quickly, and let me go." She was shaking his arm as she spoke, her face very near his own.

Peter saw suddenly that the colour in her cheeks was artificial, and that beneath it she was very white. Her eyes had dark circles under them. Her eyes were very blue.

"Give it me. Give it back to me," she said.

"I haven't got it, Sylvia," said Peter gravely.

There was a knock at the door. It opened. Mrs. Jones appeared. "The taxi 'as come," she said.

"All right. We'll be down in a moment."

Mrs. Jones sniffed, withdrew, went slowly down the stairs.

"What taxi?" said Sylvia.

"Yours. You can't stay here. You oughtn't to have come."

"As if I cared!"

Peter took her by the arm.

"We can talk in the taxi," he said. "I'll take you home."

In the taxi Sylvia was silent. Twice she took out her pocket-handkerchief and dabbed her eyes. Once, when Peter began to speak, she said, "No, wait, wait," in a muffled voice. He became aware that she was crying. He was angry with Sylvia, and angry with himself. Sylvia was really crying. The long wait, the hours without food, terrified recollections of this morning's interview with Hendebakker, terrified anticipations of another interview with him tomorrow—these things brought the tears of acute self-pity to her eyes. The recollection of Hendebakker, the sheer strength and weight of the man, his rough, hard voice, filled her with panic. She shrank from the memory of what that voice had said, but no shrinking saved her from remembrance. "You never thought that Anita would count those loose diamonds, did you? Well, *she* didn't; but I did. D'ye get that? I did. You never thought three or four of them would be missed, did you? Well, now, that's just where you slipped up, and I've got the man you sold them to right under my hand and ready to swear to you any day of the week. And *now* will you do what I tell you, my dear?" Sylvia shuddered from head to foot.

When the taxi stopped and he had paid the man, Peter said:

"Look here, I'll come and see you tomorrow and tell you all about it."

Sylvia gave a little cry that was half a sob.

"As if I should sleep a single wink!" she said. "We've got to have it out."

Peter went in with her. Sylvia's room was full of yellow roses; they smelt very sweet. She switched on all the lights, and turned impatiently on Peter.

"What have you done with the Jewel? I gave it you. I want it back."

Peter stood over her, very large. He felt a brute, but was angry enough not to mind.

"It wasn't exactly yours to give, was it?" he said.

The real crimson rose to Sylvia's cheeks.

"How dare you?" she cried.

Peter laughed.

"If it comes to that, how did you dare?" he retorted.

"I don't know what you mean."

"I'm quite sure you know what I mean. You took the Jewel from your father, and you were going to give it to that brute Hendebakker." Sylvia stared at him, flushed and curious.

"How did you know, Peter? How *did* you know?"

He said nothing. After a minute she put out her hand rather timidly and touched him.

"Peter, you're angry. Oh, don't be angry with me. Please, please don't—I'm so miserable."

She was crying again quietly. Peter began to mind being a brute.

"Look here, Sylvia, what's the use of all this?" he said.

Sylvia made a sudden movement towards him.

"Peter, give it back to me," she whispered.

"My dear girl, I haven't got it—I told you I hadn't."

"Then—where is it?"

"I sent it back to your father, of course," said Peter. "And look here, Sylvia, I may as well make my position clear. I've no idea how much you know about the Jewel, its history, and so forth; but my position is this, either the Jewel belongs to your father or it belongs to me, and I'm hanged if either of us will let Hendebakker have it. I think you'd better get that quite clear."

"I don't know—I don't know anything," she sobbed. "Peter, I'm—I'm utterly wretched."

"Oh, for the Lord's sake, Sylvia, don't cry." He patted her shoulder. "Look here, my dear girl, I mean—oh, I say, Sylvia, what is the use of crying? You'd much better make a clean breast of the whole thing and tell me why you did it."

Sylvia leaned against him, and felt that his arm was strong and comfortable.

"He—he told me it was only a copy," she sobbed.

"Who did?"

"Virgil Hendebakker."

"Good lord, you didn't believe him?"

"Of course I did—anyone would have. How was I to know which was the real one? I thought it was only a sort of joke—I did really. And now my father will never forgive me. Why, he wouldn't even let me explain. And you—you hate me for it." She trembled as she spoke, her head against his shoulder. She looked up at him for a moment, and then down again. Her eyes were very blue indeed.

"I don't hate you," said Peter gruffly.

"Don't you?" said Sylvia, with a quiver in her voice. "Are you sure? I—I didn't mean to cry or make a fuss, but I'm very unhappy and—and worried."

"What's worrying you?"

Sylvia turned from him. "What's the good?" she said hopelessly.

"Well, I might be able to help."

She half put out her hand, and drew it back again.

"No, it's no use. I must just go under. Nothing much to make a fuss about after all, is there?" She faced him with the tears running down her cheeks. "I shan't be the first or the last, shall I?"

Peter put his hands on her shoulders.

"Don't talk like that, Sylvia," he said quickly. "There's always a way out. I'll stand by you; I swear I will."

"Will you? *Can* you? No, you don't care enough. You did once, but you don't now. You used to be fond of me long ago."

"I'm fond of you now; you know I am. Besides, I'd do my best to help any woman out of a hole."

Sylvia looked up at him with brimming eyes.

"Peter, are you really fond of me—really?" she said.

"Yes, I am," said Peter. "I said so just now."

"And you'll help me?"

"I'll do my best."

She came just a little nearer.

"Peter, only one thing will help—and oh, I do want help so badly— you don't know how badly. Peter, you said perhaps the Jewel was yours. What did you mean?"

Peter frowned.

"My father left it to me in his will," he said.

"Then it's yours, it's really yours?"

"I'm not sure."

"But—I don't understand." She stared at him in frank astonishment. "If it's yours, why did you send it back to my father?"

"I tell you I'm not sure; but, anyhow, your taking it—" his frown deepened—"it was a beastly thing to do. What made you do it?"

"I've told you," said Sylvia. "But if it's yours, Peter, can't you get it?"

"I don't know. Don't let's talk about it any more."

"But you'll help me?"

"Yes, I'll help you."

Sylvia put her arms round his neck and kissed him.

Chapter Twenty-One

SYLVIA WAS HAVING breakfast in bed next morning when she was called to the telephone. She recognized her father's voice before he announced himself.

"That you, Sylvia? Oh, all right. I only want an address—young Waring's address. Oh, and by the way, is he on the telephone? Good. Just give me his number—will you—and I'll ring him up."

Sylvia gave him the address and the number.

"What do you want with Peter?" she asked, with an attempt at lightness.

She heard Coverdale laugh.

"Oh, just a little matter of business," he said, and rang off.

She went back to her room, frowning. The Jewel had reached her father, and he wanted to thank Peter for sending it back. If that was all, would he not have written? Why was he so pleased at being able to telephone? Was he going to try and see Peter?

The telephone bell rang again; Hendebakker this time, hard and cool.

"That Lady Moreland? Well, have you got it?"

"No," said Sylvia. "No."

"Well, now, that's a pity." There was no change in the tone. "Suppose you come round and see Anita right away. She's just wearying to hear all about it. Ask for her, and come right up to our private suite."

He rang off. Sylvia leant against the wall for a moment, her heart beating hard. She had her orders, and knew very well that she must obey them.

In a little over half an hour she was being ushered into the drawing-room of the Hendebakkers' private suite at The Luxe. Anita was not there; Virgil P. Hendebakker was. He waited until the door was shut, and then said sharply:

"Well, what about it?"

"I couldn't get it," said Sylvia.

"Why?"

"He hasn't got it—he sent it back to my father."

Just for a second the large, smooth surface of Hendebakker's face changed. It seemed to crumple up, as the smooth surface of water will change and become convulsed by some violent, unseen force. The bright eyes alone remained unaltered; their gaze never shifted from Sylvia's face. It was all over in a moment, and Hendebakker said in his usual voice:

"He did that? He had the Jewel, and he sent it back to Dale? If that don't beat the band!"

"He sent it back at once—early, before I could see him. It wasn't my fault."

"Oh, I'm not blaming you—not for that. As to your blame foolishness in giving it to him at all, you've got to make that good— you know that without my telling you—you've *got* to make it good."

"I don't see how I can," said Sylvia, with a sort of gasp. And as she spoke, an inner door opened and Anita Hendebakker came in. She wore a thin wrap of exotic scarlet embroidered all over with blue and violet butterflies.

"Sylvia! But what a surprise!" she said.

Hendebakker waved her back with the smooth, well-kept hand which had the scar upon it.

"Presently, Anita; just now I am busy."

She cast one glance from him to Sylvia, and went out again.

"What will she think?" said Sylvia hotly.

Hendebakker smiled.

"Anita never thinks," he said. "It would not be worth her while; I would have no use for a wife who let herself think about my affairs. Anita knows when she is well off. And now—you were saying that you did not know what to do next. You have seen this young Waring? You are quite sure he sent the Jewel back?"

"Oh yes. And then this morning ..." She told him about the telephone call from Sunnings.

Hendebakker began to pace up and down the room.

"I think he must want to see him, or he would have written," she concluded.

He nodded.

"That's right smart of you. Yes, it's likely. I'll see to it. Well, now, this is what you've got to do. Is this young man in love with you?"

"Oh, well ..." Sylvia shrugged her shoulders.

"What's that mean? That he is, or that he isn't?"

She shot a furious glance at him.

"How do I know?"

"You quit this foolishness and come to business. Is he or isn't he?"

"I don't know. I don't think he knows himself. He's fond of me."

"Has he told you so?" His tone was businesslike in the extreme.

"Yes, he has."

"When?"

"Last night."

"When you were sobbing on his shoulder, I guess." Her discomfiture appeared to please him. "Well, you keep right on that way—plenty of sob-stuff—and 'I'm a poor, weak woman with no one to protect me'—with a dash of 'There's no one in the world like you.' That's the goods. You keep right on until you've got him so that he goes down on his knees and begs you to take the Jewel for a keep-sake."

"He's got to get it first," said Sylvia a little scornfully.

"If he don't I shall." Hendebakker's laugh was quite genial. "And now, my dear, you sit right down and get that young man of yours on the 'phone."

"Why?"

"Well, I'd just as lief know whether he's going to see Dale or not; guessing's not good enough, and you can get it out of him all right. Fix it so he'll have to say what he's doing."

"He won't be in," said Sylvia, rather sulkily.

"You sit right down and try. There's nothing like trying."

He set a chair as he spoke, and pushed the table instrument nearer to her. Sylvia took off the receiver, gave the number, and frowned when she heard Peter's voice saying, "Hullo."

"It's Sylvia," she said. In spite of the frown, her tone was sweetness itself.

Hendebakker laid a piece of paper on the table before her. Across it he had scrawled in blue pencil, "Repeat his answers so I can follow." She nodded and went on speaking.

"It is you, Peter, isn't it? Yes, it's Sylvia. I was wondering—" she broke into just a hint of self-conscious laughter—"well, just wondering if we were going to meet today. I can't remember if we fixed anything. Oh, you can't! You're going where? Oh, out of town—to the *Gaisfords*'? Did you really tell me that? How stupid of me! Do you know, I can't remember it a bit. Was it last night? My dear boy, I was so tired I didn't know what I was doing. But—but, as a matter of fact, my father rang me up this morning, and I got an idea that you were going to see him—a matter of business, he said—no, he didn't tell me what it was, only that he hoped to see you at Sunnings—oh, you *are* going there? What about the Gaisfords, then—lunching with them on your way? My good Peter, how frightfully energetic!"

She paused, and looked at Hendebakker. He nodded, and laid another scrawl before her; "Fix it for him to come and see you as soon as he gets back." She glanced at it, and spoke again.

"Peter, when am I going to see you? You will come soon, won't you? You know, after last night I'm just relying on you—I can't say how much. You don't know what it is to feel that there's someone you can trust and who'll see you through...." She paused for a moment, and then added, "Peter, don't tell Father I asked about your going down to Sunnings—he mightn't like it—he's like that. Well, good-bye, dear boy, see you tomorrow perhaps."

She rang off and turned to Hendebakker for approval. He gave it unstintedly.

"That was a right smart bit of work," he said.

He patted her shoulder approvingly and walked to the inner door. "Anita," he called.

Chapter Twenty-Two

PETER LUNCHED with the Gaisfords at Merton Clevery. He listened to Major Gaisford's jovial and richly embroidered anecdotes, and duly admired the infant Jimmy.

Mrs. Gaisford was very amiable. She had grown plump and placid, and she was disposed to smile upon Peter.

"You must come and stay with us at Chark instead of now," she said graciously. "I was sorry your visit had to be put off, but this whole place does want painting so dreadfully, and my cousin Monty Ferguson's offer of his house at Chark was too good to be wasted; so we're really off tomorrow for a month. Do you know Monty at all? He swears Chark will be *the* golf-course of the future, and I'm sure he's only lending us the house because he thinks James will be converted and go about cracking it up. But there it is, you must come down and see it for yourself—any time, you know. There's lots of room. Just send a wire and come."

After lunch Peter asked Rose Ellen to walk across the moor with him. He could catch a train at Hastney Mere, and they could talk. They climbed the sandy lane together and when Rose Ellen had said three things without receiving any answer she looked sideways at Peter, beheld him wrapped in frowning silence, and spoke no more. They walked on. Overhead the sky was hazy and flecked with innumerable little clouds. A light wind blew across the moor.

Peter was thinking very hard. It was always easy to think things out when he was with Rose Ellen; she understood, she always understood even when you didn't tell her anything. Most girls would be talking now, but Rose Ellen just walked on beside him in that understanding silence.

Peter was thinking about Sylvia. He was not quite sure of where he stood with Sylvia. Last night now—of course she was nervous and overwrought, but she had certainly kissed him and clung to him. Peter frowned horribly. He tried to recall exactly what he himself had done. To the best of his recollection he had patted her shoulder— had, in fact, gone on patting it for some time. He had also kissed her somewhere on the point of the cheekbone, after which Sylvia had kissed him again and cried a good deal. To be sure, she had told him on the telephone this morning that her own recollection of what had happened was very hazy. That looked as if she did not attach very much importance to those kisses. On the other hand, she had said things about relying on him, and about his having promised to see her through. He had certainly said that he would help her; but just what helping Sylvia might involve.... He broke off his thought with a jerk. There was no doubt at all that Sylvia wanted someone to look after her pretty badly. There was no doubt at all that, in some sort, he had pledged himself to look after her. He walked beside Rose Ellen, thinking hard.

It was when they left the moor that he began to talk about Sylvia. The path ran downhill, turned, and brought them into the beach-wood where they had slept as children. The drift of last year's leaves was under their feet, and this year's first exquisite green stretched between them and the sky.

Rose Ellen stopped suddenly.

"Did you come down here to talk to me about Sylvia?" she said.

Peter nodded without looking at her.

"Are you going to marry her, Peter?"

Peter had stopped too. He pushed the beech leaves with his foot.

"I—don't—know," he said at last.

Rose Ellen met the blow with a great courage.

"Are you thinking about it, Peter?" she said. There was a pause. "If he would only speak," thought Rose Ellen; "if he would only tell me—if I really knew! Peter, Peter, speak!" Her hands came together, held one another tightly.

"I have thought about it," said Peter, speaking very slowly. Then, more quickly and in a low voice, "She's in trouble—very unhappy, I'm afraid—she wants someone to look after her—I've been trying to think it out—if it's my job, I mean—I don't know, but I think perhaps it is."

Rose Ellen's colour deepened. She never took her eyes from Peter's face. They were clear and deep, like shadowed water.

"I see," she said. "I wonder if that's a good reason for marrying anyone."

"I think it might be. Don't you think so, Rose Ellen?"

Rose Ellen's hands held one another. She said:

"No, Peter de—ah."

"You mean I'm not in love with her. That's what I don't quite know. I was once—frightfully. I told you. Do you remember? But you see I was just a fool of a boy. One takes things so damned hard at seventeen, and—and—well, I'm twenty-five now; and there's been the war and all that; and one's probably got past that intense sort of feeling. And perhaps it's my job—I don't know—I'm not sure."

Rose Ellen looked at him. At that moment her love for him was an agony of mother-love. Her heart was full of tragic tears, and yet more tragic laughter over Peter, who was too old for love at twenty-five.

"So—so—I think I'll be getting along," he said. "I—wanted to tell you. You always understand, and—well, I'll write."

For some reason Peter found himself unable to go on. He had meant to talk the whole thing out with Rose Ellen in a calm and reasonable manner; but he couldn't do it; he could not go on talking, or stay a moment longer in the beech-wood. A wave of unbearable agitation seemed to have broken over him. He did not understand it, and he had no power to control it. He caught at Rose Ellen's hands, gripped them very hard, tried to speak, choked, and flung away.

Rose Ellen watched him go. She heard the beech leaves rustle under his feet. She watched until the turn of the path hid him and he was gone. Peter was gone—gone to Sylvia Moreland. All her life he had been there—just Peter—and now he was gone.

Rose Ellen put out her hand and felt for something to lean against. There was one of the great beech trunks not far off. She went and leaned against it. It was very strong. Its roots were safe in the soil, and its lovely green branches stretched out to the wind and the rain and the sun. She stood there, and looked at the path by which Peter had gone. He had passed the bend where the bushes jutted out and the primroses grew on the bank. She could not hear his footsteps any longer. It was no use looking at the empty path any more.

She leaned against the tree, and was glad because it was so strong. That was the hollow where Peter had heaped the leaves for her head and covered her with his coat. Rose Ellen looked at it, and remembered all that Peter had been to her, all that Peter had meant to her, all that Peter had done for her. Quite suddenly her reserve and her self-control broke. She began to cry, and to talk out loud in little broken sentences, as people do sometimes when their trouble is very great and they think that they are quite alone.

Peter went on down the road. He walked at first with great strides, but by degrees his pace slackened. At first his one thought had been to get away, but after a minute or two he began to recover his balance, to wonder at himself, and to consider what had made him behave so strangely. Rose Ellen must have thought he had gone crazy.

He slowed down, and presently came to a standstill. He had meant to talk the whole thing out. The only part that he had thought would be difficult was breaking the ice, and that hadn't been difficult at all. Rose Ellen's quiet, "Are you going to marry her?" ought to have made it quite easy for them both. That was what bothered him. They had begun to talk all right in just the understanding, friendly way which he had planned—and then—what had gone wrong? It wasn't Rose Ellen's fault; he was quite clear about that. It was something in him, Peter—a rush of indescribable emotion and pain; it had come upon him when Rose Ellen had said, "I wonder if that's a good reason for marrying anyone." Yes, it had begun then, and he had said, "Don't you think it might be?" and with Rose Ellen's answer, the pain and the emotion had become unbearable. Yet, after all, what had she said? Only three words, only, "No, Peter de—ah." But when she said those three words he had looked at her just for a moment. Quite definitely Peter traced his hurt back to the moment when he looked into Rose Ellen's eyes and saw the patience in them. He hadn't see her look like that since the day when she walked towards him down the hard asphalt at St. Gunburga's.

Peter turned, and began to walk back along the way by which he had just come. He had ceased to care about his train, or Roden Coverdale, or the Jewel. That look in Rose Ellen's eyes would have brought him from the ends of the earth. His only necessity was to find out what had brought it there. He couldn't bear it. He walked back quickly.

It was when he came to where the primroses grew on the broken bank and some bushes overhung the path that he heard a sound that took his breath. It was a sob, and words. He stood still at the turn of the path and saw Rose Ellen. She was leaning against a beech tree, half turned away from him, not looking at him at all; and she was speaking, but not to him; and she was crying as he had never seen her cry. Anguish had broken through the patience in her eyes; the tears ran down, the very bitter tears.

Peter stood, and heard Rose Ellen speak.

"My Peter de—ah. No, not mine—no, I don't want him to be mine—I don't—it's not for that—only for her to love him—to be good to him—Sylvia, if you can, if you will—I won't mind, I'll be glad." Her voice dropped, shaken and despairing. "She won't—*she won't*—she hasn't got it to give—oh, my Peter, my Peter de—ah, oh, my Peter *de—ah!*"

Something broke in Peter's heart. He knew that he belonged to Rose Ellen, and that she belonged to him. They had always belonged to each other, and he had not known it. He had not seen her because she was so near. She had known, but he had not known.

Rose Ellen was not speaking any longer. Her face was hidden against the tree. Peter would have given all the world twice over to have comforted her; but something held him back, something stronger than his passion of pity and love. It was as if he had come into a holy place and seen holy things that were not meant for him to see. And then he was pledged in some sort to Sylvia. He must put that straight before he could go to Rose Ellen.

He turned, and went down the path that led to Hastney Mere.

Chapter Twenty-Three

PETER PICKED UP the bag which he had left at the junction, and travelled down to Sunnings. He found quite a lot to think about. He thought about what a fool he had been. He thought of how near he had been to losing Rose Ellen. He might have shut a door between them which he would never have been able to open again. He had, as it were, had his hand upon that door, ready to slam it, too. It really didn't bear thinking about.

The train went on; stations came and went; porters and newsboys shouted; people got in and out. Peter sat still, and went on thinking. He didn't want to sit still. He wanted to do something that would bring him nearer to Rose Ellen. What he really would have liked to do was to dash across the platform, burst into the telegraph office, and write with a stubby pencil on a neatly divided telegraph-form, "Rose Ellen, I love you terribly. I'm coming back at once." This being impossible, he sat in his corner seat and appeared to slumber.

Coverdale met him at the station with a small car which he was driving himself. He nodded without offering his hand, and talked pleasantly of indifferent matters until they had reached the house.

"Dinner is in half an hour," he said, then: "And I think, if you don't mind, we'll keep our real talk for afterwards."

Peter assented, and was shown to his room.

After dinner, in the library, Coverdale plunged straight into the middle of things.

"I'd like to say that I very much appreciate your coming," he began. "I had reasons for not wishing to come to Town just now, or I shouldn't have troubled you. And, quite seriously, I wanted to see you very much. You are, as a matter of fact, my dear Waring, that most remarkable phenomenon, a really honest man. I won't say I haven't met one or two before; but I'm not certain that I would have trusted any of them with the Annam Jewel. Tell me now, why did you send it back?"

Peter didn't answer at once. At last he said:

"Well, if it's yours, I don't want it; and, if it's mine, I'd rather get it myself."

"I see." Coverdale's tone betrayed a hint of amusement. "Well, well, that's very admirable; and I'm naturally a good deal obliged to you, both on my own account and on Sylvia's. But you say 'if it's yours', 'if it's mine'. May I ask what you mean by that?"

Peter looked him straight in the face and said:

"I have my father's notes, sir."

Coverdale nodded.

"Yes, I thought so. I thought there'd be something like that. Your father's notes on the history of the Jewel, and the circumstances which he conceived gave him some claim to it?"

"His brother left it to him by will," said Peter.

"Yes, I knew that. The question is, Waring, how much do you know?"

"I think," said Peter, "that you had better read my father's notes, and then you'll see." He held out the shabby book as he spoke. "I expect there are gaps that you can fill, and I'd rather have the whole thing cleared right up and settled."

Coverdale took the book with a "Thank you, Waring," pushed his chair a little nearer to a lamp, leaned back, and began to read. The lamplight showed his fine, dark face, the hair grey at the temples. When he turned a leaf it shone on the sensitive, well-kept hand.

Peter looked and wondered. If this man were Dale, then there were many gaps to be filled.

Coverdale finished reading, and closed the book.

"Entirely one-sided, of course, but very interesting," he said. "By the way, there's one point I'd like to rectify. Your father says that I fired at him point-blank when he sprang out of bed. As he himself admits that he was light-headed at the time, perhaps you'll take my word for it that I did no such thing. I had no intention whatever of firing at an unarmed and wounded man. Your father jumped at me, knocking my arm up, and my revolver went off into the blue. I may say that if I had fired at him, I should have hit him. It was, of course, a most unfortunate occurrence, as it led Henders to fire and hit. He had sworn not to use his revolver—that's the truth, though you may not believe it. And as to the rest of it—well, I can tell you a good deal if you'd care to hear."

Peter had picked up a paper-knife from the table near. It was a mere sliver of ivory, carved at one end into a tracery like fine lace. He sat forward hi his chair, balancing the paper-knife, twisting it.

"Of course I'd like to hear," he said almost roughly.

Coverdale nodded, got up, and began to pace the room. He walked to the window and back, then halted, stood awhile with his back to the fireless hearth, and spoke.

"Yes, I expect you'd like to hear. I know I'd like to speak. Queer, how you carry a thing for years, hardly thinking about it, and then feel the need to talk it out!" He paused. Peter looked at the ivory knife, but it did not occur to him to speak. After a moment Coverdale went on:

"I'm afraid I must be personal. If you're bored, say so—but the whole thing really hangs together. It really begins with my father. He went to China in the Diplomatic Service. When I was six there was a blazing row. He married a Chinese lady, and took up a semi-Oriental way of life. He was a man of brilliant talents and odd theories. I had a Chinese tutor until I was twelve. My father himself taught me the English school subjects. When I was twelve he sent me home. I was at Eton for six years. Then he sent for me to come out East again. Four years later he died, and I discovered that he had been living on capital—there wasn't much left, and what there was had to go to my sisters, both older than myself. They had been living in England since my mother's death. I'm really making this as short as possible, but I want you to understand the position. There I was at twenty-two, with a passion for Chinese manuscripts and Chinese antiquities of all sorts, no money and a widening breach between myself and my father's people." He shrugged his shoulders. "I set out to turn my knowledge into money. Some years were good and some were bad. I made enough to keep me, and I made a certain name for myself. I had a flair. I called myself Dale chiefly because it was shorter than Coverdale—I had no motive for concealment then. When I was nearly thirty I married Sylvia's mother—a missionary's daughter—Sylvia is very like her. That's really where the thing begins. She hated the East; she simply hated it; she wanted to get out of it and go home; it got worse after Sylvia was born."

He stopped speaking, and walked again twice up and down the long room, then took up his tale, speaking in a dry, cool voice which showed no trace of emotion.

"I had come across a reference to the Annam Jewel years before—just the merest hint. Afterwards in two other very ancient manuscripts I found passages which gave a further clue. Finally, just when the pressure of my personal affairs was becoming unendurable, I met Henders. He described the Jewel to me, and asked me whether I believed that it existed. I was very cautious, but I saw that he knew something. He told me he got his information from James Waring. Well, he brought Waring to see me; and the upshot was that we agreed to go into the job together. Now, what I want to lay stress on is this—Waring and Henders knew next to nothing; Henders only knew what Waring told him; and Waring knew no more than that the Jewel existed somewhere—he knew that it was unique—he described it. He'd been in Annam for some time—had, in point of fact, practically gone native—and he'd picked up the sort of vague stories which are associated with any famous object, especially if it is very much venerated, as the Jewel was. The point is that he didn't know where it was, and of course Henders didn't either. Neither of them had anything more than vague stories, whereas I had the exact knowledge. The second manuscript gave an account of how the Jewel came to be taken to Annam. And the third, a much later one, gave a description of the Jewel in its shrine—it was written by a Chinese monk for the edification of his abbot.

"You see, I knew where the Jewel was. They didn't. You know, of course, that Annam means 'The Hidden Way'. Well, the way to the Jewel was hidden—I knew that from the manuscript. The whole thing fired me. There was the value of the Jewel, and the pressure of my affairs; and there was the fascination, the appeal to the other side of me—the side that cared for the Jewel because it was beautiful, and unique, and very, very old—that was the strongest really. Henders was mad keen too. He was an expert in precious stones—you know that—and he was also one of the most ambitious men I've ever met. He always had his mind set to get where he is now—at the top, where he could move men and pull strings. He saw his chance in the Jewel.

Waring just wanted the money. Well, I went in with them—I didn't like either of them but I went in with them. I knew that the Jewel had been taken to Annam and had become the centre of a cult there. Well, we went there. Henders made a fake Jewel from the description. It was very rough, but he thought it might be useful."

"Is this it?" said Peter.

He dropped the paper-knife, dived into a pocket, and held out the sham stone which had come to him from his father. Coverdale picked it up, held it to the light, and tossed it back.

"Yes, that's it. Your father mentions it too. I suppose he kept it. Well, as it turned out it wasn't used. Waring gave us the slip. He found out where the Jewel was—there was a girl mixed up in it—and as soon as he found out where it was he gave us the slip—went right back on us. And I'll say this, Waring, that if ever a man deserved what he got, it was that uncle of yours. He played a pretty mean trick on the girl he got his information from, and she came to her death through it; and he went right back on his partners."

Peter slid the false Jewel back into his pocket, and retrieved the ivory knife. He had no observations to make upon the character of his Uncle James.

"Well, he got the Jewel," said Coverdale. "I don't know how, but he got it; and Henders killed him for it. I wasn't there—you needn't believe that if you don't want to, but I just give it to you as part of my statement—I wasn't there because I'd had bad news. I got a message to say my wife had gone—an American tourist with lots of money. She'd left Sylvia with her native nurse and gone. Well, the rest is more or less as your father has it. I got back to find Henders raging; and I was pretty mad too. I didn't see what right Henry Waring had in the matter at all, and I agreed to go with Henders and get the Jewel back from him, only stipulating that there should be no more violence. Well, you know what happened."

Peter nodded half absently. The scene described by his father rose before him. Henders with his light, cold eyes and his oath to use no violence, and the revolver in his hand—the hand with the scar upon it. The ivory paper-knife snapped in two; the sharp end fell to the ground.

"We got off that night," said Coverdale. "We got clear away to the States. I took Sylvia with me. We went to the States because Henders said he knew he could get a job there through a cousin of his, and, once he was in with the trade, we should be able to sell the Jewel. Now, I want you to take this in—I had the Jewel in my care, and Henders made two attempts to steal it before we landed. He didn't succeed, because I had taken his measure. I always knew I couldn't trust him an inch—that's where I was an out-and-out fool, to go into a deal like that with two men that I couldn't trust."

He threw out his hand with a sharp gesture, then crossed to his old place, and sat down.

"I'm nearly done," he said. "Henders got his job. I kept the Jewel. He used to come and ask me to let him look at it; he said it fascinated him. I know now that he was trying to make a copy. He used to sit and stare at it whilst I kept him covered—we'd got through with pretences by then, and he knew I didn't trust him. Well, in the end he tried to cheat me. He changed the false Jewel for the real one under my very nose, and almost took me in. He had chosen his time well, a dark day and the evening drawing in. But"—Coverdale laughed—"I told you I had a flair; my eye was deceived, but not my hand. I knew the thing for a fake as soon as I touched it. We had a scrap. I was off my guard, and he got my revolver. It was the narrowest escape I've ever had, for he certainly meant murder. That's his mark."

He touched the faint line of a scar that ran back from the left cheek-bone.

"Well, after that I didn't think I was under any obligation to him. I didn't think he'd give up the game, but the next thing I heard was that he'd been arrested—Michel's old game of picking out a valuable stone here and there and substituting a copy. His past record came out, and he got a heavy sentence. Before the trial was over I got news that a cousin of my father's had left me Sunnings and a goodish bit of money, so I cleared out. I'd my own reasons for never wanting to see the States again. Well, that's the story—all but one thing. Henders has a hold over me—I needn't go into it; it's to do with my private affairs— but, in the last resort, he could get me extradited to the States if he thought it worth while, and that's why I'm off."

Peter looked up quickly.

"Off?" he said.

"Yes. It's partly because I'm bored, but partly because of Henders. I shouldn't really enjoy standing my trial in New York, where Henders could get out a warrant against me if he chose. And I've a hankering to go back to China. I've sold Sunnings, and I'm off."

"Soon?" said Peter.

"Today, or tomorrow, or the next day," said Coverdale with a wave of the hand.

Peter was silent for a moment, then he leaned forward and said:

"What about Sylvia, sir?"

Coverdale's look became intent.

"You have a faculty for getting right there," he said. "It's quite a good faculty in its way. My own habit of mind is rather discursive, I'm afraid; but I was about to put that very question to you. Shall we consider it put?"

Peter got up. He looked very large.

"I don't quite know what you mean by that," he said.

Coverdale smiled his charming smile.

"It was a little crude, eh? Let me put it into a rather more civilized shape. You're pretty good friends with Sylvia, aren't you?"

"Yes," said Peter. Then, after a pause, "But why did you think so?"

Coverdale laughed.

"Oh, my dear Waring, you don't do me justice, you really don't. Sylvia gives you the Jewel, and you ask me my reason for supposing that you are friends."

"She was frightened," said Peter.

Coverdale broke in upon his rather measured speech.

"Yes, she was frightened, and therefore acted on instinct. Without thinking she turned to you, gave you the Jewel. The question is, what do you mean by being friends? Are you fond of her?"

"Yes, I'm very fond of Sylvia," said Peter. "And I'm very sorry for her, too. She's most frightfully unhappy; and that brute Henders—"

Coverdale regarded him with a slightly whimsical expression.

"Yes, yes, just so," he said. "Well, that being the case, I have something more to say. It's about the Jewel. If I keep it, Henders will rake the East for me until he finds me; and, as I desire a little peaceful seclusion for study, I do not propose to take the Jewel to China. On the other hand, I certainly do not propose to let Henders have it. There remains—yourself. Quite seriously, I have been thinking of making you a present of the Jewel with my blessing, and—you say you're fond of Sylvia and frightfully sorry for her ..." He broke off, with that easy gesture of the hand. "In point of fact, my dear Waring, I am suggesting that the Jewel might be Sylvia's dowry. I might almost be a mid-Victorian father asking your intentions, and before you answer you may just as well have a look at what you're being offered."

He unbuckled his wrist watch as he spoke, opened the back, and shook the Annam Jewel out upon the table. It lay just under the lamp and burned there like a flame. Coverdale touched it with his finger, and said, speaking only just above his breath:

"Ten years ago I couldn't have left it to you or to anyone else. I never wanted to sell it, you know. I believe I'd rather have starved. I wanted to keep it, to know that I had it—the rarest thing in the world, the only one. I don't really know that I can leave it now." His voice went away to a whisper.

Peter found himself speaking in gruff, decided tones.

"It's most frightfully good of you, sir, but I'm afraid you misunderstood about Sylvia and myself. We're just friends, and I'd be frightfully glad to be of any use to her, or to look after her, or anything of that sort, but—"

"No wedding bells?" said Coverdale. He touched the Jewel again. "Not even for this?"

Peter frowned and squared his shoulders.

"Of course you don't mean that seriously," he said. "I'm afraid I didn't make myself clear just now. Sylvia and I are great friends, and I hope we always shall be. I'm quite sure she has never thought of me as anything but a friend. She knows very well that I think no end of her, and all that; but I've always been more or less engaged to somebody else."

"Well, well," said Coverdale regretfully. "You've always been engaged, have you? That's very persevering of you."

He put the Annam Jewel back in the empty watch case, and strapped the watch upon his wrist.

The telephone bell rang sharply from the far corner of the room.

Chapter Twenty-Four

COVERDALE WAS ACROSS the room in a minute. He stood with his back to Peter, listening. Once he said, "You're sure?" and a little later, "All right, I'll make a push for it." He rang off, and came back with a queer look on his face; it suggested exhilaration, sarcasm, excitement—just a shade of each.

"Well, Waring," he said, "I suppose you're sure about that answer of yours? You won't have time to reconsider it, because I'm off. Now's your chance, or never. The Annam Jewel, going—going—gone." He tapped the face of his watch as he spoke.

"Well, it isn't everyone who can say they've had such a chance and refused it. Anyhow, I've just had word to hurry up. A friend's giving me a lift on his yacht, and he thinks we'd better hurry; he says Henders is moving. I've been ready for a day or two, so it makes no difference to me. I just take my little two-seater and disappear. You must make yourself at home and accept my apologies. I really should have liked to have had a little more talk with you; but there it is."

"You're going now?" said Peter. "Now—at once?"

"I expect to be clear in fifteen minutes or so. I'm not anxious to meet Henders. To tell you the honest truth, Waring, I'm afraid I might lose my temper."

He smiled, and began to walk towards the door. With his hand upon it, he turned.

"Oh, by the way, there's just one thing. I told you Henders could get me extradited on an old warrant. I don't know if you'll believe me, but I'd like to make a statement. I went to the States to find a man, and I found him, but I didn't lay a finger on him. I dare say you can guess who he was. He was killed in suspicious circumstances, but I didn't kill him. I cleared out because circumstances made the case look pretty black for me; and what I couldn't face then and won't face now is having all my private affairs made public and served up in the gutter press. That's why I'm running away from Henders. Well, so long."

He nodded to Peter, smiled again with that sudden charm, and went quickly out of the room.

Peter was left alone with his mind in a very bewildered condition. That Coverdale was gone, really gone, seemed difficult to believe; and yet, as the minutes passed, he began to believe it. He looked at his watch. It was something short of ten o'clock. He wondered if Coverdale had left the house. He picked up his father's notebook, crammed it into a pocket, and on the impulse went to the glass doors which opened upon the terrace, undid the bolts, and went out.

It was a May night, soft, windless, moonless, and dead dark. He went to the edge of the terrace, listened, and through the silence caught the hum of a car. The drive lay before him, winding to the left. A car coming from the garage would pass him here. He waited, but the hum died away in the opposite direction. Peter walked to the end of the terrace, and listened again. There was nothing to hear but the faint, indefinite sounds of the night. The strangeness of the whole thing came upon him strongly. Coverdale's story; Coverdale's personality; Coverdale's flight; Sylvia and the Jewel—these impressions ran into one another, mixed, blended, fused, and again dissolved even as the colours met, and fused, and dissolved in the Jewel.

Peter felt a desire to get away from the house, from all these trees, into an open place where he could walk on for miles unhindered. Whenever he was disturbed in mind he had this urgent need to walk, to get away from things, to go fast and far. He turned down the drive, and found it as black as pitch. It irked him to have to grope, to find his feet on grass, or to plunge into bushy undergrowth.

He had just extracted himself from a holly thicket when a sound came to him. He could not have told what sort of sound it was, or from what direction it came, so misleading was the darkness. He took a vigorous stride forward and tripped over a wire-rope which had been stretched across the drive knee-high. He exclaimed, tried too late to jump it, and came down with a crash. In an instant there fell upon him the enveloping folds of a heavy rug. There was a knee in the small of his back. He shouted, and got his head up; and then the rug was in his mouth, hairy and horrible, and his face was being pressed down into its folds until he could hardly breathe. He tried to roll over, to kick, but there was a weight on his legs—a weight and the pressure of a rope. The blighters were roping him up! Peter jerked, strained, got an arm free of the rug, and hit out into empty darkness. Then his wrist was caught, his arm wrenched backwards and roped against his body. He tried to shout again, felt himself turned over and dragged across grass and amongst bushes, where one man proceeded to sit upon his head and another upon his knees. Muffled by the rug, there came to Peter's ears the voice of Virgil P. Hendebakker speaking urbanely.

"Very sorry indeed to incommode you, Mr. Waring, but business is business. Now this little business talk of ours can be quite pleasant and friendly if you're willing to have it so. I'm considerable of a judge of men, and if you'll give your word of honour not to call out, I'll have my men take that rug off your face and sit you up. If you're willing, just kick with your feet."

Peter kicked out at once. He was boiling with fury, and the rug tasted perfectly filthy—long, stringy hairs on it, and a flavour like goat and tobacco. The men who were sitting on him got up, the rug came off, and Peter felt himself sat up with a tree at his back.

"That's better," said Hendebakker. "Now, Waring, you know what I want. Have you got it?"

"No, I haven't!" said Peter fiercely.

"You're sure of that? Word of honour, now?"

"I haven't got it."

"Well, now, I think I'll just make sure of that."

He switched on an electric torch, handed it to the man who stood nearest him, and proceeded to search Peter with scientific thoroughness. When he had finished he said:

"Well, I've sized you up all right. That's a consolation for not getting what I came for. Now, if you'll give me your word not to get violent, my men shall untie you. I don't ask you not to go to the police, because I guess you're intelligent enough to have thought out all the reasons against letting the police in on this job—ladies should be kept out of police courts. Well, now, your word of honour."

"For what?"

"What I said—no violence. You finish your walk, and all past friends."

"You're a damned swine, Henders," said Peter.

Hendebakker laughed good-temperedly.

"Never lose your temper in business," he said. "It's always a handicap. You give your word?"

"Yes," said Peter.

A minute later he was free. Hendebakker and his men were gone. Peter listened, and heard the faint sound of their going. He judged them to be making for the house. Yes, of course, that's what they'd do. Well, Coverdale must be well away by now; but just as well to make sure. If he were anywhere about, he must be found and warned.

Peter stretched himself, and began to grope among the bushes. He had rather lost his sense of direction. A few steps brought him to a bank, and as he stood with his shoulder against it, someone laughed in the darkness just above him. There was a rustle in the bushes, and the sound of a man scrambling down the bank a yard away.

"Well, Waring, we meet again," said Roden Coverdale.

"You nearly met Henders too," said Peter grimly.

Coverdale laughed again, the gay, irresponsible laugh of a man on holiday.

"Not so nearly as you think. I ran my car out by the back way and down the lane over there. Then I climbed the bank. I had just a fancy to see if Henders was going to pay me a visit—I'd had information, you know. Your little show was rather unexpected. I'm afraid I congratulate myself on not having come down the drive. I'd have taken a hand, only I knew Henders wouldn't be fool enough to hurt you—it was the Jewel he was after, naturally, and as soon as he found you hadn't got it he'd be off after me. I'm afraid he's going to be disappointed. Well, I'm really off this time."

"Yes, I think you'd better hurry," said Peter. "Henders doesn't seem to waste much time over his jobs."

"No, he doesn't, and that's a fact. He's pretty efficient...." Coverdale paused, and then said in a tone touched with hesitation, "I suppose you won't take my hand; there's no blood of your kin on it—I told you the truth there, and—well, I've liked you a good deal, and I'm sorry you won't come into the family."

A curious emotion rose in Peter. He could see nothing but the darkness and black shapes of trees. He put out his hand and grasped the "thin hand, very strong", which Henry Waring had described. It lay cool and slim in his grip for a moment, then withdrew, leaving something behind it, something like a round pebble, hard and very cold. Peter made a movement, heard the rustling of the bushes, the snapping of a twig, and a half-laugh that came from the bank above him. A voice in the dark said:

"No conditions this time," and then: "Good-bye, Peter. Good luck to you."

He leaned against the bank and called cautiously:

"Coverdale, wait!"

For answer he heard the sound of retreating footsteps. A minute later a car slid past on the other side of the bank. Roden Coverdale was gone.

Peter stood alone in the dark, with the Annam Jewel in his hand. From the first moment he touched it he knew it for what it was. He remembered Coverdale's assertion that he had recognized the fake Jewel as a fake when he touched it. Peter knew why. The real Jewel felt quite different to anything that he had ever handled before; it was hard, and it was cold; it was very cold.

Peter took out his handkerchief, knotted the Jewel into one corner, and rammed it down into his pocket again. Then he climbed the bank, pushed through some bushes which grew upon it, and dropped into the lane below. His one concern was to get as far from Sunnings as possible. He had no fancy for meeting Henders again that night. It would be frightfully inconvenient if he were to kill Henders—and he felt a good deal like killing him if he got the chance. He swallowed his rage with difficulty every time he thought about the wire rope, and the man who sat on his head, and the taste of that beastly rug.

He crossed the lane, climbed a fence into a field, and made for a footpath which he remembered. It ran across three fields and came out upon a wide common. Peter pounded along, and the anger began to go out of him. Once clear of the trees, he could see his way. There was a soft, even darkness everywhere which gave things a vague look; but one could see where the hedges ran, and where the skyline ended. There were no stars.

Peter walked on and on—five miles from Sunnings—eight—ten—twelve. He was quite out of his reckoning, and simply took the ways that lay before him. He thought of a great many things as he walked; of James Waring, who had wanted money and had cheated, and lied, and gambled away his life for the Jewel; of Henders and his ambitions which the Jewel was to serve; of Coverdale and his passion for the beauty of the Jewel. What had the Jewel done for any of them?

It was two in the morning when he stopped walking and realized how far he had come. He had no idea of where he was, and, had he wished to return to Sunnings, he could certainly not have retraced his steps. He was in evening clothes, and one of his thin Oxford shoes was nearly through in the sole.

He made his way into a wood that ran back from the road, and found a sheltered place where dry leaves rustled underfoot. He lay down, and went instantly to sleep.

Chapter Twenty-Five

THE SUN WOKE HIM. The slope of the wood was towards the east, and, as he sat up and stretched himself, he saw the sun lying like a round ball of yellow fire on the crest of a rising line of low hills. The sky was faintly, mistily blue. Three little wreaths of cloud showed like puffs of smoke on the horizon, as the sun rose they began to glow; the sun turned rose-colour, and the rose-colour changed to gold; the blue brightened.

Peter got up, walked about, and began to wonder what he should do next. He barred going back to Sunnings; anyhow, a dozen miles across country in broad daylight and in these clothes couldn't be thought of. There must be a village somewhere about, and in a village, doubtless, some sort of cap and overcoat could be procured. If he could get his evening clothes covered up, he could go back to town and telephone to Sunnings for his bag.

It was the Annam Jewel that bothered him. Most definitely he did not wish to take it back to town with him. He hadn't particularly wanted to have it; but, having got it, he meant to keep it out of Hendebakker's clutches. To take it back to town seemed a good deal like asking for trouble.

He came out into the sun on the edge of the wood, undid the knotted corner of his handkerchief, and set the Jewel in the light. No, he'd be hanged if he'd let Henders have it. It was his.

Then and there the idea came to him. He would send it to Rose Ellen for safe keeping; and Rose Ellen who always understood—could she fail to understand that Peter and the Jewel were both hers for the taking? The idea pleased Peter very much. He couldn't go to rose Ellen yet. He couldn't say, "Rose Ellen, I love you most frightfully— I've always loved you though I didn't know it—and I shan't ever stop loving you again for a moment." But he could send her the Jewel. You didn't need to say things to Rose Ellen; she always understood.

He sat there with the Jewel on the palm of his hand, and turned it this way and that while he made a plan. After a little while he got up and went back into the wood. There was plenty of moss between the gnarled roots of the trees. It was fern moss, brilliantly green. He spread out his handkerchief, and piled the moss upon it. Then he picked wood violets and primroses, a little bunch of each, and stuck them in the moss to keep them fresh. He put the Jewel in an old envelope which he folded into a small square. Then he hid the little package under the moss, knotted the handkerchief at the four corners, and took the road. It was about six o'clock, and a very fine morning.

He walked about until eight, keeping as much as possible to the fields. At eight o'clock he entered a village which possessed a railway station, and was therefore certain to have a post office. The post office was also a baker's shop, and Peter's heart yearned towards the loaves of bread and the currant buns of yesterday.

A stout woman in blue-and-white checked apron was washing down the step. She had cheeks like the largest sort of red apple and very round blue eyes. Her front hair was controlled by eighteen metal curlers, which astonished Peter very much. Over the curlers she wore a man's tweed cap which kept on slipping to one side.

"Good morning," said Peter. "I want to send a parcel—registered."

The woman rose on her knees, and surveyed him with pardonable surprise. She saw a very large young man, with a shock of fair hair standing wildly erect. "Evening clothes too, and all burst at the shoulder, if you'll believe me," as she afterwards told her son William's wife. "And his tie round under his ear, and a nan'-kerchief full of moss and flowers and such stuff in his 'and."

"You don't say!" said William's wife.

Mrs. Merewether stared at Peter, and Peter repeated his remark. As he repeated it he smiled.

"I do want to send a parcel," he said.

"Not till nine o'clock, you can't," said Mrs. Merewether, still on her knees.

Peter looked at the loaves.

"I say," he said, "I suppose you couldn't—I mean of course I couldn't expect you to sell me a cup of tea unless—I say, you don't sell cups of tea, do you?"

"No—" said Mrs. Merewether; after a pause she added—"sir."

"But you sell loaves and—er buns."

Peter smiled again, and Mrs. Merewether was suddenly reminded of the days when William would get into a scrape at school and come to her to be got out of it. She got up and looked reprovingly at Peter.

"I've been out all night, and I'm most dreadfully hungry," he said.

Mrs. Merewether wiped her hands on her checked apron, and led the way indoors. She took Peter through the shop into a parlour that smelt of new linoleum and turpentine. The windows were tightly shut. There was a table with woolly mats on it, four horsehair chairs, and a sofa with a pink-and-green crochet antimacassar. There was an aspidistra on the window-sill, and a very large tortoise-shell cat on the hearthrug.

Peter put the handkerchief which contained the Annam Jewel on the horsehair sofa, and watched Mrs. Merewether replace the woolly mats with a tablecloth. She brought bread and a pat of butter. Then she went away and fried bacon—Peter could hear it sizzling—the smell of it mingled pleasantly with the smell of the turpentine and the linoleum.

145 | THE ANNAM JEWEL

When Mrs. Merewether brought in the bacon, she said, "That's a cut off William's pig, and a fine pig it were." When she came in with the tea, she stood with the milk-jug in her hand, and remarked abruptly, "Bad company's been the ruin of many a young feller—that and drink—and what I says is, pull up while you can and before you're made to. Lor, if I haven't forgotten the mustard!"

Peter had finished the bacon by the time she came back.

"I say, that was excellent bacon," he said. "William's pig must have been a champion. Now look here. Do you think—I mean have you got such a thing as a box to spare? Those flowers"—he pointed at the handkerchief—"I want to send them to a lady, to a young lady." And suddenly, to his horror, Peter discovered himself to be blushing.

Mrs. Merewether instantly jumped to a conclusion which she afterwards imparted to William's wife. "Come over me in a flash it did, just in a flash. 'You've been misjudging of that pore young man.' I said to myself. 'It's not drink and bad comp'ny, but a tiff with his young lady that's sent him walking about all night like a loony in his evening clothes.'

"Fair off his nut he must have been; but there's some gels is never 'appy unless they're tormenting of their chap."

"That's right," said William's wife.

Peter filled a soap-box with moss, laid the Annam Jewel in its folded envelope at the bottom and put the primroses and violets on the top of it. There was still room in the box, and before he realized what was happening, Mrs. Merewether had produced a large bunch of blue forget-me-nots and a very little bunch of bright pink ones.

"Nice things to send to a young lady, I always thinks," she said. "Can't come amiss, ferget-me-nots can't. Kind of hits you slap in the face the meaning does, don't it—fer-get-me-not? And the pink ones— they're not so common, and my old granny, she always called 'em no-nevers. Pretty, ain't it?" She repeated the two names lingeringly.

"Fer-get-me-not. No-never. Sweet, I call it. You tell your young lady, and see if it don't fetch her. It would me when I was a gel. I'll get you some paper and string and some sealing wax."

Peter found a pencil and a half sheet of notepaper in one of his pockets, and wrote to Rose Ellen:

Dear Rose Ellen,
Don't unpack this box until there's no one there. It is in a
bit of paper under the moss. Keep it safe for me till I come,
and don't tell anyone. I'll come as soon as I can.

He signed it "Peter", frowned, and added a postscript.

The primroses and violets are out of a wood, but the
forget-me-nots were in the post office garden. The woman
says the pink ones are called "No-never".

Peter was rather pleased with this postscript. He hoped very
much that Rose Ellen would understand it. He thought she would. He
sealed the parcel with bright violet wax, using his father's ring. The
impression came out clear and distinct: "Be Ware".

Chapter Twenty-Six

Peter came back to town in an aged mackintosh belonging to Mrs.
Merewether's husband. He hoped fervently that it would rain, but the
day remained obstinately fine and clear, and he was thankful to bury
himself in a taxi.

Arrived at his rooms, he had a bath, and telephoned to Sunnings
for his bag.

Sylvia Moreland spent the morning shopping. She returned to
her flat at one o'clock to find a letter waiting for her from her father.
It contained a large cheque, some good advice, and a message. The
message was for Mr. Hendebakker. Sylvia read it several times before
she went to the telephone and rang up The Luxe.

Her foot tapped impatiently as she waited. After an endless delay
she heard Hendebakker's voice saying, "Hello."

"It's Sylvia Moreland speaking. I've had a letter from my father."

Hendebakker coughed. It was a signal that he was not alone.

"I'll be coming round," he said, and rang off at once.

It seemed a long time to wait until he came. Sylvia was both
nervous and angry. She was also full of curiosity. Hendebakker's visits

to her flat were, of design, so rare that she knew he must consider a letter from her father of vital importance. He arrived at last. His genial smile disappeared as the maid closed the door behind him.

"What does he say? Give me the letter," he said sharply. "What's the postmark?"

She handed him the envelope. It bore a London mark, and he threw it aside impatiently.

"The letter!"

"It's private," said Sylvia.

"Nix!" said Mr. Hendebakker emphatically. "Quit fooling and give it me."

Sylvia handed it over. He turned so that the light fell upon the page, and read it through carefully. As he read, he summarized the contents in a businesslike manner. No heading. Written with a fountain pen—his own—on paper which wasn't his own. Written, in fact, after he got away. A cheque enclosed. Parental admonition. And at the end, the message:

> Tell Hendebakker that I haven't taken the Jewel with me after all. I should hate him to waste his valuable time coming out to China after me, especially as I'm hoping for a little peace and quiet myself. Tell him I pledge my word that the Jewel remains in England. I'm neither taking it with me nor having it sent after me. I don't want it. I'm through. Tell him this, word for word.

That was all.

Hendebakker looked up from the letter, and met Sylvia's eyes, blue and curious.

"Do you think he really hasn't taken it?" she said.

Hendebakker nodded.

"There'd be a catch with most men, but not with Dale," he said. "When it comes to a business deal Dale's straight—everyone in China knew that. I'll take his word for it that he hasn't got the Jewel, and that means"—his voice became extraordinarily smooth and gentle—"that means young Waring's got it after all."

Sylvia started. But Hendebakker was not noticing her. He locked his hands behind his back, and began to pace slowly up and down, still holding the letter, still speaking in that quiet way.

"I was a blame' fool not to think of it. Yes, Waring's got it for a cert. Yes, Waring's got it. I'll call any man a liar who says he hasn't. Now, now, now—let me figure it out. He hadn't got it when I searched him, but he's got it now for sure. I guess I *was* a fool not to tumble to it as soon as I found the tracks of Dale's car in the lane. He came on Waring there, after I'd searched him, and gave him the Jewel. And Waring's got it—it's all creation to a dime he's got it."

He fell into silence, but went on walking up and down. The hum and the jar of the street traffic seemed to sound louder and louder as the silence continued. Sylvia leaned on the back of one of her black chairs, and fidgeted with the gold tassel of a bright-blue cushion.

At last Hendebakker turned towards her, swinging round suddenly and sharply, and fixing his light eyes full on her face.

"Is he back in town?" he asked.

"Who?"

"Young Waring."

"I've no idea."

"Find out. Ring him. Ask him to tea or dinner—anything for an excuse—and when you've got him, make him talk if you can. Get going. Do it now."

Sylvia did as she was bid. He followed her to the telephone, and stood there while she listened. He could hear the sound of a voice without distinguishing words. After a moment she rang off, and turned to him.

"He came back this morning, but he's out. She doesn't know when he'll be back."

They returned to the drawing-room.

"Now," said Hendebakker, "you attend very carefully. Just as soon as you've had your lunch you'll go round to Deakin and Blash, the house agents, and you'll ask them about houses for sale."

He sat down at her little escritoire and began to write, talking as he did so.

"This is what you're to ask for—accommodation, grounds, etcetera. You're looking at houses for a friend who's coming home from, say, Egypt. If they don't mention Keith Lodge, say you heard it was going. It's on Wimbledon Common. Say you'd like to look over it; and bring the keys away with you. When you've got them, come to The Luxe and have tea with Anita."

He handed her the sheet of instructions.

"Get that off by heart and give me the paper back," he said.

Sylvia found Anita alone at tea-time. They had tea, and talked clothes and scandal.

"Virgilio, he is out," said Anita. "As if I knew where! Never do I know what he does—but I am not jealous." She laughed complacently, and they went on talking.

Mr. Hendebakker strolled in as they were finishing tea. Five minutes later Anita got up and went out of the room. Hendebakker watched her go with a nod of approval. Then he said:

"Have you got the keys?"

Sylvia took them out of her bag and handed them to him.

"Any difficulty in getting them?"

"None whatever. I should think the house had been on the books for years. The young man in the office said as much; he said he was afraid the place was very neglected and overgrown."

"It is," said Hendebakker. "He's right on the spot about that. Now, Lady Moreland, I want young Waring at Keith Lodge tonight—say ten-thirty. It isn't real dark then."

Sylvia exclaimed; drew back.

"What do you mean?"

"Just exactly what I say. I want Waring there at ten-thirty p.m., and it's up to you to get him there. I don't care how you do it, but he's got to come."

"And when he's there?" said Sylvia in a low, strained voice. She was watching Hendebakker, and her heart fluttered when he smiled,

"Well, my dear, I rather think of doing a deal with him," he said pleasantly. "Yes, I rather think we shall be able to do a deal."

"I won't do it," said Sylvia, with a sudden lift of the head. "I won't. You can't make me."

Her thoughts were racing. Hendebakker meant to get Peter down to that lonely house and then, by some violent means, get him to give up the Jewel. She was to be the decoy. But if she refused, defied Hendebakker—why—yes, why shouldn't she and Peter join forces? Peter—she was really fond of Peter if he had the Jewel and she stood out, they might make a good bargain with Hendebakker yet. She thought he would pay to get the Jewel—perhaps quite a large sum, enough to clear her. She must see Peter, persuade Peter, and for the moment put Hendebakker off and gain time. All these thoughts flashed through her mind as she looked into Hendebakker's face and saw its expression change to anger. Her eyes fell before his. She caught her breath and put her hands before her face.

"Mr. Hendebakker, please—oh, you know I've done everything you've asked me to; but I can't, I can't do this."

"Can't you?" said Hendebakker. He caught her wrists and pulled her hands down with a jerk. "Can't? Won't?" he said. "You do a bit of thinking. What about standing in the dock for theft? You do as I tell you, or I'll put you there."

Sylvia burst into tears of rage.

"Let me go," she sobbed. "How dare you?"

Hendebakker dropped her hands, turned from her with an ugly sound, and walked right across the room and back again. He had himself in hand when he returned.

"See here," he said; "you're all worked up, and you had me so that I was pretty near being worked up myself. Now, that ain't business. This is a business deal. You go right home and think over what I've said. You can take an hour. When you've thought it out, ring me. Mind you, I came near to losing my temper; but I meant what I said. You'll do as you're told, or you'll stand in the dock for stealing Anita's diamonds. Just go right along home and think about the headlines in the Society papers, and what being in prison will be like. They'll cut your hair, you know, and you'll not see a looking-glass for five years or so. You go along and think it out."

Chapter Twenty-Seven

SYLVIA WENT HOME shaken by fear and anger. Hendebakker terrified her; not his threat only, but the man himself—his cold eyes, his ugly temper, his brute strength, his self-control. The last was what frightened her most. To see him smile in a pleasant, friendly fashion when, not a minute before, she had had a glimpse of the wild beast behind bars—this set her shaking.

Her thoughts turned to Peter. She had flirted with Peter, but she was really fond of him, and the idea of getting behind Peter, of getting him to stand between herself and Hendebakker, grew and took definite shape. She might do worse than marry Peter Waring. Of course, he would have to give up the idea of burying her in the country on that ridiculous horse farm of his. If they could get a substantial sum out of Hendebakker, they could live in Town. Peter could keep his interest in the farm if he liked, and run down occasionally—it was quite a good plan for a man to have something to do. Yes, she might do worse than marry Peter—if he really had the Jewel and they could make decent terms with Hendebakker.

She came face to face with Peter half a dozen yards from the entrance to her flats.

"Oh, I'm so glad to see you," she said.

Peter, turning in with her, explained that he had been busy with his uncle's solicitor all the afternoon, and had just been told that she was out.

His uncle's solicitor—had he given him the Jewel? The thought passed quickly through her mind as she laughed and said:

"Well, I'm in now, and quite specially pleased to see you, because— oh, Peter, I've got such a lot to talk to you about."

Peter followed her into the drawing-room, and thought, not for the first time, that if Sylvia was as extravagant about other things as she was about flowers, it was no wonder that she got into debt. There were sprays of orchids like white butterflies in a very old cloisonné jar of the colour of faded turquoise; where the fire had burned a few nights ago was a bank of blue delphinium; the Ming vase held yellow roses; not a flower in the room but was out of season.

"Peter, did you see my father?" said Sylvia eagerly. "I've been longing to see you, because I've had a letter from him, and—now, what did I do with it? No, it doesn't really matter, but, tell me, did you see him?"

"Yes," said Peter, "I saw him."

Sylvia stopped turning over the papers on her writing-table, and came to him with her hands out.

"You know, he misjudged me quite dreadfully the other night, and—and I'm afraid you did too—and I was so upset that I couldn't explain properly. I can't bear to have you think badly of me, Peter; and I want you to know just how it happened. I don't know what you thought, but it was quite simple really.

"I was dining with the Hendebakkers, and we were talking about the Jewel—Anita had it on as usual—and Mr. Hendebakker said that my father had a copy of it, and that it would be interesting to see them side by side. He said the copy was really wonderful, and offered to bet that it would take us in. We all got quite excited about it, and Mr. Hendebakker said what a pity it was that he and my father had quarrelled years ago. He said he couldn't ask him to let us see the copy because of the quarrel. You see how simple it was really, don't you? I dare say it was stupid of me, but I said I'd borrow the copy and bring it to The Luxe for them to see; and that's just what I did. I never thought my father would know—and he wouldn't have known if I'd had a scrap of luck. When I saw him come into the lounge at The Luxe I thought I should have died of fright. I don't know what made me give you the Jewel. I was simply too frightened to think."

She paused, and looked at him with depths of appeal in her blue eyes. "Peter, you *do* see how it was, don't you?"

"It was the Annam Jewel that you gave me," said Peter, "it wasn't a copy."

"I *know*. I know now, but I didn't then. Mr. Hendebakker deceived me. I believe he really meant to change the stones—at least, I'm afraid that's what he meant to do. Is it very uncharitable of me to think so?"

"I don't think I should bother about that," said Peter.

"No, but I do bother about my father. Oh, do you know, I never thought he would go without saying good-bye like that. It—it hurts rather. Has he really gone, Peter?"

"Yes, he's really gone," said Peter.

"Peter, you're being maddening. Do talk to me. Do tell me about it. Can't you see how much I want to know?"

"Well," said Peter soberly, "what do you want to know, Sylvia?"

She put her hand on his arm.

"Why, the whole thing, of course—why you went there; how you got on; what you talked about. And—oh, Peter, *did* he give you the Jewel?"

Peter laughed.

"How can I keep my head when you ask me umpteen questions at once?" he said. "I went down there because he asked me to. We got on very well. We talked about China, and the United States." He laughed again.

Sylvia shook his arm.

"You don't tell me the only thing I want to know," she said. *"Did he give you the Jewel?"*

"Why should he?" said Peter innocently.

Sylvia stamped her foot.

"You're being horrible," she said. "After all, I am his daughter. I don't think you need be so secretive. He told me in his letter that he wasn't taking the Jewel with him, and *naturally* I thought—"

"Yes, you thought—"

"I thought you might have it. Oh, Peter, have you—have you got it?"

Peter hesitated for just the fraction of a second. Then he said:

"No, I haven't got it."

"But he gave it you—I know he gave it you."

He hesitated again.

"I don't think I want to talk about the Jewel," he said at last.

"But I do, Peter. It's important, it really is. You see, I happen to know that Mr. Hendebakker would give a really fabulous sum for it. And if we could make a bargain with him ..."

She broke off because of what she saw in Peter's face. He turned very white, and said in a carefully restrained voice:

"Hendebakker will never have the Jewel. We won't discuss it, if you don't mind."

Sylvia looked at him wide-eyed, and fell back a pace.

"Good gracious, how *ridiculous* you all are about the thing!" she said. "You're as bad as my father; he wouldn't discuss it either. Anyone would think—" she laughed a pretty little ringing laugh—"Peter, you look like thunder, and it's not a bit becoming to you."

She laughed again, kissed the tips of her fingers to him, and went across the room to where the butterfly orchids hovered above their turquoise jar. She pulled out one of the sprays and came back, a teasing smile on her face, sharp offence and determined curiosity in her mind.

"Do you like orchids?" She touched his hand with the spray.

"I don't know," said Peter. "Not very much. I like primroses better."

He thought of the beech-wood; last year's leaves with the primroses breaking through them; Rose Ellen with the tears raining down her face. Sylvia and her orchids seemed very remote.

"I adore them," said Sylvia. "I like expensive things, you know. I'm a wicked, extravagant woman; I like things that other people haven't got. That's why I want the Jewel."

Peter began to frown, but changed his mind. Instead, he looked into Sylvia's blue eyes and laughed frankly.

"Pax," he said. "I'm sorry I was cross just now. I felt cross. I really won't talk about the Jewel—anything else you like, but not the Jewel."

Sylvia curled herself up in a chair.

"Well, what shall we talk about?" she said. "It's rather like a game, isn't it? The forbidden word. Isn't it a funny thing that as soon as you're told you may talk about anything you like, you don't want to talk about anything at all? I think you can do the talking. You haven't really told me what you did whilst you were out of Town. By the way, weren't you going to see the Gaisfords?"

"Yes, I lunched there," said Peter.

"All that way for lunch?"

"I wanted to see Rose Ellen," said Peter simply.

Sylvia looked at him over her spray of orchids. Her eyes narrowed a little, her lips smiled.

"She isn't really related to you at all, is she?" she said.

"No."

Peter had one elbow on the mantelshelf. He was not looking at Sylvia or thinking of Sylvia. He was thinking about Rose Ellen, who was really no relation. With his left hand he picked up a little jade fish, balancing it precariously upon two fingers. It was made of white mutton-fat jade, its eyes bulged, and it had three tails. Peter bent a gaze of frowning intensity upon the fish, and went on thinking about Rose Ellen.

"It was an odd thing, your mother adopting her like that." Sylvia's tone was a meditative one. "I suppose she never found out who her people were or anything?"

"No," said Peter. She was his Rose Ellen, only his.

"It must be so strange not to have any relations," said Sylvia, "especially for a girl. You see, it's really bound to stand in the way of her marrying—I mean supposing some really dreadful relations were to turn up—one never knows, does one? You know, I thought of that the day you brought her here; and I felt sorry for her. She's pretty too—I think she's *quite* pretty. Don't you?"

Peter dropped the jade fish into the bank of blue delphiniums which filled the hearth. He said, "Yes," rather shortly as he stooped to pick it up.

Sylvia's temper had been rising steadily. An odd antagonism seemed to be growing between them. She began to break the white butterflies from her spray, but still she smiled.

"Peter, how monosyllabic you are. You forget you were to do the talking."

Peter put the jade fish back upon its carved ebony stand.

"I didn't like what you were saying very much," he said bluntly.

"My dear Peter, what was I saying? Anyone would think you were in love with the girl."

Peter looked her full in the face, and said:

"I am." Then he went on speaking quickly and with great simplicity. "That's why I didn't like what you said—about her getting married, and not having any real relations. You see, it doesn't matter at all—it simply doesn't matter."

"You're in love with her," said Sylvia. She spoke mechanically. She was suddenly so angry that she repeated her last words, hardly knowing what she said. How dared Peter Waring stand there and tell her he was in love with another woman? She stripped the orchid spray of its last blossom, and let it drop.

"Yes," said Peter. "I wanted to tell you, Sylvia, because we've been pretty good friends. I think I've always cared for Rose Ellen; but I only knew it yesterday. It's odd how those things happen, isn't it?"

"Very odd," said Sylvia. She got up as she spoke. "Very odd indeed. No wonder you didn't want to talk about the Jewel." She laughed—it is easy to laugh if you're angry. "A man in love has only one topic of conversation. What a good thing I happened to strike it!"

Peter looked rather puzzled.

"I'm sorry," he said. "I'm afraid I'm boring you. I thought you would be interested."

Her smile flashed out, her brilliant, elusive smile.

"But of course I'm interested," she said.

Chapter Twenty-Eight

"I DO NOT LIKE Sylvia Moreland so well as I did, Virgilio," said Anita Hendebakker.

She stood in the middle of the room, looking at her husband's back as he sat bent forward over a writing-table. She threw him a glance, half pettish, half startled.

Hendebakker grunted. After a moment he swung round in his chair, pen in hand.

"I didn't just get that," he said.

Anita tapped with her foot. She wore an odd, sheath-like garment of heavy gold tissue embroidered in a design of black lilies. A rope of pearls fell to her knee.

"I say, Virgilio, that I do not any more like Sylvia Moreland as once I thought I did."

"Well," said Hendebakker, "that's bad news for Sylvia, I guess."

The carnation deepened in Anita's cheeks.

"It is bad news for me," she said, "and you know, very well you know, Virgilio, why it is that I like her not any more. It is because I think—yes, *well*, I think that it is you who like her too much."

"And what makes you think that?" said Hendebakker, smiling pleasantly.

Anita retreated a step or two.

"It is no use you to look at me like that. When I am angry I am not frightened; no, not even when you smile." Her bosom heaved, her colour came and went, her eyes confessed the fear that she denied. "It is too much Sylvia with you, I tell you. You go out, and I do not know where you go; but I suspect. She comes here, and you send me from the room that you may talk with her. She calls you on the telephone, and, if I answer, it is you she asks for; and while you speak to her, again I am sent away. I say, Virgilio, that I bear it no longer."

Hendebakker got up. As he came across the room towards her she retreated until at last she could go no farther. She stood against the wall, her head thrown back, her eyes wide and dark. He spoke gently.

"You won't bear it?"

She breathed a trembling "No."

"Well, now, what will you do?"

Anita went on looking at him. All at once he put a hand on her shoulder.

"Say, Anita," he said, "d'you ever think? If you do, right here's the time when it's going to be useful to you. Five years ago now, in New York—you do some thinking about that."

Anita stared.

"Five years ago, in New York, what were you?"

He shot the words at her with a sudden violence which was terrifying. "How'd it suit you to go back? Think you'd enjoy it now? If you're a fool, I reckon you're not such a fool as that. I reckon you know when you're well off."

The colour died out of her face. She closed her eyes. Hendebakker put his arm round her, and half lifted, half guided her to a chair. Then he took her hand and patted it.

"You're a mighty pretty woman, Anita," he said, "and you've done pretty well for yourself. When you want to think, you think about that. *Quit thinking about my business.* You'll be liable to get wrinkles if you don't, and I'd hate to have you lose your looks. Sylvia Moreland is *business.* You freeze on to that."

The large dark eyes opened, gazed at him. She lifted her hand timidly and caught the lapel of his coat.

"Business?" she breathed.

Hendebakker nodded.

"Never mix business with pleasure," he said. "That's been my motto right along. You freeze on to business, and business'll freeze on to you. That's what I've done, and that's why we're staying at The Luxe with money to burn. The man that mixes up business with pleasure is going to come a most almighty smash. I'm not such a blame' fool; and you ought to know better than to think I am. The amount I love Sylvia Moreland needn't keep you awake at night, Anita, and that's a fact."

"How do I know that you speak the truth?" said Anita. "Perhaps you do, perhaps you do not. Who knows with a man?"

Hendebakker laughed.

"If you can't know, you can guess," he said. He kissed her. "You quit being jealous; it don't suit you; and what's more, it don't suit me."

Anita threw her arms about his neck with a sob.

"Ah, I have been jealous," she breathed. "I have suffered. I have waked in the night. I have said, 'If he loves me no more, my life is over.' Is it that you love me no more, Virgilio?"

"No, it isn't, and you know it isn't," said Hendebakker, laughing again. "But don't you start interfering in my business deals, or there'll be bad trouble. I don't take that from anyone. So you quit and be a good girl."

As he bent to kiss her the telephone bell rang sharply. He pushed Anita back into her chair, and went over to the writing-table.

"Hullo," he said, "hullo," and heard Sylvia Moreland's voice saying:

"Oh, is that you? I've rung up."

He glanced over his shoulder at Anita. Her large, lustrous eyes were watching him; her hands played with her pearls. With a shrug of the shoulders he turned back to the telephone.

"I reckon you have. It's Hendebakker speaking."

"Yes; I've rung up to say I'll do it—I mean I'll do what you asked me to do this afternoon." There was a note of defiance in Sylvia's tones.

"That's sensible of you," he said, and heard her laugh, a hard, angry little laugh. She went on speaking at once.

"He's been here. He's only just gone. I'll do anything you want me to."

"Good! Did you fix anything up?"

"No. I thought it would be better if it looked like a sudden impulse, as if I had just thought of asking him to go."

"Can you get him later?"

"Yes. I've found out that he will be at his club this evening. I can ring him up there about ten o'clock. I know just what to say."

"You're sure he'll come?"

Sylvia laughed again.

"Oh yes, he'll *come*," she said. "Chivalry's his strong suit, you know—and I'm going to be in horrible trouble. He'll never let me trek off to Wimbledon all by myself to see a monster of a man who's blackmailing me."

"Oh, that's the stunt, is it?"

"Don't you think it's a good one? I thought it was." There was that odd mingling of triumph and nervousness in her voice.

"I think you're a real good liar," said Hendebakker admiringly, "real smart. I wouldn't presume to offer any suggestions. You have him there at ten-thirty, and I'll take off my hat to you. Now, you listen a minute. At ten minutes to ten there'll be an ordinary taxi waiting at your corner. The driver will be one of my men. Just to make sure, you ask him his name. If he says Robinson, that's right. He'll take your orders until you get to Keith Lodge."

"And then?" There was more nervousness than triumph now.

"Now, don't you get rattled. This is a plain business deal. We come to terms, and all go home again to bed."

"And if he won't?"

"He will," said Hendebakker cheerfully. "Don't you fret about that—he will. In the seclusion of that rural retreat we shall come to terms."

"But if you *don't*?"

Hendebakker hung up the receiver and rang off. Anita was still watching him.

"To whom did you talk, Virgilio?"

"I talked to Sylvia Moreland."

"Ah yes, something told me so—something here." She laid her hand upon her bosom.

"Well, it told you right. You're getting smart, Anita."

He came quite close to her, bent down, kissed her—and then, with his face quite near to hers, he said with a sudden drop in his voice:

"Don't you be too smart, Anita. It don't pay."

Chapter Twenty-Nine

PETER WAS WRITING letters at his club when Sylvia rang up. Mrs. Jones had mended his dinner jacket rather under protest. She sniffed when she took it from him, and sniffed again when she brought it back neatly brushed and with the burst seam repaired. Both sniffs accused Peter of midnight roystering, and intimated, without the actual use of words, that Mrs. Jones didn't hold with such goings on.

Peter went to the telephone rather resignedly. He was in the middle of a letter to his partner, and had no wish to be interrupted. He wished he had not told Sylvia that he was spending the evening at the club. Later on he was to wish it again, and a good deal more fervently.

"Oh, Peter, is that you?" said Sylvia's voice; and Peter said that it was. "Oh, I'm so glad, so thankful you're there still. Peter ..." Her voice choked for a moment. "I—I'm in the most dreadful trouble."

Peter very nearly said, "Again?" but restrained himself, and tried to infuse a proper amount of sympathy into his "What is it? What's the matter?"

"I can't tell you on the telephone, but my affairs have come to a crisis."

"What? Since I saw you?"

"Yes, I was frightened then, but I've had a most dreadful letter since, and—and a telephone call. Peter, isn't it what they call blackmail when someone says you must go and see them and pay up at once or they'll do perfectly dreadful things to you?"

"It might be," said Peter guardedly. "Is anyone doing that to you?"

"Oh *yes.*" There were tears in Sylvia's voice. "Peter, he says I must come and see him tonight, or—or he'll do the most dreadful things. And, oh, Peter, I'm afraid to go by myself."

"You mustn't *dream* of going." Peter was very emphatic.

"I must. I must go. I don't want to, but I can't help myself. But I don't want to go alone. I don't think I can face it. And you said—you said you'd help me. Oh, Peter, will you come with me? Will you?"

"Look here, Sylvia, there can't be all this urgency. I'll come round tomorrow and go into it with you. It's perfectly ridiculous your thinking of going to see anyone at this hour of night."

"You don't understand." He could hear her voice trembling. "You simply don't understand. I must go. The only question is, will you come with me, or have I got to go alone?"

Peter was feeling justly annoyed. How women did panic over business! But, of course, he couldn't let Sylvia go and interview some brute of a money-lender by herself. He said without enthusiasm:

"Oh, I'll come," and heard her give a sort of gasp before she answered:

"I'll call for you, then; I've got a taxi."

The ring-off followed immediately. Peter went back and finished his letter. He had meant to polish off half a dozen more, but he supposed that they would have to wait.

When he got into the taxi beside Sylvia he was feeling a good deal ruffled. He began to express his feelings.

"You know, my dear girl, this is the most awful rot. It is really."

"What is?" said Sylvia coolly.

"Your charging off at this time of night to go and do business with some beastly money-lender. Who is the brute, anyway?"

"His name's Robinson," said Sylvia, "and he isn't exactly a money-lender. He's—he's—I don't exactly know how to describe him."

The taxi was going along at a good pace.

"I don't want you to describe him; and I don't want you to go and see him. I want you to let me take you home. If it's absolutely necessary, I'll go and see him myself. But it's all nonsense your running after the man at this time of night. I can't see where this frightful hurry comes in."

"I must go," said Sylvia in a low, despairing voice. "I must go. I'd give anything in the world to go home again, but I can't. If I don't see him tonight, it's all up."

"I don't believe it," said Peter crossly.

"You needn't." Her voice was full of sadness. "You can stop the taxi this minute, and get out and go home. I oughtn't to have asked you to come; it was stupid of me."

Peter was very angry. He thought Sylvia a most unreasonable woman, and he would have liked to take her home and lock her in her flat out of harm's way. This course being impossible, he told her gruffly not to talk nonsense, to which Sylvia replied by slipping one of her hands into his and saying, in a voice shaken by emotion:

"You *are* coming with me, then? Oh, I knew you wouldn't fail me."

Peter took his hand away.

"If you insist upon going, of course I'll come with you. Where does this man hang out?"

"It's a house at Wimbledon," said Sylvia.

"Wimbledon? Good lord, Sylvia!"

"It's his own house," said Sylvia meekly. "He's going abroad tomorrow, so it's my only chance of seeing him personally. I do dread being put off by a clerk who says he has no authority. I do think a personal interview with the man who has really got the whole thing in his hands—well, it means so much more, doesn't it?"

"I don't know," said Peter. "I should have everything in writing if I were you." Then, after a pause, "You know I'm absolutely in the dark. Who is this fellow? Do you owe him money?"

"Y—yes," said Sylvia. She dreaded Peter's downright questions, but for the moment she could think of no way of escape from them.

"How much?"

"I—I don't like to say."

Peter prayed for patience.

"My dear girl, what do you want me to do? Am I to talk to this man for you? Or am I just to stand by whilst you talk to him?"

"Yes, I think so," said Sylvia.

"All right. I just wanted to know, that's all. Then I won't ask you any more questions."

They drove on in silence. It was dark, cloudy, and rather airless. Presently they left houses behind them, and emerged upon a stretch of common.

"Do you know the place? Are we nearly there?" said Peter.

"I've never been there," said Sylvia rather faintly.

As she spoke the car left the main road, turned in amongst trees, and followed a long, winding drive. Keith Lodge stood by itself in large wooded grounds. The drive was a very long one, and there were trees everywhere. At times the overhanging branches barely cleared the top of the car. They drew up with a grinding sound on a gravel sweep. The driver jumped down and opened the door.

Peter felt Sylvia's ungloved hand tremble in his as he helped her out; her hand was very cold. His heart smote him for his ill-humour, and he gave her arm a little reassuring pat.

"It'll be all right. Don't worry," he said, and heard her draw a sharp breath.

She made no other reply, and they went up to the front door in silence.

Peter thought the house very dark and forbidding. The windows on their right were shuttered. A pencil of light came through a knot-hole. The fanlight above the front door showed a faint glow. Otherwise the house was in darkness. With his hand on the knocker, he turned.

"Look here, Sylvia, I don't like the look of this place," he said. "There's something fishy about it. Why on earth does the man want to see people at night? You'd much better let me bring you down tomorrow at a reasonable hour."

She reached past him, caught at the knocker, her hand on his, and knocked sharply. Her hand was not cold now, but burning hot.

"No, no, we can't go back," she said.

She had not looked behind her, but she knew very well that the taxi-driver had followed them. There was certainly no going back.

"Go and sit in the car," said Peter. "I can see the man."

As he spoke the door opened, not widely; about a foot of tessellated pavement showed in a dimmish light.

Peter put his hand on Sylvia's arm and asked:

"Is Mr. Robinson at home?" He spoke to the merest silhouette of a man standing there in the narrow opening.

The man drew back, the door opened a little wider. With a sudden jerk Sylvia freed herself and passed quickly into the hall. Clear in Peter's memory there rose the very feel of that wet and windy night, twelve years ago, when little Rose Ellen had pulled her hand from his and run to meet adventure at Merton Clevery. He stepped forward, following Sylvia as he had followed Rose Ellen, and sharp across the moment of dreamy recollection there struck the sound of his own footsteps and Sylvia's, echoing as footsteps only echo in an empty house.

Chapter Thirty

PETER HAD ONLY a momentary impression of the hall as a large, square emptiness made visible by the small flicker of a candle-end that guttered and went out in the draught of the closing door. There was no wind, but the hall door had slammed. Peter took a quick stride away from it. The door had not shut of itself; and, with every sense alert, he was aware that someone had come in after him and was there, close to him in the dark. He could hear the sound of breathing, the sound of stealthy movement.

He called aloud, "Sylvia, where are you?" and at once changed his position. There was no answer, no sound but the echo of his own voice coming back to him from empty spaces. And then, with swift unexpectedness, two things happened. Right in front of him a door opened inwards upon a lighted room; and at the same moment someone rushed him from behind and impelled him violently forward.

Taken unawares, he broke into a stumbling run, and so came into the lighted room, and heard the door fall to behind him. Hendebakker's voice rang sharply in his ears:

"Hands up, Waring. Hands up, or I fire!"

Peter got his balance, and, falling back a pace, put up his hands.

The room was large, some thirty feet by forty. It was entirely unfurnished, and its parquet floor stood thick with dust. There were wooden shutters. The walls were panelled, and the paint, which had once been white, was stained and discoloured. On one end of the white marble mantelpiece was a portable electric lamp. Against the other end leaned Virgil Hendebakker, his dark coat smeared with dust and an automatic pistol in his hand. The pistol was pointed at Peter.

"Good evening, Waring," he said cheerfully. "I'm real sorry to bring you so far, but business is business."

Peter measured the distance between them, and decided that a rush was not good enough. In a smaller room he would have tried it; but thirty feet gave Hendebakker too many chances. He went back another pace, leaned against the wall, and said:

"Where's Lady Moreland?"

Hendebakker smiled.

"I guess you needn't worry about Lady Moreland," he said. "It's real nice of you, but you're wasting your time doing it. Lady Moreland's got as good a notion of looking after herself as any young woman I ever met. It's Sylvia Moreland first, and the rest nowhere."

"I suppose," said Peter, "that you didn't bring me here to discuss Lady Moreland—did you?"

"I did not. I wanted to talk business with you. I don't have to tell you what the business is either, I reckon."

Peter said nothing. After a moment Hendebakker went on:

"I'm free to confess that you and Dale were one up on me at Sunnings. Now, Waring, you take notice of what I say. No one stays one up on me for very long—and why? Because I make it my business to get square. I'm a pretty efficient man of business, and when I set out to do a thing I do it."

"You're a pretty good hand at blowing your own trumpet, aren't you?" said Peter.

"Fair," said Hendebakker. "Fair. Only a fool thinks he can do without advertising nowadays. Now, Waring, where's the Jewel?"

Peter was silent.

"Waring," said Hendebakker, "you make me tired. I'm not bluffing; I've got facts to go on. Dale sent me a message to say he was leaving the Jewel behind him. Well, you may think it strange that I'd take his word for it; but that's because you don't know Dale as well as I do. I suppose it's the same with all of us; there are things we'll do, and there are things we won't do. Why, there's a thing or two I wouldn't do myself. So that's where it is. Dale wouldn't lie about the Jewel. I knew that; so, as soon as I got his message, I knew for sure that he hadn't taken it with him, and I knew for sure that he hadn't passed it on to his daughter. She'd have been ready enough to do a deal with me if she'd had anything to bargain with." He laughed rather grimly, and added, "It's up to you. What about it?"

"Do you generally talk business like this?" said Peter. "Because I don't. Put down that damned revolver of yours if you want me to talk."

"It's an automatic," said Hendebakker, "and I rather think I'll keep it where it is. It feels handy. But, if you'll pass me your word that you're not armed, you can put your hands down. I've had mine up for half an hour or so before now and it's mighty uncomfortable. Are you armed?"

"No, I'm not."

"Well, then, put them down. And now, to resume—what about it?"

"As far as I'm concerned, nothing," said Peter, putting his hands in his pockets.

"That," said Hendebakker, "is unwise. Come, Waring, what's the good of the Jewel to you? You can't sell it; you can't wear it; you can't hide it. I tell you I mean to have it."

"Very well, then, get it, Henders," said Peter. "I can't stop you, can I? I can't sell it; or wear it; or hide it, as you say. Go on and get it, and be damned to you."

"Now what's the good of losing your temper over a business conversation?" said Hendebakker. "It's right down foolish. Come now, Waring, I said you couldn't sell the Jewel, but that's where I was wrong. You *can* sell it to me. I'll give you five thousand for it—not dollars, pounds—five thousand pounds."

"No, thanks, Henders."

"Ten," said Hendebakker. "I never thought you'd take five, but ten—say, Waring, figure it out to yourself—ten thousand pounds at five per cent or more against a Jewel that'll never be anything but trouble for you, and bad trouble at that. You're not such a blame' fool as to hesitate?"

"Nothing doing, Henders," said Peter quite cheerfully.

"Fifteen thousand pounds," said Hendebakker, stretching out his left hand, palm upwards, as if it held the money. "It's a fancy price, but, if I choose to pay for my fancy, it's nobody's business but my own."

Peter laughed suddenly.

"Go it, Henders," he said. "Why stop at fifteen thousand?"

Henders' outstretched hand dropped to his side. Peter, watching, saw it clench till the knuckles whitened. He wondered at the man's self-control, for, if his hand betrayed him, his face did not; nor did his voice as he said:

"Well, what's your price?"

"Haven't got one," said Peter. "There's nothing doing, Henders, and you'll save us both a lot of trouble if you'll take that as final."

"That so?"

"That's so."

Their eyes met in a long, hard stare. Then, with great suddenness, Hendebakker pulled out a whistle and blew it twice. The door opened instantly and two men came in, the taxi-driver and another.

"Tie him up," said Hendebakker; and there ensued what Peter afterwards described as a scrum.

The moment Hendebakker spoke, Peter swung round upon the nearer of the two men, aiming a blow at his jaw. As he swung, his foot slipped on a splash of candle-grease, and he came down, grabbing at the man and bringing him with him. Before he could recover, the taxi-driver was on him, wrenching his right arm backwards; and quick upon that Hendebakker came up at a run, and the muzzle of his pistol was jammed against Peter's ear. The first man scrambled up, produced a rope, and secured Peter's arms behind his back.

"Now, get up and march," said Hendebakker, and gave him a push with his foot. Peter stumbled to his feet.

The taxi-driver fetched the lamp, and they came through the hall to a dark and steep stairway which led to the basement. Peter was furiously angry, but he had his wits about him. He made no further struggle, because, as long as his legs were free, there was just a chance of something turning up; also he felt that he would prefer walking to being carried down that steep stair.

They arrived in an echoing basement; a huge, deserted kitchen with a rusting range; large, dim passages; a stone-flagged hall; and a door opening upon another stair, steeper still, with narrow steps which hardly gave room for a man's foot.

"I reckon it isn't every house has got such mighty convenient cellars," said Hendebakker.

He looked round approvingly as he spoke, motioning to Robinson to hold up the lamp. There was an open space at the foot of the stairs. To the right a long stone passage faded into gloom.

"Right along there," said Hendebakker, "and the second door on the left. It isn't locked—yet."

The door opened outwards, and, the man Robinson going in first with the light, Peter came into a small, close cellar some ten feet by seven or eight.

"Now tie his legs," said Hendebakker. He did not speak again until Peter, with his legs roped together, had been deposited in a sitting position with his back against the cellar wall. Then, the men having gone out and shut the door, he said reprovingly:

"You're a mighty foolish young man, and you're giving me a lot of trouble. There's no reason in this foolishness, and the sooner you quit and come to terms, the better for us all."

The electric lamp stood on the floor. Its searching light illumined the little square room, with its walls of whitewashed brick and floor of heavy flagstones. Across the narrow space Peter glared at Hendebakker.

"You will answer for this, Henders," he said at last.

"Now, what's the use of that sort of talk? I guess you're soothing yourself with the thought of me in the dock, and you in the witness-box, and one of your judges giving me a seven years' stretch. Well, that's just dope—you take it from me, it's just dope. Why, if there's one feature of this Jewel business that stands out more than another, it's the plain fact that none of the parties in the case have ever been in a position to go to the courts about it. There was Dale and me. He robbed me, for sure—took the Jewel and went at a time when he knew I was having trouble and couldn't come after him. Do you suppose I wouldn't have had the law on him if I could? Why, of course I would; but I just wasn't in the position where the law was worth a dime to me, and Dale knew it. You may say that's neither here nor there, but take your own case. I'm free to admit that you've a better legal case than either Dale or I have, and a better record too. But just you think a moment. We'll say you're sore about Lady Moreland; you've a right to be, but how'd you like it if it were she that was in the dock? You can't touch me without you touch her—you can't do it. If you ever move hand or finger against me over this business I'll take mighty good care that she gets half of whatever's coming to me."

"What a damned swab you are, Henders!" said Peter.

"Now, you go easy, and listen to me. Your friend Lady More-land's in this game up to her very neck—right up to her neck she's in it. Who got the keys of this house from the agents? Lady Moreland. Who brought you here? Lady Moreland. Who let me know you were going to Sunnings? Who told me for sure that you had the Jewel? Lady Moreland."

The realization that Henders was speaking the truth rushed in upon Peter in a bitter flood. Sylvia had gone back on him, had given him away at every turn. She was Hendebakker's tool, in it up to her neck, as he had said.

"Courts of law aren't the only place where one can settle up," he said grimly.

"That's so," said Hendebakker. "That's why we're here. Now, let me put the case quite plainly to you for a moment. This is an isolated house, standing—well, I dare say you noticed how far it stands back from the road. It's been empty, I understand, for something like seven years; and I'm told it has a real lively reputation for being haunted. These cellars are way down underground, as you know. Just taking these facts into consideration, how long do you suppose you might stay here before someone happened in upon your bones? Quite a time, I should judge; but I'll be interested to have your opinion."

"Are you proposing to murder me?" said Peter. "I should think twice about it, if I were you. Murder is risky work in this country."

Hendebakker laughed.

"Murder you, Waring? Not I—I'm not such a fool. This is a plain business deal. All I want is to come to terms. This highfalutin talk about murder makes me tired. It's all very well on the movies, but in a plain business matter it makes me tired." He paused, and then added, "Mind you, Waring, I'm not saying that you mightn't get me so that it was a question whether you got damaged or me. If such was the case, you could make a pretty safe bet as to who would get hurt—it wouldn't be me. Now taking these facts into consideration, don't you think you had better come to terms?"

"What's the programme if I don't?" said Peter.

"You'll get an interval for reflection," said Hendebakker. "You can do some real good reflecting down here; nothing to disturb you; nothing to eat; nothing to drink; nothing to do, except to fix up your pride so as it'll let you take a mighty good offer."

Peter said nothing.

"There's one thing I'd like you to get your mind clear about," said Hendebakker. "There's just three people beside myself know where you are, and I don't want you to lay up disappointment for yourself by thinking that any of them are going to be a mite of help to you— they're not. Lady Moreland won't go back on me, because she daren't; and I'll tell you why. She took some loose diamonds that Anita had lying about, and she tried to sell them—I can put my hand on the man she tried to sell them to—and she knows just what'll happen to her if I ever have the least grounds for thinking she's not square with me. Then there are my two men. Perhaps you're relying on them. Maybe you think they won't go to extremities, or that you can bribe them. Well, you can't. You can count them out for the same reason that you can count Lady Moreland out. I don't employ any man I'm not sure of; and I'm sure of those two, because I could get 'em fourteen years tomorrow. See? And now I'll be going. Sure you haven't thought better of it?"

Peter remained silent.

"Well, well," said Hendebakker, "you do some thinking."

He opened the door and went out, leaving the lamp in the middle of the floor. After a moment he came back. He had in one hand an empty beer-bottle, and in the other about an inch of candle. He set the beer-bottle in the corner farthest from Peter, jammed the candle-end into the open neck, and set light to the wick.

"That's to let you down easy," he said. "Well, so long, Waring." He picked up the electric lamp and went out, locking the door behind him.

Peter listened to hear whether the key was withdrawn, but the only sound that came to him was the sound of Hendebakker's heavy step going away down the flagged passage. The sound grew fainter and fainter until his ear could no longer catch it. A dull silence settled.

Chapter Thirty-One

MR. HENDEBAKKER went upstairs, passed through the hall, and out at the front door. When he came to the taxi he stopped, swung his light up, and caught a glimpse of Sylvia's startled face.

"Come back into the house," he said.

"I don't want to," she breathed. "It's a dreadful house; it frightens me."

Hendebakker put down his lamp, opened the taxi door, and held out his hand.

"Come along," he said. And Sylvia came.

When they were in the hall again, and the door was shut, he said:

"You've done some good work tonight, and I'm pleased with you."

"Then let me go home," said Sylvia. "Oh, Mr. Hendebakker, *please* let me go home."

"All in good time. You've got to talk to young Waring first."

"I can't!" The words were a cry, spontaneous and terrified.

"Oh yes, you can. You've got to, anyway. He won't talk to me, but I rather guess he will to you."

"What have you done to him?" said Sylvia.

"Nothing. Only tied him up so's he can't damage himself or anyone else. He's an obstinate devil, and he won't talk. I want to get his tongue going. Now, he's riled with you, and when a man's riled he's liable to talk pretty freely. What you've got to do is to get him talking. Maybe he'll let slip where the Jewel is. He hasn't got it on him; I'll take my oath to that; and I don't believe he's banked it. If you ask me why, I tell you I don't know; but no one who has the Jewel ever wants to put it away in a bank. They want to keep it where they can get at it and look at it. I thought Dale had banked it, but he hadn't. I don't know where it was, but he hadn't banked it; and I don't believe that Waring has either. He's only had it twenty-four hours for one thing. Now, you come along with me and do your best to make him talk. You can pile on the sob-stuff and register as much remorse as you think he'll swallow. But get him going."

At the corner of the passage which led to the cellar Hendebakker stopped.

"I'll be right here, round this corner, where the light doesn't show," he whispered. "I don't want him to suspect I'm around. You keep along by the wall till you come to the second door. The key is sticking in the lock."

"I can't," said Sylvia. "It's so dark."

Hendebakker pulled out a pocket torch and put it into her hand.

"That make you feel any better?" He gave her a push in the direction of the cellar. "Get a move on."

Sylvia came to the cellar door, and stood there with her hand upon the key. She was afraid to go on, and doubly afraid to go back. When she dared delay no longer, she turned the key with a wrench and pulled the door towards her. It creaked as it swung open. She stood on the threshold, and saw Peter propped in a sitting position against the opposite wall. The light from her torch cut through the faint candlelight and showed her his face, very white, smeared with blood and dust, and his eyes fixed on her with surprised contempt.

173 | THE ANNAM JEWEL

She shuddered. Her hand dropped to her side. The torchlight made a little, shining ring upon the stone floor.

"What do you want?" said Peter.

"I—I came," said Sylvia, speaking slowly and vaguely. She rested her free hand upon the jamb, as if she needed support. "I—came—to—oh, Peter, have they hurt you?"

"Not yet," said Peter grimly.

Sylvia came slowly into the room. She closed the door, extinguished her torch, and slipped it into an inner pocket of the wrap she was wearing. She was bareheaded; her hair was bright in the candlelight. She came forward with an inarticulate murmur of distress.

"Why have you come?" said Peter.

"I had to," said Sylvia in a choked voice. "Peter, what—what must you think of me?" There was a pause.

"I expect I'd better not say," said Peter at last.

She cried out as if he had struck her, and dropped on her knees beside him.

"Peter, don't! I can't bear it. I know what you must be thinking. But he made me do it. I didn't want to, I had to. Oh, can't you understand a little bit? Haven't you ever been so afraid that you had to do what you hated doing? Haven't you ever been afraid like that?"

"No, I haven't," said Peter.

Sylvia was crying. She kept her hands before her face because she could not bear to look at Peter. Something tugged at her heart. Pain, terror, remorse—she had no need to act these things; they possessed her. Behind her sheltering hands the tears ran down.

After a minute, Peter said:

"Good lord, Sylvia, why did you do it? I thought we were pals."

Sylvia let her hands fall, and looked at him with lovely, tear-drenched eyes.

"You won't ever believe that I care," she said. "You can't believe it, but it's true. I care more than you do."

"Well, you've a pretty rotten way of showing it. Look here, Sylvia, what's the good of talking? The point is, what are you going to do now? You haven't got a knife about you, I suppose, or a pair of scissors?

If I could get these ropes off, I'd make that swab Henders sit up. I suppose you couldn't have a go at the knots?"

"I can't," said Sylvia, in a despairing voice.

"You mean you won't? Good lord, Sylvia, are you going to let the brutes murder me?"

Sylvia shrank back.

"Peter, give him the Jewel," she said, very low.

Peter set his jaw.

"I'm hanged if I do."

"But, Peter, what's the good of keeping it?" she said. "Even if you get away now, it would only be the same thing over again."

"I'll take my oath it wouldn't."

"It would, it would. You don't know Mr. Hendebakker. The Jewel's a sort of superstition with him. He'll never, never rest until he gets it."

"Nonsense!" said Peter. "You've let the man come over you with his bullying ways. If you'll help me to get out of here, I'll jolly well show Henders that this sort of game can't be played twice. No, Sylvia, listen, and for the Lord's sake don't cry. You can't possibly give your mind to what I'm saying if you keep on crying. You're frightened of Henders, and you've just sopped up what he said about your getting into trouble if you don't do what he tells you. To start with, is it true that he's got a real hold over you? I suppose it must be, but I just want to make sure. He says you took some loose diamonds belonging to his wife, and that he can prove it by the man that you tried to sell them to. Now, I don't want to hurt your feelings, but *is* that true?"

Sylvia turned her head away. He saw the colour run up to the very roots of her hair. She said nothing.

"I'm sorry, Sylvia, but we've got to the place where nothing but plain speaking is much good. Is it true?"

She looked at him then, flushed and on the defensive.

"It was a trap, I'm sure it was a trap. She had a handful of the wretched things; she took them out of her jewel-case and threw them on the table. One rolled off on to the floor, and she never even bothered to pick it up. How was I to suppose she'd count the stones? I don't believe she did, either. It was a trap, I'm *sure* it was."

"I dare say it was, but the fact remains that you did take them."

"I was so dreadfully hard up," said Sylvia, looking down. "I didn't think she'd miss them, I didn't really."

Peter restrained himself. There was either nothing to say or too much. After a moment he said:

"Let's get back to the point. You propose to let Hendebakker murder me because he's got this hold over you and you're afraid of getting into trouble."

"No, no!" said Sylvia. She put out her hands as if pushing something away from her.

Peter frowned.

"It's not 'no', it's 'yes'," he said. "But what I want you to understand is this—if you help me to get away, I'll see that you're safe as far as Henders is concerned. Don't you see that I shall have a far stronger hold over him than any that he has over you? Tying people up in cellars and threatening to starve them to death is not the sort of thing you can do in Wimbledon without getting into trouble. Don't you see, Sylvia? You must, surely. Get me out of this, and Henders won't dare look the same side of the street again. You'll be rid of him for good."

"You don't know him," said Sylvia. "I daren't, I simply daren't."

Peter was silent for a moment.

"Look here, Sylvia," he said at last. "I take it you don't absolutely want Henders to murder me. I mean you'd rather I got off as long as you're quite safe yourself. Well, if that's the case, I'll show you how it can be done. You go home, and when Henders is well out of the way, find my uncle, Miles Banham. He's at The Luxe, and you can get him on the telephone. You can ring up from a public call-office if you like, and you needn't give your name. You needn't appear in any way. You need only tell Miles to search the cellars of this house. Will you do it?"

Sylvia shrank back in real terror.

"Peter, I couldn't. Don't ask me. He'd know at once—I mean Mr. Hendebakker would know at once. Oh, Peter, *do* try and see my side of it. I don't believe you realize my position a bit. If you did, you'd see how impossible it is for me to go against him. I can't do it, I can't indeed."

Peter looked at her without speaking. He could not trust himself to speak, but the look went home.

"Don't, Peter, don't!" said Sylvia, springing up. "It's cruel of you to look at me like that. I can't bear it. It's not my fault if your wretched, obstinate pride won't let you take Mr. Hendebakker's offer. Why, he told me he'd give ten thousand for the Jewel."

"Fifteen," said Peter.

"And you refused it? Fifteen thousand pounds! You can sit there and tell me you refused fifteen thousand pounds! Why, it's madness, it's just madness!"

Peter laughed.

"Peter," said Sylvia, coming nearer, "let me go to him; let me tell him you'll come to terms. If you won't do it for your own sake, oh, won't you do it for mine? Why, I'm wretched, simply wretched. And if anything happened to you—if he really hurt you—I don't see how I could get over it. Peter, you were fond of me once—you were *very* fond of me; you said you would give me the Jewel—yes, you did; you know you did. And all I ask now is for you to tell me where it is. Peter, *please*, where is it?"

Peter laughed again, an angry, bitter laugh.

"Go on and guess," he said. And quite suddenly Sylvia put both hands up to her head and drew a long, startled breath.

"You've sent it to her—to Rose Ellen. That's what you've done with it," she said in an odd, whispering voice. Then, aloud and triumphantly: "Yes, of course you have. Why didn't I think of it before? I was to have it when you were in love with me; and now, of course, it's for her. You've forgotten all about offering it to me, and you've forgotten all about being in love with me. You're in love with Rose Ellen, and she's got the Jewel." She spoke faster and faster, retreating across the cellar until she came to the door. As she pushed it open, Peter called out in a voice which she had never heard from him before:

"Sylvia! For God's sake, Sylvia!"

The candlelight was leaping and falling; the wick, with only half a round of wax adhering to it, was fallen sideways against the neck of the bottle. The shadows rushed up to the roof and dropped again. The light flickered once, and twice.

Sylvia stood on the threshold and laughed.

"It's true, it's true, it's true," she said; and, as Peter called out again, she jumped back and slammed the door.

He heard the key turn. The light went out.

Chapter Thirty-Two

SYLVIA RAN ALONG the dark passage, and as she ran she heard Peter call again and yet again. Her one concern was to put the stairs and lighted spaces between her and this darkness, those cries. It was only when she reached the corner and found a pitch blackness everywhere that she realized that Hendebakker was gone. She had left him here with the electric lamp, and he was gone. In that frantic moment Hendebakker, who had been her terror, became her only help and safety—and he was gone. Her fright was so great that she completely forgot the little torch in her pocket. She was alone in this dreadful underground place where her footsteps rang hollow and Peter's voice still followed her.

She leaned, half fainting, against the wall, her sense of direction lost, her every faculty numb. Somewhere beyond her there was a scurry and a squeak, and as she started in the direction of the sound, two tiny, greenish points like pin-pricks of light showed for an instant and were gone. A sound between a gasp and a scream came from her dry throat. As if in answer to the sound, light shone suddenly, and Hendebakker came round the corner, walking briskly and holding his lamp shoulder-high.

He took Sylvia by the arm, and half pushed, half led her as far as the foot of the stairs, where he had perforce to shift his grip and give her more support. When they reached the kitchen level she turned on him, gasping and as white as a sheet.

"Oh, why did you go? You promised to stay," she cried.

"It's real nice to be missed," said Hendebakker. "And I rather guess it's the first time you've ever felt that way about me, so I'll make the most of it. You needn't be riled, though—I wasn't very far. You didn't really think, I suppose, that I'd be willing to take your own account of your interview with Waring—did you? I've a great deal too much respect for your powers of invention. When it comes to lying, I'll give you best every time, though I'm a pretty fair performer myself."

"Where were you?"

"In the next cellar. There's a mighty convenient ventilator in the partition, and I think I may say that I didn't miss a word of your conversation. I found it very interesting."

Sylvia put out an impulsive hand.

"Then you heard what I said at the end. She's got it—I'm sure she's got it—he's sent it to her."

"This Rose Ellen—who is she?"

"A sort of adopted sister, and he's just discovered that he's in love with her—he told me so this afternoon, and I was an idiot not to guess then that he'd given her the Jewel."

Hendebakker threw the light on her face, and saw it eager and intent.

"That's very interesting," he repeated. "I'd like to know what makes you think he's sent her the Jewel."

"I don't think it, I *know* it," said Sylvia. Her foot tapped the floor impatiently. "I know it because I know Peter Waring—he's like that. He was in love with me once, and he would have given me the Jewel then if he'd had it. I tell you I *know* he has sent it to Rose Ellen."

"Well, it's likely," said Hendebakker. "I'll look into it in the morning. What's her name, and where does she live?"

Sylvia gave him the address at Merton Clevery, and watched him write it down.

"Now we'll be getting home," he remarked.

Sylvia touched him on the arm.

"Are you going to leave him there?" she asked, pointing downwards; and, as Hendebakker nodded, she gave a sob and said, the words tumbling over one another." Oh, Mr. Hendebakker, don't—not in the dark—and his hands tied—and there are rats! Oh, please, *please* don't leave him there alone."

Hendebakker burst out laughing.

"Would you like to keep him company?" he said; and then, "He ain't a girl; a rat or two won't hurt him. You're too softhearted, but I reckon it's a little late in the day for that. You just come along home."

They went off separately: Sylvia in the taxi, with Robinson driving; Hendebakker in his own car with the other man.

Sylvia sat huddled in a corner, and cried most of the way home. Her own flat, lights, and some supper revived her, but later on in the darkness terror came upon her again. Peter was in the cellar with his hands tied. It would be horribly dark there, and horribly, horribly still—unless the rats came. She shuddered from head to foot and switched on a light with a rosy shade. Her pretty room sprang into view. An inlaid mirror caught the light and reflected it. All the hangings were mauve and blue, exquisite, delicate, spotless. Sylvia looked at them, and saw bare walls of whitewashed brick, stained with mould, and a rough door whose hinges were red with rust. Peter was in the dark. She shivered and pulled up her eiderdown. Peter couldn't move or use his hands. The cords would be cutting into his wrists. There was a smear of blood upon his forehead.

Once she actually got out of bed and went to the telephone. If she dared ring Miles Banham up, if she only dared! She stood with her hand on the receiver for ten minutes, trembling and shivering. Then, like the thrust of a knife, came the remembrance that Hendebakker had heard Peter ask her to ring his uncle up. He'd know at once. It was impossible, it was quite impossible.

She went back to bed in helpless misery. Peter would never forgive her. She liked to be admired; she liked people to like her; and Peter would never admire or like her again. Her heart was broken with self-pity.

"Oh, what have I done that such dreadful things should happen to me?" she wailed.

The pleasant, rosy glow filled the room. Sylvia buried her face in her hands—and through the twilight which they made she saw the accusing stare of Peter's eyes.

Chapter Thirty-Three

PETER HEARD Sylvia's scream; he heard Hendebakker's muffled tread. Both sounds died on the heavy air, and he heard no more.

An access of uncontrollable rage made him struggle fiercely with his bonds, but this too soon passed, and he leaned against the wall with a bitter realization of impotence. The men who had tied him up knew their work. No strength or struggle of his would avail. He would only exhaust himself, fret his strength away, and struggle towards the nightmare of madness. His thoughts raged in a furious mutiny against his will.

Henders—if ever he got free! Peter saw red when he thought of Henders. And Sylvia—blackness and bitterness were in the sound of her name; her fluent lies; her tears; her appeals for his help. He felt, not anger, but a sick revulsion. People whom one knew, one's pals, didn't do things like that. But Sylvia had done them—and he had thought of marrying her! If it hadn't been for Rose Ellen, he might have thought that he was in love with Sylvia; he might have asked her to marry him. It was just as if he had been walking along some pleasant, familiar path, and then suddenly there was no path—nothing but emptiness. Peter felt himself on the edge of that emptiness, looking over it into horrible blank space. If it hadn't been for Rose Ellen—and with that a most dreadful fear rushed upon Peter and shook him. Rose Ellen— Sylvia had guessed what he had done with the Jewel; by some devilish intuition she had hit upon the truth; and she would tell Henders; she had gone from him hot-foot to tell Henders! He knew it. He was sure of it. The terror rose about him like swirling water. It took his breath and drowned his reason. He had sent the Jewel to Rose Ellen and had brought her into most dreadful danger. Henders would go down there, and—anything might happen.

Peter wrestled with this terror, and presently thoughts came to his aid. Henders would look for Rose Ellen at Merton Clevery, and she would not be there; she would have gone to Chark with the Gaisfords. This was the first thought. It came to him with all the force of a shock that it was today that the Gaisfords were going to Chark; it was only yesterday that he had stood in the beech-wood and seen Rose Ellen's tears; it was only yesterday that he had gone to Sunnings. Why, the Jewel would not reach Rose Ellen until tomorrow; he had sent it off from Mrs. Merewether's post office that morning, and it certainly would not reach Rose Ellen at Chark until tomorrow.

It seemed simply ages since he had sat on the outskirts of the little wood and watched the sunrise dazzle on the Annam Jewel, simply ages since he had hidden the Jewel in a nest of moss and covered it with forget-me-nots. What was it the woman had called the pink ones? "Never"—no, that wasn't right—"no-never"; it went in a sort of jingle:

Forget—me—not ... no—never.
Forget—me—not ... no—never.

Peter's thoughts were slipping from him into a dreamy place beyond the cellar. They slipped a little farther, and suddenly he was walking with Rose Ellen between hedges of forget-me-nots that had grown thirty feet high and were arched overhead like church windows. The flowers hung down and brushed Rose Ellen's hair. She picked a great handful, all bright-blue like the sky, and held them out to Peter, and said: "Forget me not. You won't, will you, Peter de—ah?" She really said "Petah", and he loved her very much for saying it like that.

In his dreams Peter wanted to find a bunch of the pink no-nevers, and to give them to Rose Ellen. In the odd way in which things go in dreams, he couldn't say, "No, never," unless he could find a bunch of the flowers, and he knew that, unless he could find them, Rose Ellen would begin to cry again, her heart would break, and she would go away, and Peter would never be able to find her any more. He looked everywhere for the little pink no-nevers, but wherever he looked there were only blue forget-me-nots, and he saw Rose Ellen's face change and grow sad. He tried to call her, but he could not speak. Then suddenly there was a bunch of the pink forget-me-nots growing high up where he must climb the hedge to reach them, and the hedge had thorns in it like rose thorns, only longer and sharper. He climbed, and the thorns tore him. He grasped the flowers, and same down with a crash because the hedge wavered and fell in. Peter said, "No, never," and tried to give the flowers to Rose Ellen, but she wouldn't take them. She cried out, and Peter saw that what he held was the Annam Jewel. "No, no!" said Rose Ellen. "I hate it!" Peter woke up with a great start. The cords were cutting his wrists.

It took him a minute or two to clear his thoughts, but after that minute he set himself to think in real earnest. He had to get to Rose Ellen, and he had to get to her before Henders did. The terror had departed. He meant to get out of the cellar and to reach Rose Ellen. He had no idea how it was going to be done, but he meant to do it. Twelve years ago he had stood outside St. Gunburga's and made up his mind to take Rose Ellen away and to find her a home. Peter at twenty-five was not very different from Peter at thirteen. The end still came before the beginning; he saw first what he meant to do, and wrestled afterwards with the ways and means of doing it.

He had to get out of the cellar. He had to get his arms and legs free. How? Peter had no idea. He frowned ferociously in the darkness, and set himself to visualize the cellar as he had seen it by the light of Henders' electric lamp. Three walls of brick, barely covered with very ancient whitewash; high up in the left-hand wall the grating of a ventilator; opposite to him, the door with rusty lock and hinges. The door did not fit very well; it cleared the uneven stone of the floor by three-quarters of an inch or so, and there was a wide crack on the hinge side. Above the door, two feet of brick and another ventilator. On the right, in the corner, the beer-bottle which Henders had used as a candlestick. A flagged floor, very dusty. A few straws lying about. That was all, that was absolutely all. There was nothing else in the cellar of any sort or description except Peter himself, sitting propped against the wall which faced the door, his legs roped together and his hands secured behind his back.

It came to this, then, that the only movable things in the cellar— the only things that were not structurally part of it—were Peter, the straws, and the beer-bottle. The beer-bottle—Peter's mind became concentrated on the beer-bottle, and all at once an elusive memory slipped in amongst his thoughts and, as it were, played hide-and-seek with them. It was there, and gone; back again for an instant, and then once more just out of reach. It had something to do with St. Gunburga's, with his getting Rose Ellen out of St. Gunburga's; it had something to do with the wall. Peter made a sudden grab at the slippery memory and held it. *There was broken glass on the top of the wall.* He had put his coat on the glass. Why? To keep it from cutting his hands. *To keep it from fraying the rope.*

Peter gave a shout that echoed through the cellar. Broken glass and a rope. A rope might be frayed by broken glass! Oh, blessed beer-bottle! Oh, blessed, blessed beer-bottle! Peter dismissed dreams and memories, and settled down to a practical consideration of the problem before him. He sketched an ordered programme.

(1) The beer-bottle must be broken.

(2) He must use the broken glass to cut through the cord that bound his hands.

(3) Having freed his hands, he could easily get the rope off his legs.

(4) He must kick out the lock of the cellar door.

He reckoned that the first half of the programme would certainly take time, and that it must be well past midnight.

Before doing anything at all he had to get across the cellar. It was really quite easy to roll across a flagged floor with your arms roped behind you and your legs tied—easy, but horribly unpleasant. Peter got a straw down his neck, and a great deal of dust up his nose; he also took some skin off his hands. He arrived at the door, and lay in a most uncomfortable position, flat on his back, with the greater part of his weight on his hands. It was not so easy to get into a sitting position; his elbows being tied together, he could not use them to raise himself. The obvious alternative was to lever himself up by swinging his legs from the hips. This brought him up with his left shoulder against the jamb of the door. It also took all the skin off his knuckles, which had necessarily played the part of a fulcrum. As his feet came down they knocked the bottle over. It fell and rolled just out of reach. He shuffled forward inch by inch until his feet touched it. It was lying between him and the wall in very much the position he desired. He pushed it until it was right in the corner, with its base flat against the left-hand wall.

He sat still and considered the important question of where to break it. A kick with his heel on the shoulder, he thought; that would probably bring the neck away whole and provide some good jags of glass. A second kick would break the body of the bottle if he should find it necessary to have splinters or fragments to work with. Better break too little than too much to start with.

He made sure that the bottle was in the right position, leaned his shoulder against the wall, and kicked out cautiously. The bottle neck slid from under his left heel, and the bottle pivoted and rolled away from the wall intact. He pushed it back, measured his distance as well as he could, and let drive again. This time his heel struck the shoulder and smashed it. The bottle was broken, and he had now to turn himself round and shuffle backwards along the wall until he could feel for the glass with his hands.

The bottle had broken, as he had hoped, without splintering much. Feeling gingerly behind him with his bound hands, he found that about two-thirds of the shoulder had come away in one piece with the neck; the remaining third lay by itself, a sharp, irregular fragment; the base of the bottle was unbroken.

With his right hand he picked up the bottle-neck and, using it as a handle, tried to bring the sharp edge of the shoulder to bear on a strand of rope about three inches above his left wrist. The position was a most dreadfully cramped one, and he soon became aware that his wrist was a good deal more vulnerable than the rope. The glass slipped continually, and he could get no real purchase—the edge scratched at the rope without fraying it, and whenever it slipped he cut himself. He let the bottle-neck slip from his numb fingers and began to think again. There was probably an easier way of doing it. If there wasn't, he must have another go. He hoped with some earnestness that a better plan would turn up.

After a bit he stood the end of the bottle up on its base, and tried to saw the rope by moving his wrists to and fro across the uneven edges; but the bottle slid and toppled. All the same, the idea was a good one. If only he could fix the bottle in some way so that it could not move! Peter shook his head impatiently. No use to consider impossibilities. He couldn't fix the bottle, because there was nothing to fix it with.

His mind came back to the big splinter of glass. If he could fix that somehow. Where? Between the flagstones? He leaned sideways and felt with blood-smeared fingers. No, the cracks were filled with cement. With the word crack, he thought suddenly of the door. There were cracks there and to spare—one on either side. Yes, something might be done with the door.

He picked up the splinter, and shuffled forward with it until he came to the jamb of the door. With his back towards it, he felt for the crack on the lock side, and tried the bit of glass in it—turning, shifting, pressing until it jammed and remained wedged. About two inches of glass now stuck out, with a curved, irregular edge. Getting as close to the door as he could, he set his roped wrist against this edge, and brought all the pressure he could to bear on it, so as to fix it still more firmly in position. Then he got to work. By hunching and dropping his shoulders he kept the rope grating against the jagged edge of the glass. In a less awkward position, and with the use of his eyes, the job would have been an easy one, but as it was—well, he set his teeth and was thankful that it was possible at all. The shrugging movement gave him so little play, and involved so much sustained effort, that there were moments when achievement seemed terribly remote. Yet slowly and surely the cord was fraying. Up, down—up, down—up, down— the monotony was suddenly broken by the piece of glass slipping. Do what he could, Peter could not wedge it firmly again. He had to shuffle over to the corner and break what remained of the bottle. It took him three journeys and a great deal of patient effort before he could fix another piece of glass at all firmly in the crack.

The edge of this second bit was not so conveniently curved. As the cord wore through, it became increasingly difficult not to cut himself. Up, down—up, down—up, down—it was frightfully hard work, and a thirst was upon him like all the thirsts in the world rolled into one. He would almost have given the Annam Jewel for a drink of water. The cellar was hot and airless. His mouth was full of dust.

He had been hunching and dropping his shoulders since the year one, and an interminable stretch of time lay before him in which he must continue that slow sawing of rope on glass. If only the glass would hold now! The second strand was through, and the third was well on its way—very difficult not to cut oneself. The first bit of glass was a much handier one—pity it hadn't stayed the course. Up, down— up, down—up, down. Oh, lord, how much more of it? The glass was slipping again; he felt it give, and had to work it back into place, using one of the un-frayed turns of the rope to push with. Then on again until suddenly the last strand gave, and the glass gashed his wrist. He could hardly believe it.

For a moment he leant back against the door. The cessation of effort was grateful beyond words. And then a dreadful thought brought him bolt upright. Suppose he had only cut the rope between two knots and should find himself in the same case as when he began. Not being one of those who allow themselves to be hypnotized by possibilities, he began at once, by jerking and wriggling his arms, to bring one of the cut rope-ends within reach of his groping fingers. Nothing moved. He got the cords against the raised edge of the door jamb and rubbed them on it. An end fell down, brushing his finger-tips. He strained his arms apart, and felt the lashings give a little. He could now work his arms one against the other. His hands were loose. The strain on his elbows slackened. The ropes fell to the floor. His arms were free. He drew in his breath and stretched.

The first stage had been accomplished. He had now to untie his legs. For the moment his hands and arms felt as if they did not belong to him. He went on stretching and moving them until he could feel for and loosen the knots about his knees. When his legs were free, and he could stand, he stamped about the cellar, and would have shouted as he stamped, had he been quite sure that Hendebakker had left no one on guard. Of course, it would save him trouble if somebody opened the door; but, on the other hand, he felt he would rather kick out the lock than risk a charge under the muzzle of an automatic pistol.

When his legs and arms were more or less his own again, he took his bearings carefully, and prepared to deal with the door. He longed for shooting-boots instead of Oxford shoes, but he hoped for luck and kicked out. His heel missed the lock, landing just above it. His shoes scraped on the edge of the iron casing. He lost his balance and sat down hard upon the stone floor. The second kick got home, but the lock held. The third kick smashed it, and the door swung out.

Peter came into the pitch blackness of the passage, and stood there, listening. The door swung back towards him, creaking. He caught it by the edge, and waited, his ears on the stretch. If there was anyone in the house, the odds were that he would have heard that last crash; and yet—Peter remembered that the kitchen floor lay between him and the living-rooms, and he doubted whether a man on the ground floor could have caught any sound from the cellars. Anyhow, no one was coming down. He waited another minute to make sure of this, and then, letting go of the door, he crossed the passage to the opposite wall and began to feel his way to the corner.

He remembered that there was a sort of square hall, and that the steps ran sharply upwards about a yard or two from the turn. He came round the corner, and went on groping forward until he hit his head. The stairs were nearer than he had thought.

He reached the kitchen floor, and had rather a hunt for the next flight; the darkness was confusing, and he could not remember his position. He was glad to come out into the upper hall and to find that the darkness here was less absolute. The fanlight over the front door showed grey.

Again he stood and listened. There was not the slightest sound in all the house; more than that, there was no feeling of human presence. After a moment Peter was so sure that he was quite alone that he walked boldly to the door of the room in which Hendebakker had trapped him, and flung it open. It was darker here than in the hall, but a faint line defined the shutters.

Peter had come to look for his opera hat. He remembered that it had dropped here, and he had hopes that it might be more or less undamaged. He found it collapsed, but not as opera hats are intended to collapse. It had been smashed in sideways, and as a hat it was no more. He left it lying there, and, making his way to the front door, he opened it and came out into the porch. It seemed like the best part of a year since he and Sylvia had stood there together.

Peter guessed that it was about three in the morning. After the dense gloom of the house it seemed quite light out here. He could see things: shapes of trees; a black belt of shrubbery; the line of the gravelled drive. He shut the front door behind him and took his way towards the road.

He would have to walk into Wimbledon, knock up a garage, get a drink—before anything a drink—and induce someone to drive him back to town. He hoped to get to his rooms before daybreak. It was, in fact, something after four and broad daylight when he tiptoed up the stairs. Peter felt that if Jones or Mrs. Jones were to emerge, his character would be irretrievably lost. He had never really discovered whether the Joneses slept in the basement or the attic. It was with feelings of relief that he reached his own room.

A look at himself in the glass increased this relief immensely. Never had he beheld anything so disreputable as his own appearance; his hair wildly uncontrolled and caked with dust; his face—which he had vainly tried to clean with a handkerchief—greyish and smeared with blood; his clothes beyond description. He shed them hastily, rolled them into a bundle, and consigned them to the depths of his clothes-basket.

His left wrist was a good deal cut and scratched, and his knuckles badly barked. None of the cuts was deep, but there was a general effect of gore and grime. He decided that he must have a bath if the roof fell in. Afterwards he would look up a train for Chark, and perhaps get a couple of hours' sleep. If he got a train about nine, that would do. Henders would be off on a false scent to Merton Clevery; a train about nine would get him to Chark by eleven. He must pin a paper on his door, asking Jones to call him at eight.

He had his bath; found that the eight forty-five reached Lenton, the station for Chark, at ten-thirty-seven; pinned up a paper asking to be waked *without fail* at seven-thirty; and in two minutes was deeply, dreamlessly asleep.

Chapter Thirty-Four

ROSE ELLEN received the Annam Jewel at breakfast. She sat facing a sunny window. The light fell in patches on the polished floor.

"Toppin' day," said Major Gaisford for the tenth time. "What I say is, by all means go to the sea if you're goin' to have fine weather. If you're not goin' to have fine weather, stay at home."

"But one can't always tell, dearest," said Mrs. Gaisford.

"If you're not sure of fine weather, stay at home," said Major Gaisford. "Rosie, the marmalade is with you. Pass it along, if you can spare it. I say, it *is* a toppin' day, what?"

Mrs. Gaisford said, "Yes, dearest, it is, isn't it?" And then, in an undertone to Rose Ellen, "Now, what do you think about Jimmy's tunics? That blue linen you got—if we use the width of the stuff, we could get out four instead of three. Now, don't you think we *could* use the width? Nurse says we can't; but you know how dreadfully obstinate she is about cutting things out. I *can't* see why we shouldn't use the width. Can you?"

It was at this moment that the door opened and Levitt came in with the post. Mrs. Gaisford had a letter; Major Gaisford had a bill; and Rose Ellen had the Annam Jewel.

"Susie says," announced Mrs. Gaisford—"oh, dear, I do wish she'd write plainly—Susie says—James, you're not listening—Susie Lamont says that she can come to us from the twenty-ninth to the third—or is it can't? James, does she say that she *can* come or that she *can't* come? It might be either. I do think people should be made to cross their t's."

Major Gaisford began to hum and haw over the letter. Rose Ellen was looking at what the post had brought her. It was a parcel—from Peter. She couldn't think why Peter should have sent her a parcel—registered too. It wasn't her birthday.

"I shall have to wire and ask her which she means," said Mrs. Gaisford, resignedly. "Can—can't? No, it's no use, I shall *have* to wire. She'll be horribly cross, but it can't be helped."

She turned her attention to Rose Ellen.

"Why, child, who's sent you a registered parcel? And why don't you open it?"

"I think it's only flowers," said Rose Ellen. "It feels damp and smells mossy."

Major Gaisford burst out laughing.

"Whoever heard of registerin' flowers?" he said. "Flowers? Rubbish! Open it, Rosie, and let's see these precious flowers of yours."

"They're from Peter, aren't they?" said Mrs. Gaisford. "He writes such a good *plain* hand—I do wish everybody would. I shall *have* to send that wire, and Susie will be dreadfully annoyed."

"Peter—ha, ha, from Peter, are they?" said Major Gaisford. "She's blushin', my dear, she's blushin'. They *are* from Peter. Rose by name and Rose by nature, what?"

"Now, James," said Mrs. Gaisford. She shook her head at him, but he was spreading marmalade on buttered toast and chuckling to himself.

"Careful young man to register 'em, what? Open 'em, Rosie, and let's have a look. You have to be dooced careful with flowers, you know. Toppin' idea sendin' 'em to a girl and all that; but you have to be dooced careful."

He passed his cup to his still frowning wife.

"More tea, my dear, and stronger, and less sugar—the figure, you know, the figure. Yes, dooced careful you have to be, Rosie. Why, I knew a girl—what was her name? Somethin' odd, Anstice—yes, that was it, Anstice Gale—and a feller I knew was gone on her—don't know why, I'm sure, but he was. Well, this girl was dooced keen on the language of flowers and all that—had a book about it; a meanin' for every flower—and this feller who was keen on her thought it 'ud be a toppin' idea to send her some flowers; so he went and did it, and the next thing he knew, she was engaged to another feller. You see, the poor feller had put his foot in it somethin' shockin'. I forget what he sent her—dahlias or peonies or somethin'—but of course the girl went and looked 'em up in her book; and what do you suppose they meant? The poor feller never knew until it was too late that the meanin' was, 'I regard you with loathin'.' Pretty tall that, what? Shows how dooced careful you have to be, Rosie." He laughed heartily. "You just open your box, and let's see what kind of a bloomer this young feller of yours has made."

"They'll make such a mess here," said Rose Ellen.

She got up with the box in her hand. Her colour was deeper than usual. She wanted to open her parcel when she was alone. It was so odd that Peter should send her flowers. It was so odd that he should send her anything that needed to be registered. She held the box tightly, looked at Mrs. Gaisford with rather a startled, pleading expression, and said, speaking quickly and low:

"They'll make a dreadful mess in here; flowers always do."

Mrs. Gaisford nodded and smiled indulgently.

"Yes, yes, take them away," she said. "And, my dear, will you look after Jimmy for an hour whilst Nurse gets settled down a little? I thought perhaps you'd take him out to the end of the garden on the cliff. Nurse'll fetch him in at half past eleven."

"Yes, I'd love to," said Rose Ellen at the door. She shut it after her next moment, and Mrs. Gaisford turned to her husband.

"Now, James," she said, "you're not to tease, or look, or make jokes. You're to leave the child alone. I do really think there's something in it with Peter Waring, and you're to be good and not take any notice."

"Oh, nonsense! Girls like to be teased about their lovers," said Major Gaisford easily. He got up and strolled to the window.

"*Toppin'* day, isn't it?" he said.

Rose Ellen took a flat glass dish from the pantry, and went up to her own room. The parcel smelt mossy. The flowers were sure to be wild flowers—people didn't send garden flowers in moss. She would fill the glass dish with moss and stick the little wild things in it so that they should look as though they were growing. There would be violets and primroses for certain—perhaps anemones and wood sorrel. Major Gaisford was forgotten.

She came into her sunny room, and set the glass dish on the wide window-seat. The window looked across the garden towards the sea. There were pine trees beyond the flower-beds, and beyond the pine trees blue water and blue sky.

Rose Ellen cut the string of her parcel, and sat down on the window-ledge to open it—first brown paper and string; then Mrs. Merewether's box; and then Peter's letter, rather damp and mossy. Rose Ellen picked it up, but before she read it she looked for a moment at the sea, and the sky, and the pine trees. It was such a blue day. There was so much light. The air moved as if it were alive.

Rose Ellen held the letter very tightly. After her storm of tears and bitter pain there had come a calm. And now, quite suddenly, she felt that something was going to happen, something big. She was not afraid, but she felt awe. She sat with Peter's letter in her hand, and could not read it. It seemed a long time before she could read it. When she lifted it she was rather pale, but her eyes shone. She read:

Dear Rose Ellen,

Don't unpack this box until there's no one there. It is in a bit of paper under the moss. Keep it safe for me till I come, and don't tell anyone. I'll come as soon as I can.

Peter.

PS.—The primroses and violets are out of a wood, but the forget-me-nots were in the post office garden. The woman says the pink ones are called "No-never".

"Oh!" said Rose Ellen, when she had finished reading. She laughed a little, happy, shaky laugh. Then she said very softly, "Oh, Peter de—ah."

The blue sky and the light seemed to be in the room with her; it was such a sunny, sunny day. And the scent of the pines—Rose Ellen would always love the scent of the pines.

She took out the blue forget-me-nots and the pink no-nevers. Next came the wood violets and primroses, very sweet. She laid each bunch by itself, and began to lift the moss. It was fern moss, very green, the sort she loved best of all—perhaps Peter remembered how much she liked it. She lifted the moss, and found something doubled up in an old envelope.

"Keep it safe till I come, and don't tell anyone." What was she to keep safe for Peter? Her hand shook a little as she tore away the sodden paper. Then she cried out. The Annam Jewel slipped between her fingers, and lay upon the moss. She cried out, and shut her eyes. The room seemed to tremble a little. She caught at the edge of the window-seat, bent forward, and looked again.

It was the Annam Jewel. Peter had sent her the Annam Jewel. It lay there on the moss, and the sun shone on it. It was living colour. It was sky, and sunset, and golden moon.

A great many thoughts came into Rose Ellen's mind as she looked at the Jewel. Quite suddenly she pushed it down into the moss and covered it. Her eyes went back to the sky and the sea.

After a little while she got up, and filled the glass dish with water. Then she laid the moss in it, and made the little bunches of flowers stand upright in the moss as if they had roots and were really growing.

When she had finished, the Annam Jewel lay alone, with the light upon it. Without looking at it, Rose Ellen carried her little moss garden to the other side of the room and set it down on a table out of the sun. Then she went back.

Peter had said, "Keep it safe for me till I come." Peter had said, "I will come as soon as I can." She must keep it safe for Peter.

She picked up the Jewel, knotted it in a little handkerchief with a net border, and pushed it down inside the front of her brown holland dress. She put Peter's letter there too. Then she put on a shady rush hat, and went to find Jimmy.

Chapter Thirty-Five

PETER ARRIVED at Lenton at a quarter to eleven, and took a taxi out to Cliff Edge. The driver took a sharp turn to the right just before reaching Chark, and for the last half-mile they followed an unmetalled track across the rising moor. Cliff Edge had a right to its name; the space of the garden beyond it, the cliff fell sheer to the sea.

Peter paid and dismissed his taxi, and was prepared with an apology when Mrs. Gaisford came into the drawing-room. She wore the air of a woman who had been torn from her unpacking.

"No, not a bit too early, if you don't mind looking after yourself," she said. "After all, it's Rose Ellen you want to see, isn't it? Now, do you mind finding your own way down the garden? She's out on the cliff, beyond those trees, with Jimmy. I'm just going to send Nurse for him." She stood by the open glass doors and pointed. "Straight down the path past the tulip beds," she said.

Peter walked down the path between beds of orange, and lilac, and rose-coloured tulips. Where the flower-beds ended there was a shrubbery. Beyond the shrubbery there were seven pine-trees. The path took a winding turn and came out on the real edge of the cliff. The ground was very uneven; yellow patches of sand showed between the tussocks of coarse grass. A heaped parapet of rough stones guarded the dangerous edge. Beyond it was the sea.

Peter saw Rose Ellen. She was leaning against the parapet with one arm about the infant Jimmy, who had fallen asleep. He slept, as many children do, with his eyes only half shut; some of the blue showed through the lashes, and looked all the bluer because his cheeks were so red. Rose Ellen's head was bent so that the shade of her hat fell upon Jimmy's face.

Peter stood still for a moment, and looked. Something tugged at his heart. Rose Ellen looked up and saw him.

There was just a moment of silence, and then Rose Ellen said, "S-s-h!" and held out a little, brown left hand. Before Peter could say anything, there was a sound of footsteps and a rustle of starched linen, followed by the appearance of Jimmy's nurse. She removed Jimmy, still sleeping. Peter sat down on the grass beside Rose Ellen.

"Did you get it?" he said. "My parcel, I mean. It ought to have come. Did you get it?"

Rose Ellen looked at him with a very little smile which began by being teasing, and then trembled into sweetness.

"I got your flowers," she said.

"You did? Did you like them? Did you find the Jewel?"

Rose Ellen nodded.

"Why did you send it to me?" she said.

Peter frowned. He might tell Rose Ellen that he had sent her the Jewel because he wanted her to have it—he thought of doing this—he began to dig little holes in the sand and to frown at them ferociously. Or he might tell her that he had sent her the Jewel because he knew that it would be safe with her. But then she might not understand— even Rose Ellen might not understand.

"Oh, Peter, your hands, your poor hands!" said Rose Ellen in a quick, distressed voice. "What *have* you done to them?"

Peter's indecision passed. He rolled over, with his elbows on the ground and his chin in his hands.

"It's nothing," he said, "only scratches. But I've been going rather strong in the adventure line ever since I left Merton Clevery. It doesn't feel like two days; it feels like years. And I want to tell you all about it. That's why I've come."

"Is it all about the Jewel?" said Rose Ellen.

"Some of it's about the Jewel."

Peter was not going to commit himself. He had made a plan. First of all he was going to tell Rose Ellen about the Jewel and his adventures; and then he was going to tell her how frightfully he loved her. He couldn't think how he hadn't known it all the time. There was something so dear about Rose Ellen. Now that he was with her he felt as if nothing could ever go wrong again. Rose Ellen made you feel like that.

"Tell me, Peter de—ah," she said.

"I want you to read my father's notes first. I got them when I was twenty-five, with a sham Jewel. Read it, and you'll see."

He dragged the exercise-book out of a pocket and laid it on her lap. Rose Ellen opened it and read in silence. While she read, Peter watched her face. Rose Ellen was frightfully fascinating to watch, because her colour kept changing; all the changes were beautiful. It came to Peter as a sort of surprise that Rose Ellen was beautiful.

She finished reading, and looked at him across the open page.

"Peter, it's dreadful," she said. "Oh, Peter, I hate it."

She put her hand to her breast, took out the little knotted handkerchief with the net border, and set it on the grass at arm's length.

"Yes, it makes you feel like that," said Peter. "It's all rather beastly, really. I want to tell you about it—the rest of it. These two men whom my father speaks of—Henderson and Dale—well, one of them is this man Hendebakker that the papers are so full of, the new millionaire; and the other is Mr. Coverdale." He paused, and then added, "Sylvia's father."

Rose Ellen cried out softly. Her hands took hold of one another.

Peter began to tell her the whole story. It was always easy to talk to Rose Ellen, because, even if she didn't say a single word, you felt that she was going with you all the way.

The beginning was the most difficult part. Sylvia—he didn't want to talk about Sylvia, but he couldn't leave her out, not to Rose Ellen. The scene at The Luxe when Sylvia gave him the Jewel, got three short sentences. The scene in the beech-wood, when he saw Rose Ellen's tears and knew how much he loved her, did not get a sentence at all. He went on with a rush to his visit to Sunnings and Roden Coverdale.

"He was awfully decent to me. He told me things. I'd like to tell you all about it, if you don't mind."

Rose Ellen didn't mind; she said so. Peter went on. He gave her Coverdale's story in full; passed hastily over his own encounter with Hendebakker; and then rather spread himself on his tramp in the dark, his night in the wood, and the superlative excellence of Mrs. Merewether's bacon. As he talked he dug little sandpits, making patterns of them.

"She was *frightfully* nice to me," he said. "She thought I was a lost soul, but she fed me and gave me William's overcoat—at least, I'm not sure if it was William's or her husband's. I *was* a sight; you've no idea what I looked like. It does seem ages ago. I mean it seems like last year since Coverdale shoved the Jewel at me in the dark. I hope he got away all right. I liked him most awfully, you know; it seems odd, but I did." He began to make a little rampart all round the sandpits. It was about three inches high, and he took great pains with it.

"And—and Sylvia?" said Rose Ellen. She hadn't meant to speak, but the words seemed to say themselves. She said, "And Sylvia?" and caught her breath lest she should say any more.

"That's the perfectly beastly part of it," said Peter gloomily. "All the part about Sylvia's absolutely rotten. I don't want to talk about it, I couldn't talk about it to anyone but you; it's too beastly."

He was looking at his sand wall and not at Rose Ellen. He did not see that she was getting paler and paler. In very short, jerky sentences he gave her to understand that Sylvia had fetched him from the club, and that they had gone to a house in Wimbledon where Hendebakker had trapped him.

Rose Ellen could hardly bear it. The part about the cellar was dreadful. It was all dreadful. She couldn't bear it. She cried out. Peter told her not to be a little mug, and proceeded to illustrate his escape. It made him rather sandy, but he showed her how he had broken the bottle and used the glass to free his wrists. He was by now a good deal pleased with his escape.

"I only wonder there's any skin left on my hands at all," he said in conclusion.

But Rose Ellen came back again to Sylvia.

"Peter, how could she? I can't bear it. She went away and left you—in that horrible place with that horrible man? Oh, Peter, why?"

"She's afraid of him. He's a brute, you know, and he's got a hold over her. It's simply beastly, but I'm afraid she took some diamonds belonging to his wife, and he knows it."

Rose Ellen said, "Oh!" in a shocked whisper, and looked away. There was something she must say, and she didn't know how to say it. She caught at her courage, and said in the merest breath of a voice:

"I want to say something—I must say it, but I'm frightened."

Peter put his left hand over her left hand and gripped it. He had to come nearer in order to do this. He felt Rose Ellen's hand tremble under his.

"What is it?" he said. "It doesn't matter what you say. Just tell me what it is."

"Were you engaged to her?" said Rose Ellen. She had turned quite white; the words came with a rush, "Were you engaged to her?"

"No, thank the Lord, I wasn't," said Peter.

"But—you—were—in—love—with—her?"

"You know I wasn't. Rose Ellen, *you* know I wasn't."

She shook her head.

Peter's grasp tightened on her little shaking hand.

"You must know. You always know things. You know I love you frightfully."

Rose Ellen shook her head again.

"Well, I do," said Peter fiercely. He looked at her with a most fearful frown; and then, with no warning at all, he dropped his head upon her hand and began to sob.

In a moment Rose Ellen was bending down to him, her free hand stroking his hair, her voice soft and broken.

"Peter de—ah, oh, my Peter de—ah, oh, don't—oh, Peter, don't."

"I'm such a damned fool," said Peter in muffled tones.

"You're not, you're not. What is it, darling? Tell me. Tell Rose Ellen."

Peter kissed the hand that was wet with his tears, choked back a sob, sat up, and caught Rose Ellen in his arms.

"Oh, Rose Ellen, you do, don't you?" he said. "You do love me? I'm a damned fool, but I love you *frightfully*."

Chapter Thirty-Six

"YOU DIDN'T SAY if you liked my flowers," said Peter presently. "Did you like them? Did you? Did you know what I meant when I sent them?"

Rose Ellen nodded, with her head against his shoulder.

"I liked the bit about the pink ones immensely," said Peter. "I never heard it before. I had a dream about it when I was in that beastly cellar. There was a hedge of the blue ones as high as a house; and you said, 'Forget me not'; and I wanted to say 'No, never'; and I couldn't, because I couldn't find any pink ones. It sounds mad, but it was like that in the dream. I want you to say it now. Look at me and say it."

Rose Ellen sat up and looked at him. There was a lovely carnation colour in her cheeks. Her eyes were like peaty pools with the sunlight on them; they shone as they looked at Peter.

"Forget me not," she said, and then quite suddenly she hid her face, and Peter's arm was round her again.

"No, never," he said. "No, never, never, never. There, I made up my mind I'd say that to you. And when we're married you shall have a bunch of the blue ones, and I'll have a buttonhole of the pink no-nevers. I think that's a top-hole idea, don't you?"

Rose Ellen sat up and looked at him again, very seriously this time.

"But I haven't said I'm going to marry you, Peter de—ah," she said. Peter hugged her.

"Little liar. Years and years ago you said you would. Don't you remember when we ran away? You said you wanted to be really and truly Rose Ellen Waring; and I said you'd better marry me, and you jumped at it, you simply jumped at it."

"Peter, I didn't."

"You did. Don't you remember?"

199 | THE ANNAM JEWEL

"You forgot," said Rose Ellen, very low.

"It was there all the time really," said Peter, "and I'm never going to forget any more. When will you marry me, Rose Ellen? It must be soon, or the forget-me-nots will be over."

"I haven't said I'll marry you, Peter," said Rose Ellen again.

"But you will." He laughed, and then he stopped laughing because there was something in her face which he didn't understand.

Then Rose Ellen said a very surprising thing. She said quite gently and firmly:

"I'll marry you if you'll give me the Annam Jewel, Peter."

"I've given it to you already," said Peter. "Why? Why did you say that, Rose Ellen?" He frowned, and his voice changed.

Rose Ellen picked up the little handkerchief with the net border and unknotted it. The Jewel fell upon a bare patch of sand, and lay there in the sun.

"You didn't think I wanted it to keep?" she said. She looked at him in distress. "You didn't think that? Peter, whom does it really belong to?"

"I suppose," said Peter, "that it really belongs to me; at least, I don't suppose it belongs to anyone else."

"What did you mean to do with it?"

"I don't know," said Peter. "We might sell it—it's worth a lot of money, you know. Henders offered me fifteen thousand for it, only I think he's a bit cracked about it. Anyhow, I'm hanged if I'd let him have it at any price. But we could sell it to someone else. What do you think?"

Rose Ellen shook her head.

"Why not? The money would be quite useful."

Rose Ellen's hands were holding one another again.

"Oh, Peter, give it to me," she said. "As long as it's anywhere in the world, people will go on doing dreadful things because of it. Look at your uncle, and your father, and Mr. Hendebakker, and Sylvia. If we sold it, there would be more dreadful things—more people stealing, and murdering, and cheating because of it. Please give it to me, Peter de—ah."

"But what will you do with it, Rose Ellen? You say 'as long as it's in the world'. You can't take it out of the world. What would you do with it?"

"I should throw it into the sea," said Rose Ellen, with calm decision. She rose on her knees, and beckoned Peter to look over the parapet. "Do you see that pale line in the water? Look, you can follow it quite a long way. I always think it looks like a piece of ribbon. It comes in round the point there, and then goes out to sea again. Well, it's a most dreadfully strong current. They call it the Smuggler's Race. No one can bathe here because of it; anything that gets into it is never seen again." She caught his arm with both hands. "Peter, if I were to throw the Annam Jewel into that current, I think it would be out of the world."

Peter stared at the Smuggler's Race. It fascinated him, that pale, bright ribbon rushing mysteriously faster than the surrounding water. The tide stood high against the cliff. It would be easy to drop the Jewel into that swift stream and be rid of it.

After a moment they turned away. The Jewel lay on the sand where Rose Ellen had dropped it.

"It's very beautiful," said Peter regretfully.

"Yes," said Rose Ellen. She picked it up and held it in the palm of her hand. "It's not its fault," she said.

They stood in silence and looked at it. Then Rose Ellen spoke again.

"Peter," she said; and Peter came close to her and put an arm about her shoulders. "Peter, I was thinking—"

"What were you thinking?"

"About something in your father's book; he said your uncle kept on saying it." She repeated the words very low:

"'The blue is the Celestial Heaven; the red is the Elemental Fire; the green is the Living Earth; and the gold is the Ray of Wisdom in the heart of man. Can these things be taken by violence?'"

Her voice trembled and stopped. She leaned against him, and he held her tight. "Peter," she said at last, "do you see? It's beautiful, but it's not so beautiful as the sky, and the sunset, and all the little green things that grow in spring; they're much more beautiful really, and people don't steal and kill and tell lies because of them; they're for everybody." She gave a little laugh. "Nobody murders because of a red sunset, or tries to steal the sky, Peter de—ah. The Jewel's only a picture, and I like the real things best. Will you give it to me to throw away, Peter de—ah? I can't marry you unless you do, I can't really."

"Good morning, Miss Mortimer," said Virgil P. Hendebakker. "I'm real sorry if I intrude."

Rose Ellen stepped away from Peter, with the Jewel in her hand. Neither of them had heard Mr. Hendebakker come down the path between the tulips; his step had been light upon the gravel, and silent on the sand. He stood a few yards away, and smiled, as who should say, "I, too, have been in Arcady." Peter looked at him with a scowl.

"You've nothing whatever to say to Miss Mortimer," he said. "You get out of this, and quick, Henders, or you'll be sorry."

"Now, Waring," said Hendebakker, "you're riled—and I'll allow that you've reason to be riled. As soon as I found you'd gone I came after you to finish our little business conversation. You made a real smart getaway, didn't you? You're one up on me over that." He waved a hand towards Rose Ellen. "I presume that you've put Miss Mortimer wise, and that she's in on this deal." His eyes were fixed upon the Jewel. Rose Ellen closed her hand upon it.

"The Jewel belongs to Miss Mortimer," said Peter. "I've no business with you, Henders, and you've no business here."

"Now, now," said Hendebakker soothingly, "just one moment, if you don't mind. I'd like a word with Miss Mortimer. Very happy to meet you, Miss Mortimer." He bowed. "Now, about this Jewel—why can't we come to terms? You're liable to have trouble if you keep it. What do you want with a thing that'll only bring trouble? I offered Mr. Waring fifteen thousand last night in peculiar circumstances. Well, I'll rise to twenty. It's a crazy price, but you can have it. Now, I put it to you, isn't twenty thousand pounds a whole sight better than you freezing on to a thing that's bound to get you into trouble?"

Rose Ellen spoke, not to Hendebakker, but to Peter.

"Is it really mine?" she said. "Have you given it to me?"

Peter nodded without speaking. His heart beat hard against his side. He knew what Rose Ellen was going to do, and he found the moment an emotional one.

Hendebakker was puzzled. There was something in the air; he did not know what; but there was something.

"Is it a deal?" he asked.

Rose Ellen spoke to him for the first time, looked at him for the first time.

"No," she said; just the one word, clear and hard as crystal.

She turned then, quietly and without haste, moved a step nearer to the parapet, and, before Hendebakker had the slightest idea of what was going to happen, she lifted her right arm and threw, as Peter had taught her to throw in the long-ago days when they were brother and sister. She threw, and the throw was strong and true. The Jewel left her hand, rose a little, flashed once in the sun, and fell clear into the blue rush of the Smuggler's Race. It was gone; with the merest flicker of spray it was gone; the pale current took it, and it was gone.

Rose Ellen laughed. She said, "Oh, Peter de—ah," and clapped her hands. She turned to him laughing, with the lovely colour in her face and happiness in her eyes.

In the same moment Mr. Hendebakker lost his temper suddenly and completely. For an instant Peter saw what Sylvia had once seen. Something made him look—for all his life he was thankful that something made him look—and he saw a horrible fury break up the genial smoothness of Hendebakker's face. Peter made a dash at him, saw his hand go to his hip; and, as the hand went up again and a shot rang out, he closed with the man, and they came down together on the sandy grass.

Rose Ellen cried aloud and ran towards them. She had seen the pistol aimed at her. Her ears rang with the noise that had made her cry out. She did not know that she owed her life to Peter's rush— Hendebakker didn't miss what he fired at. She reached the struggling figures. Peter had his knee on Hendebakker's chest, and was strangling him; he was as white as a sheet, and he knew nothing in the whole world except his desire to kill Henders here and now. Rose Ellen was calling to him, catching at his shoulder; she was trying to prevent him from killing Henders; she was calling to him in an agony; her arms were round him, she was trying to get between them.

"Peter, I can't bear it. Oh, Peter, you're hurting me, you're hurting *me!*" It was the voice and almost the words of the little Rose Ellen who had pleaded for the life of her doll. "I can't bear it, Peter."

And just in time, voice and words pierced through Peter's madness to Peter's self. His hands relaxed their dreadful grip. He stared at Hendebakker for a moment, and said in a hoarse whisper:

"Have I killed him?"

Rose Ellen said, "No—no—no," with a sob between each word. She pulled him towards her, and when he got to his feet she leaned against him and wept bitterly. After a moment he put his arms round her and they stood there until he asked:

"Are you sure I haven't killed him?"

"No—no—no," said Rose Ellen again. "Of course you haven't. Look for yourself."

She stepped back, and Peter saw that Hendebakker had rolled over and, still gasping and choking, was trying to rise.

Rose Ellen made a swoop, picked something up, and ran to the parapet. When she came back Hendebakker was sitting up and rubbing his throat.

"You've got me beat," he said at last. "You've got me beat."

He looked at Rose Ellen as he spoke, but it was Peter who said in a slow, controlled voice:

"Henders, if you had hurt her—"

"Well, I didn't," said Mr. Hendebakker. His voice came more easily now, and he spoke with a singular composure—afterwards Peter gave the man credit for his self-command.

"Well, I didn't," said Mr. Hendebakker. "I'm liable to lose my temper, and I'll admit I lost it just now." He stroked his throat, and swallowed.

"Nobody's sorrier than I am, for it's clean against all my principles. Losing your temper don't pay, and it's dead against my principles. Now, if I had shot Miss Mortimer just now—well, she'd have been at the end of her troubles, and I'd have been right at the beginning of mine. I'm real glad you spoilt my aim, real glad. See?"

"Look here, Henders," said Peter. "I've had about enough of you. You get out."

"All in good time," said Hendebakker.

He controlled a disordered collar, and smoothed his hair. Then his hand went to his hip, and he looked about him.

"Where's my automatic?" he said coolly.

"I threw it into the sea," said Rose Ellen in tones of clear severity.

"Did you now?" He gazed at her with some admiration, and she flushed.

"It's the best place for it," she said, with a touch of heat. "With your sort of temper you ought never to carry a revolver, never."

"Now that's real good sense," said Hendebakker.

"Henders, get out," said Peter. "I've had more than enough of you."

Hendebakker got slowly to his feet, and dusted his trousers.

"Lucky I've got my automobile outside," he said. "I should hate to travel in a train looking this way. Yes, I'm going, Waring; but before I go I've got a proposition to make to you. You needn't fall in with it if you don't like, but it might be worth your while. Miss Mortimer, you're a real sensible young lady, and I put it to you—do any of us want this business talked about?"

"No, we don't," said Rose Ellen. "Peter, we don't, do we?"

Peter frowned. He was still very white.

"What do you mean, Henders?" he said sharply.

"Well, it's this way," said Hendebakker. "The real Jewel's in the sea, and no good to anyone. The observation I was going to make is this—are you a card-player, Waring?—the king's good enough if no one has the ace. Anita sets a good deal of store by the Jewel, and I set a good deal of store by Anita. I'd be real glad to have her go on thinking that she's got the Annam Jewel; and, as I put it to Miss Mortimer just now, what do you stand to gain by talking? Is it a deal? I'll make it worth your while."

Peter set his jaw.

"Henders, if you don't get out, I'll kill you. I swear I will," he said.

Rose Ellen's hand tightened on his arm.

"Peter," she whispered, "we don't want to talk. Tell him we won't if he'll leave Sylvia alone."

Peter hesitated. It went so horribly against the grain to make a bargain with the man. After a moment he said rather jerkily:

"We don't want to talk: but you've got to leave Lady Moreland alone. D'you hear? If you annoy her in any way, I'll see to it that everyone knows your Jewel's a fake."

Hendebakker burst out laughing.

"You're pretty much of a fool, Waring, aren't you?" he said. "You don't owe her much, and that's the bedrock truth. It's mighty bad business to pay what you don't owe. But, as far as I'm concerned, it's a deal. You hold your tongue about the Jewel, and I'll hold mine about the lady. Well, so long, Waring. Miss Mortimer, I'm very pleased to have met you."

He bowed ceremoniously, picked up his soft felt hat, dusted it with care, put it on and walked away.

They watched him out of sight, and stood in silence for a while. Then Peter said, "Rose Ellen," in a shaken, uncertain voice, and she turned to him with both her hands out, palm upwards, empty.

"I've thrown away twenty thousand pounds, Peter," she said between tears and laughter. "And, oh, Peter, I'm so happy. And oh, Peter de—ah, I am so rich."

Peter couldn't speak at all. He went down on his knees, and hid his face in those soft, empty hands.

Epilogue

THE JEWEL LAY in the Shrine. There was light about it. The Shrine was full of light. The Jewel shone. It shone with the four great colours: blue of the Celestial Heaven; crimson of Elemental Flame; green of Immortal Spring; and the golden Ray of Wisdom.

The place was full of light.

The love of Rose Ellen lay in the heart of Peter. It shone, and made a light there. It was clear as the Celestial Heaven, and warm and pure as Flame. It was one with Immortal Spring, and at its heart was the golden ray of Wisdom.

The Jewel lay in the Shrine.

THE END

Made in United States
North Haven, CT
12 April 2022